RUN, KISS, REPEAT

JAMIE EVERLEE

First paperback edition April 2020

Book design and Illustration by Caroline Teagle Johnson

ISBN 978-1-7347345-0-8 (paperback)

ISBN 978-1-7347345-1-5 (ebook)

To my sister, my first reader,
my husband, my biggest supporter,
and my kids, my motivation

PROLOGUE

Harrison pulled at the tight collar of his tuxedo. He felt like the top button of his shirt was trying to strangle him. He hadn't worn it in a long time, so he wasn't sure if maybe it was too small or if he'd just become accustomed to his street clothes. Back when he had first started his security company, when he was both the muscle and the brain, attending events like this had been something he did routinely. He couldn't deny he missed having an excuse to have his gun attached to him. Although he was certain he wouldn't need to use it. Not in this stale ballroom, filled with even staler doctors.

Recently his team had messed up the last handful of events. In the past week alone, they'd botched the security at an organized boycott at the university. Peaceful protests had quickly escalated to violence, and there had been a handful of injuries brought on by his own damn team. The local media had covered it extensively. Harrison hadn't been around; he'd seen it on the news himself.

This client, the Minnesota Association of Medical

Doctors, had heard about the altercation and called to cancel two nights earlier. Even though the group was a small client on the scale of everything, Harrison had decided long ago that he wouldn't burn any bridge. So he'd assured them he would personally staff their event, and that they had nothing to be concerned about. They had nothing to worry about in the first place, but that was just his opinion. After some recent mass shootings, the president of the association felt certain his annual fundraising dinner would be a target of the next one. He didn't clarify if he expected a disgruntled patient to break in, or if a doctor would lose their marbles and turn to violence, but Harrison figured both were unlikely.

Harrison scanned the crowd. Everyone was busy sipping chardonnay. He could use a drink himself; it would be a long night. Part of him hoped there would be at least a bit of excitement at the event so he could have something to do— maybe break up a fight over whose Tesla accelerated faster.

He spotted Dr. Larkspur approaching him. He had his hands tucked in his pockets as he ambled over.

"Mr. Williams, good to see you," Larkspur said, sticking his hand out to him.

Harrison returned his handshake. Larkspur was exactly how Harrison had pictured him from their phone and e-mail conversations. He was in his sixties, slightly balding, with a slim build. His reading glasses sat a bit too far down his nose.

"You too, Dr. Larkspur." Harrison continued scanning the crowd. He *was* looking for someone, just not a shooter. "Any residents attend this thing?"

"Maybe a few. But primarily we focus on those who can actually afford to pay our dues." The doctor chuckled at his own joke. It took a lot to make Harrison laugh, Larkspur was maybe one of the least humorous people he'd ever met.

"Everything going well?" Harrison asked.

"So far, yes, but you can never be too careful. Your company helping at all with finding that poor missing girl? The runner?"

"Can't say I've heard about her."

Larkspur stared at him, dumbfounded. "It's all over the news. You really should see if you can help."

"I'm sure the police have it under control." Harrison didn't feel like explaining to the man in front of him that searching for every missing person without pay wasn't what his company did.

Just then he spotted the person he was looking for: Logan. Harrison hadn't been sure if Logan would attend, but he'd known there was a chance. Logan, a few years younger than Harrison, was standing next to a pretty brunette. She had on a tight, long black dress that dipped down her back, showing off all of her curves. She seemed to radiate both confidence and sex.

Logan, on the other hand, looked as uncomfortable in his tuxedo as Harrison felt. Harrison had a hard time believing this group was full of Logan's people. Of course, if he was sleeping with that brunette, maybe he didn't have it too bad.

"Will you excuse me," Harrison said to Larkspur, who had kept talking long after Harrison had stopped listening.

Harrison walked up to Logan and his date, who were both chatting with an older couple. When Harrison looked at them closer, he realized they must be her parents. The girl was the spitting image of the older woman, likely her mother, who was dressed in a more conservative black gown, but was still striking.

"Hey there, Brother," Harrison said, giving Logan a small smirk.

He watched Logan do a double-take. Harrison definitely didn't fit into Logan's new life. At least, he knew Logan thought that. Logan's look of surprise quickly turned into a sneer, and his arms crossed in front of him.

"Harrison." He looked around before zeroing in on his brother. "What are you doing here?"

"Work. I thought I might see you here."

"I'm Emily," the brunette said, inserting herself into their conversation. She grinned at Harrison, grabbing his arm with her acrylic nails. "Logan never mentioned he had a brother."

"Is that so?" Harrison raised an eyebrow at Logan.

"Emily, you remember Dr. Davis?" her mother asked, drawing Emily's attention away from him.

He watched Logan look too, except his brother's gaze didn't go to the well-dressed man with salt-and-pepper hair nearby, but to the much younger woman at his side. She was way too young to be his date, so he guessed she was Davis's daughter. And based on Logan's expression, he knew her. Harrison had a skill at reading even the subtlest movements someone made, and there was something in the way Logan's eyes went right to her that made him think she must mean something to his brother.

She didn't have the same sexual appeal as Emily, but when he took a moment to look at her, he could see that she was actually prettier than Emily, but in a much more restrained way. For instance, he could see she was very well-endowed, but the neckline on her halter dress was much more modest. Her blonde hair was swept up, showing off her slender neck. Harrison was a sucker for a pretty collarbone. Her face wasn't covered by makeup either—maybe a swipe of mascara and some lipstick. Her posture, though, was uninviting. She seemed rigid and uptight, based on the tight smile plastered on her face.

"So seriously, what are you doing here?" Logan asked him.

Harrison stared at him. "I'm working security for a job. I'm not stalking you, Logan."

Logan rolled his eyes. "I know that. It just seems weird."

"Are you embarrassed by me?"

Before Logan could answer, Emily was back and Dr. Davis and the woman were gone.

"So what do you do?" Emily asked, her hand back on Harrison's arm.

He noticed how Logan didn't seem to care that his date was attempting to flirt with him.

"I work in security," he said.

"Like a cop?" she asked, batting her eyelashes.

"Something like that."

"Well, we're meeting up with some friends after this is over if you want to join us," Emily said. "I can't believe I didn't know Logan Williams had a brother."

"He wouldn't be interested," Logan said.

Logan was right; Harrison had zero interest in getting together with Logan and his friends. It sounded more painful than staffing this lackluster event.

"I should get back to my work. Good to meet you, Emily. Logan."

"See you around!" Her voice was cheerful. She clearly

wasn't acknowledging the fact that Logan was glaring at Harrison.

Harrison walked off. He would not grovel at Logan's feet to get him to forgive him for what had happened in the past. Hopefully, he would make things up to his brother someday, but tonight he needed to make sure nothing went wrong. His company couldn't afford any more bad press.

He finished a lap around the ballroom when he saw the blonde again. She was sitting at a table by herself. He had a sudden urge to go over and talk to her, but knew it was a stupid idea. If Logan had any interest in her, he wouldn't want to see Harrison anywhere near her. Plus, she'd probably freeze him solid with the ice queen vibes she was giving off. No, he'd be wasting his time, and he had more important matters to attend to.

"Julianne," he heard someone say to her before they walked over and kissed her cheek.

For a brief second she looked up and her eyes met Harrison's. She gave him a fleeting smile before she turned back to the other woman at the table. He would have thought he'd imagined it, except he noticed her look at him again, her cheeks ever so slightly pinker than they had been before.

Julianne. He couldn't know why, but he had a feeling he would be seeing her again.

1

Julianne was always on time. It was one of the things her attendings always commented on in rotation reviews. But today she was ridiculously late for her weekly running club. Work had gone late, then someone had a flat tire in the middle of rush hour, and now she was a good fifteen minutes behind. Her group would probably already be running and she'd just have to go by herself, which, in her mind, defeated the purpose of even being there. Besides wanting to train for a half marathon, which she hadn't even gotten around to registering for, she'd joined the club because she needed to meet some friends who weren't up to their corneas in medicine.

She noticed a nearby parking spot on the busy, tree-lined street that circled around Lake Bde Maka Ska. Julianne quickly snagged the spot and pressed the power button on her Lexus GX, courtesy of her father. She was still dressed in her green hospital scrubs, so she awkwardly wiggled her pants off in the front seat of her car before pulling on her black Lululemon leggings. She looked around outside before

taking off her shirt. She wasn't a prude, but she didn't want to
flash anyone. When she was satisfied that she was alone she
quickly replaced her T-shirt bra and scrub shirt with her
white sports bra and a gray tank top. She pulled her long,
honey-blonde hair back into a low ponytail before grabbing a
light jacket and hopping out of the car.

Her socked feet hit the cold pavement below—being late
really didn't suit her. She shoved her sneakers on before
locking the door and jogging off toward the 32nd Street
Beach. She felt all the tension leave her body when she
spotted Katie, Molly, and Lucy stretching near the rest of the
group.

Their running club consisted of about fifteen runners
who met on a jogging trail that circled around a popular lake
in the Uptown neighborhood of Minneapolis, Minnesota.
She'd joined the running club during freezing January
temperatures, and the March air, while still cool, was
welcoming.

She'd met Molly and Katie on her first day. Their athletic
ability was similar to hers, which meant they were all in
decent shape and could run without being winded, but they
weren't exactly sprinting ahead of everyone. Molly was a stay-
at-home mom to a toddler and a new baby. She had curly
brown hair she always wore in a topknot. She didn't seem to
be able to have a conversation that didn't involve babies or
poop or her favorite, poopy babies. Katie, a pretty, peppy
blonde, was a marketing manager at Target and spent "literally all of her time there." Her words, not Julianne's. So while
Julianne had been glad to meet the two women right away,
she was thrilled when Lucy showed up the following week.

Lucy had been a good twenty minutes late her first day.

This normally would have bothered Julianne, but she couldn't help but feel bad for her. She was dressed horribly for running in January—no gloves, no earmuffs, and her leggings were so thin you could see a hint of white skin underneath. Julianne had reached into her pocket, pulling out an extra pair of gloves she'd forgotten the week before and offered them to the newcomer.

"Here," Julianne said. "You'll want these."

Lucy grinned at her from behind her choppy, chocolate-brown bob and quickly shoved her hands into the gloves.

She'd learned Lucy was a freelance photographer. She took pictures of babies, families, weddings, and other adorable Instagram-worthy shots. Lucy was a few years younger than Julianne, who had just turned twenty-seven. There was something about Lucy that reminded Julianne of her sister Ella, which gave her an immediate soft spot in Julianne's heart. Julianne and Lucy had gotten together for drinks the following week and had quickly become good friends.

She'd actually become the first friend Julianne had made in years, since she had a strict policy about not fraternizing with people from work. She avoided all social outings with her fellow residents; she wanted there to be a separation between her work and personal lives. She knew all too well how they could easily become intertwined, and she was determined to not let her career, albeit her dream one, rule her whole life.

"Hey, Jules!" Lucy grinned as she jogged up to them. "You're never late—we thought maybe the hospital held you hostage."

"Basically," she replied.

Julianne was a second-year general surgery resident. Her hours were long, and the call was brutal. Training for a half marathon felt insane, especially with her hours, but she needed motivation to run. She'd learned long ago how therapeutic running could be.

Their running coach began announcing the day's run around the lake, but Molly and Katie's conversation snagged her attention.

"Yeah, it's super scary," Katie said.

"What?" Julianne asked.

"Didn't you see on the news?" Molly asked. "A girl was out running, and she's gone missing."

"Really? Like, around here?" Julianne rarely had time to check the news. Most of the time, she was lucky if she remembered to brush her teeth.

"Yeah, like five miles from here. It's really freaky," Molly said. "My husband won't even let me outside to run on my own anymore. Apparently, her Apple watch showed she was on Highway 103, and then all traces of her disappeared."

"Hmm," Julianne said, noticing Lucy's attention had strayed. She was looking at Theo, the crazy hot guy in their running club. She was pretty sure he had a girlfriend, but Lucy was a flirt, and it didn't seem to matter to her.

"Anyway, just be careful," Molly said.

Besides talking about babies and poop, Molly also liked to worry. Julianne didn't plan to make a habit of running alone on deserted roads, but she would not stop going outside. Molly and her husband lived right in Uptown, for crying out loud. No one was going to take her.

"How was your trip?" Julianne asked Lucy as they ran

ahead of Molly and Katie to make room for a woman and her two dogs coming toward them.

"Good," she replied, looking off across the lake.

When she didn't add anymore, Julianne found herself slightly snubbed at her short answer. Lucy must have noticed because she quickly smiled. "Sorry, I'll tell you more later. It's—"

Julianne cut her off. "Yeah, of course. Don't worry about it!"

They had become close over the past few months, but there was a lot Julianne didn't know yet about Lucy. Lucy had a tendency to go from friendly to closed off quickly, and Julianne didn't want to push her.

She changed the subject. "I saw you watching Theo."

Lucy laughed. "His calves, Jules! I just can't."

They both laughed as they continued on, trying to save their breath for the four miles they had ahead.

"Want to meet up Wednesday to run?" Lucy asked. "I was hoping to get in an extra run each week if I'm actually going to do this half."

The group was currently meeting Mondays and Fridays, and Julianne also knew she should run more if she wanted to complete thirteen miles in a couple of months. "Yeah, that sounds great."

"Three?"

"Yes, let's do it."

When her run was over, Julianne drove over to her father's house. She'd promised she'd come over for dinner, and if she went home to shower, she wouldn't make it in time since his new house was on this side of town. She knew he might not appreciate her sweaty workout clothes attire for dinner, but at least she was showing up.

His new house was way too large, but gorgeous. She walked up to the door and knocked. His girlfriend's small white dog began yapping. Julianne took a deep breath.

"Julianne!" the woman said. "So glad you could make it! Please come in."

Julianne walked in, stepping back to avoid the hug she knew Lauren would try to give her. She felt her hands clench briefly. Julianne had met Lauren on several occasions now, and she wasn't a fan. She was fifteen years younger than Julianne's father, and she tried to overcompensate every time Julianne was around.

"Hi, Lauren," she muttered as the white dog jumped on her legs.

"Sorry about Miss Muffet," Lauren said. "You know how she is."

Julianne just gave her a brief, forced smile before walking past her. She couldn't imagine how her father could stand someone who named their dog "Miss Muffet."

"Hello, Julianne." her father's deep voice bellowed from the kitchen.

Julianne found her father sautéing something on top of his five-burner La Cornue range. It surprised her to see her father cooking; he had definitely never done that when she was growing up. If her mom had ever been busy, it was always takeout or delivery. Richard Davis was entirely too busy to be bothered with domestic tasks. Her dad was a world-renowned gastroenterologist, the CEO of his hospital, and completely lacked all skills required for being a husband and a father.

"You cook?" She looked down into the pan in front of him. It didn't smell like it was burning, so there was that.

"Oh, yes!" Lauren exclaimed, walking up to him and wrapping her arms around his waist. "We took so many cooking classes together on our trip to France."

"I'm surprised you find the time," Julianne said, taking a seat at the island bar. Julianne would bet her life that her dad didn't normally do this when she wasn't around. This was for show. He was a workaholic that cared about two things: himself and his career. She'd known him too long to expect him to change. "What did you want to talk about?"

She'd just seen him a week ago at the fundraiser, so she didn't see why they couldn't have talked then.

"Actually, we both want to talk to you," Lauren said, coming over. Her white veneers gleamed under her pink lipstick.

Julianne stared at her father. "Are you getting married? Is she pregnant? Oh god, please tell me she's not pregnant."

He stared back at her. "Could you please be a little more respectful, Julianne?"

Julianne sighed. "I don't think that's the kind of relationship Lauren and I are ever going to have."

Lauren placed an unwanted hand on her arm. "I'm not pregnant, but your father and I are moving."

Julianne looked back and forth between them. There was something going on that she wasn't understanding.

"Okay?" she asked. "But didn't you just buy this place?"

"We're planning to move to Washington. Where Lauren's family is from," her dad said.

Julianne shook her head; she couldn't be hearing him right.

"But . . . your job? You've worked your whole life to be the CEO at your hospital."

He nodded. "I know, but it's important to Lauren that we be closer to her family, and I think maybe it's time for a change."

Julianne was at a loss for words. Her father had spent his entire life ignoring his family so he could work more. She couldn't fathom how he could now let that all go for a woman he'd only known for a year. He could have taken a break when her sister, Ella, had gotten sick. He could have taken a break when she'd died. He could have taken a break when her parents' marriage began falling apart. But he had done none of those things. He'd wanted to be the CEO. He'd wanted to be some kind of surgical god. And so that was what he'd done.

"Unbelievable," she said, hopping down from the bar stool. "I don't think I'm hungry. I should really get home."

He stopped stirring. His face was stoic; an expression she knew all too well.

"Stop it. This isn't an insult to you, Julianne," he said, his voice raising only slightly.

"Actually, it is." She stared at him and felt a brief shudder when she saw her own eyes looking back.

Anger swelled inside her. She wanted to shout everything in her head, but she refrained. It wasn't worth it. *He* wasn't worth it. He was her father, and he was one of the reasons she'd wanted to become a doctor in the first place, but he hadn't been her role model in a long time. She wanted so badly to have Ella to go to. Ella was the one person in the entire world who would have understood.

Julianne hurried out of the house, slamming the door

behind her. Her father wouldn't follow her out. He would tell her he didn't do dramatic, but really he avoided feelings at all costs. She understood. She didn't like to talk about her feelings either, but she could at least acknowledge it was a flaw. Her dad mistakenly considered it a strength in both of them.

2

J ulianne stifled a yawn as she stepped out of her car Wednesday morning, a gray thermos in one hand and her bag in another. She shouldn't even be tired; she'd gotten more than enough sleep. She had been getting up at 4:00 a.m. for the last few years, and it had become her routine. She took the parking garage elevator down to the street level before taking a slow drink of her hot coffee as she waited for the crosswalk signal to appear.

"What up, Davis?"

She recognized his voice with no need to turn around. Julianne held back an eye roll. It really was too early for Logan Williams. They weren't friends, so she ignored him. Logan gave her a lopsided grin before running across the street, not caring that the blinking orange hand was saying to not walk.

She went to the cafeteria when she made it inside the hospital. The smell of eggs and syrup wafted around her, compelling her to order both scrambled eggs and a slice of French toast before sitting down at a table. A TV played in the room's corner—everyone seemed to be looking at it, so she glanced in its direction and didn't notice Logan approaching her table.

"Shitty, huh?" he asked, pulling up a chair.

Apparently he thought they were friends. It wasn't that she disliked Logan, but if there was an award for most popular and charming resident in her year, it would be him.

"Is that about that missing girl?" she asked.

He nodded, shoving a big bite of his scrambled eggs into his mouth. "It's been a week now. If I was her family, I can't say I'd hold out too much hope."

"Hey, Logan," Emily Mitchell said, approaching Julianne's table, which was quickly becoming not hers at all. She would have to start eating breakfast at home if she wanted some peace and quiet.

Emily flipped her perfectly curled brown locks behind her back as she took a seat next to Logan. Her chair was practically touching his. Julianne noticed Logan glance at Emily's breasts. She was fairly certain Emily noticed too, but didn't seem to mind. Truthfully, there probably weren't too many women who would complain if they caught Logan checking them out. He had an athletic build and was on the verge of being considered tall—just shy of six feet. Somehow his sandy brown hair was tousled just the right way, every day. He had ridiculously blue eyes, and he looked really damn good in scrubs. She'd heard rumors that he'd hooked up with his fair share female med students, some female residents, and even one anonymous attending. Julianne didn't really believe that last one, but Logan certainly had a reputation. So Emily could keep flipping her hair at him all she wanted; Julianne had no desire to get Logan's attention.

"That poor girl," Emily said. "My mom has been freaking out about it."

Julianne cut into her French toast, taking a large bite. She tended to eat quickly. As a resident, she rarely had time for long meals.

"What about you, Julianne?" she asked.

Julianne looked up at her, her mouth full. The food muffled her reply. "What about me?"

"Does it freak you out to go running now?"

She shook her head. "No, why should it? I just run around my neighborhood or with a group."

Emily seemed satisfied by her answer, so she turned her attention back to Logan. "What does your brother have to say?"

Logan shot Emily a look that Julianne wasn't quite sure how to interpret. Julianne didn't know really anything about Logan's family. Logan had completed his undergrad and medical school in Wisconsin, but she'd heard his family was actually from Louisiana. He had just a hint of an accent when he spoke, so she assumed it had been a while ago. Unlike Logan, she had known Emily before their residency because both of their parents had also attended medical school together, and they'd been seeing each other at functions for years.

Julianne's pager went off before anyone could say anything else. It was the ER.

"Duty calls," she muttered, taking the last bite of her food before grabbing her plate and putting it on the trash vestibule.

Julianne walked into the ER and found Dr. Cavernash waiting for her.

"Hey, Dr. Davis, thanks for coming so quickly," he said. "This patient is a thirty-five-year-old male who was in a car accident and sustained significant trauma to the abdomen, resulting in a diaphragm injury and large intestine herniation. He is hemodynamically unstable with an acute abdomen."

Julianne nodded. "Is the patient intubated? Are there any other injuries?"

"Yes, we intubated him and placed two large bore IVs that are wide open," he replied. "He has abdominal bruising and possible internal bleeding."

Julianne walked into the patient's room where a nurse was changing the patient's IV fluids. She took his vitals before pressing on his stomach, feeling the telltale signs of peritonitis. She grabbed the phone on the terminal—it was time to page her attending physician. It was officially going to be a long day when she had to go to the OR before 5:00 a.m.

The surgery that morning had taken several hours, followed by another extensive case from a gunshot wound. By the time Julianne finished her afternoon rounds, she had just enough time to get home to change before her run with Lucy.

Julianne had a one-bedroom condo just west of downtown. Admittedly, it was nicer than her residency salary afforded her, but so were her car and her clothes. Her father hadn't severed their ties financially, and she'd always lived a certain lifestyle. She'd grown up that way. But lately she wondered if she would be better off not accepting help from her father. She hated feeling like she owed so much to him: her medical education, her rent, her car.

It was unseasonably warm, so Julianne had worn leggings and just a T-shirt for her run with Lucy. They'd decided last night to meet at Lake Harriett. Julianne didn't see Lucy's car as she pulled up, but she wasn't surprised.

The warm weather had attracted a swarm of runners and walkers. After stretching and doing a quick warm up of lunges and jumping jacks, she glanced at her Apple watch. Lucy was now fifteen minutes late. After another five minutes, she sent her a text but didn't get a reply. When it finally appeared Lucy wasn't coming, Julianne ran the three-mile loop of the lake on her own before heading home.

On Friday at running club, Julianne spotted Katie and Molly right away. Lucy was once again not there. It was still early, but she felt uneasy. She hadn't heard from Lucy at all since they were supposed to meet for their run on Wednesday. Julianne remembered Lucy's vague response about the vacation she'd taken and wondered if maybe she was avoiding talking to her about it. Julianne suspected the vacation had been with a guy, but Lucy didn't always share personal details. She honestly couldn't care less if Lucy didn't want to tell her any more about it. It just seemed odd that she hadn't even replied to her text.

"No Lucy?" Julianne asked them.

Molly shook her head. "Not yet."

Julianne tried to warm up but felt distracted. She noticed Theo was missing today as well. Could Theo have been the mystery man Lucy had gone on a trip with?

Their coach informed them they were doing *fartleks* that day, which was a Swedish term for the freaking worst, or better known as speed play. Basically, it was a mix of jogging and sprinting. When Julianne had been in better shape, she'd loved the challenge of a sprint, but right now they made her lungs burn and her quads scream.

After her run, Julianne got into her car, hitting the phone on her car dashboard and scrolling down for Lucy's number. The phone went straight to voicemail.

"Dammit, Lucy," she muttered.

Julianne knew she should go home, but her conscience urged her to go to Lucy's apartment to make sure nothing was wrong.

It took her about ten minutes to get to Lucy's building. It was usually tricky to find a parking spot at Lucy's apartment, so she was grateful to find one right out front. She scanned the area for Lucy's red Honda Accord, but saw nothing.

Julianne touched a button on the panel next to the door that buzzed Lucy's apartment but, as expected, no answer came. A young couple opened the main door just seconds later. Julianne smiled at them politely before quickly entering into the door behind them. She ascended the steps two at a time before walking down the hall and arriving at 208.

Julianne knocked twice before tentatively twisting the door knob. She hoped it was locked so she wouldn't have to go inside. She was nervous to see what she'd find. To be honest, while she knew Lucy decently well, there was still a lot she didn't know. She didn't know where she'd grown up. She knew nothing about her family; Lucy had just mentioned her mom once or twice in passing. She knew a couple of Lucy's friends, but they seemed to be more like acquaintances than close friends. While Lucy came off as being extremely extroverted, she kept her private life just that—private.

The door opened easily, and Julianne hurried inside. She shut it quietly behind her before looking around. She breathed a sigh of relief to see it hadn't been robbed, at least upon first glance everything appeared to be neatly in place.

Lucy's entire apartment was about six hundred square feet. While small, it was welcoming, with art plastered on every open inch of wall. Julianne appreciated art and design, but her brain didn't function how Lucy's did when it came to it. Just like Ella. Ella had passed away from cancer when she was just twelve years old. But Julianne knew Ella would never have wanted to follow their father's footsteps in medicine. Ella had been wonderfully artistic, more creative than Julianne could ever be.

Julianne approached Lucy's bedroom and slowly pulled open the door to look inside. She had been to Lucy's apartment several times but had not seen inside her room. It was small, with less art than the main apartment, and a double bed underneath a bay window. There were clothes strewn across her bed and dresser. Julianne had a feeling this wasn't a sign of a robbery. Maybe Lucy was one of those people who always had clothes thrown around their room, again like Ella. For her own part, Julianne was slightly neurotic with her closet organization.

She left her bedroom, scanning around the apartment again, and spotted a calendar on the fridge with handwritten notes scribbled on most of the dates. She glanced at the entry from last Wednesday—*Run with J!*

Lucy had definitely been planning to run with her. She glanced at her schedule for Tuesday—*Shoot with the Bently's @ 10 a.m., Run @ 7 p.m.* She quickly glanced at the calendar for any other runs Lucy had gone on. She noted several more evening runs in the past month. Lucy had never mentioned those to her.

Julianne had been begging her mind to not go there, but the missing runner appeared, refusing to move out of her vision. There was just no way that could have happened to Lucy—except why not? Lucy wasn't one to pay attention to news; she probably didn't even know about the missing girl to begin with. She had been in her own world when they'd discussed it at running club; she hadn't even commented. Lucy was used to going random places for photo shoots, so she probably wouldn't think twice about running alone somewhere desolate that others might have been more cautious about.

Julianne felt her own heartbeat quicken. Lucy was her friend, first and foremost, but that undeniable feeling that she needed protecting, that she was Ella, flooded over her. She fished her phone out of her back pocket, trying in vain to call her phone again. Still dead. She looked at her calendar to see Lucy's location today. She was supposed to have a photo shoot: *Newborn Alver @ 9 a.m. at Kingston Memorial.*

Julianne's residency was at Kingston Memorial. There was a chance she'd be able to find the Alvers to see if Lucy had come this morning. She glanced at her watch. It was now 7:00 p.m.; she could be there in a half hour.

At the hospital, Julianne swiped her badge to get inside the employee entrance. She found a quiet hallway before jumping onto an empty computer terminal, quickly logging in before anyone could question her. She just needed to find the Alvers' room. As she was finishing writing the room number, she heard Emily's voice behind her.

"Julianne? I didn't think you were on call tonight."

Julianne shook her head. "I . . ."

She was a terrible liar. She hated it.

"I'm not," Julianne said, lowering her voice. "I have a friend who is a photographer, and she was supposed to do some newborn photos here this morning. I'm worried she might be missing, so I wanted to check to see if she came to take the photos."

Emily's jaw went slack. Julianne worried she would scold her for looking up information for personal reasons, but her response surprised her.

"Oh my god. Missing? Like the runner girl?" she asked, pulling a stool up to the computer to sit next to her.

Julianne nodded. She recounted everything that had occurred since Lucy hadn't shown up for their run.

"Wow. Have you gone to the police?"

Julianne looked at her oddly. She hadn't even considered that yet. She assumed her family would need to do something like that, but she didn't even how to get ahold of them.

"Right, of course," Emily said, noticing her expression. "Sorry, I'm super into crime dramas. I guess you should just go chat with the Alvers for now. But . . ."

"Yes?"

"Did you know Logan's brother is a cop?" Emily asked.

"Really?"

She nodded. "He doesn't talk about his family. Like, at all. But it got brought up one time, so now you know."

Julianne nodded, unsure of what Emily expected her to do with this new information. She was about to get up to head to the Alvers' room when Emily spoke again.

"I'm almost done with call, and I was planning on

meeting up with the gang after at Ernie's bar. I'm sure Logan will be there if you wanted to see if his brother could help."

Julianne regretted how much she'd already told Emily about Lucy. She had no intention of involving Logan Williams in this.

"I think I'll pass."

Emily shrugged and grabbed a stack of folders on the desk before walking off.

Julianne took off toward the birthing wing. She flashed her badge at the front desk. The nurse at the front desk gave her street clothes a once-over but didn't comment. The Alvers' door was slightly ajar, so she knocked lightly before going in.

The mom laying in the hospital bed gave her a tentative smile. She was nursing her tiny infant. Her husband sat in the chair in the corner of the room, slumped over in sleep.

"Hi," Julianne said, walking over slowly. "I'm Julianne, I'm so sorry to bother you . . ."

"Are you the lactation consultant?" she asked.

She shook her head. "No, I'm actually your photographer Lucy's assistant."

Recognition lit up in her eyes.

"Oh!" the mom exclaimed. "We were so sad she didn't show up today. I tried calling her and left a message and never heard back. You could have just called—you really didn't need to come in person."

Julianne's stomach dropped. Even if she had been expecting this answer, it didn't make her any less nervous. Her face felt hot, and she wanted to run out of the room.

"I . . ." she began, but faltered. "We just wanted to apologize. I was already visiting another family at the hospital. Lucy will be in touch."

The mom gave her a quizzical look and appeared to be about to speak, but Julianne quickly exited the room.

Julianne thought about Emily's suggestion about reaching out to Logan. It seemed crazy. The chance of him being able to help her was slim at the very least, but she had to do something. She was sensible to a fault, and it made her feel that this fear was justified. And that alone was what was going to force her to get in her car and head to Ernie's.

After stopping home to change quickly out of her running clothes, Julianne stepped into Ernie's. It smelled like both popcorn and stale beer. It was dim, but she noted the vintage beer signs plastered all over the walls. She stood behind a few people waiting near the host stand to show their IDs. She tried to look around them to see if she could spot anyone she knew from her year, hopefully Emily, but it was crowded from being a busy Friday night.

She spotted Neil Hutchinson toward the back of the bar. They'd just finished a cardiothoracic surgery rotation together, and he seemed nice enough. She flashed her ID at the muscled bouncer before she began walking over to Neil, but stopped when she heard a familiar voice.

"Can I get you anything to drink, Davis?"

She paused, turning around slowly. Logan grinned at her. His teeth were extraordinarily white. Her immediate reaction was to put her walls up and have a quip to reply with, but instead she forced a smile. "Sure."

He moved over from his spot at the bar so she would have

room to stand next to him. "Are you a beer or wine girl?" he asked, his eyes searching hers. "Wait, let me guess. White . . ."

Julianne interrupted him before she lost her ability to pretend to be nice. "I'll take a beer."

She didn't love beer, but she didn't hate it. She actually would have preferred a nice glass of sauvignon blanc, but she didn't feel like proving him right.

He nodded at the bartender who was coming toward them.

"Two Grain Belts," he said before turning to her. "It's a light one, good for someone who really prefers white wine."

She'd had Grain Belt before. It wasn't at all what someone who enjoyed a nice glass of white wine would like. She raised an eyebrow but didn't call him out.

"Is figuring people out one of your talents?"

"So I've heard." He was still smiling at her, the corners of his eyes crinkled. It was unnerving.

"Well, joke's on you, because I love light beer."

Logan laughed, a real one from his stomach. Julianne felt a small, real smile creep over her face.

"Touché," he replied, handing her the beer the bartender had just sat down. "I'm not going to lie, Davis. I'm pretty shocked to see you out."

"I go out," Julianne replied. "Just not with people from work."

That wasn't entirely true. She really didn't go out much at all. She'd never been one to go to bars or clubs.

"Because you're too good for us," he stated.

Her mouth dropped open a bit. "What? No."

"It seems like it," Logan said. "Just so you know."

Unsure of how to respond, she took a sip of her beer. It

wasn't terrible. Watery, but mostly it tasted like every other beer she'd ever drank.

Logan eyed her curiously. "I think honesty is the best policy."

She'd give him that—she did, too. But she would not admit to thinking she was better than everyone else; she'd never thought that. She had simply promised herself to have at least one part of her life not revolve around medicine, unlike her father. But this wasn't exactly something she felt like explaining to Logan. "Okay, well if I'm being honest then, it's true. I don't love beer."

Before she could stop him, he'd waved down the bartender.

"No, please stop," she muttered, trying to push down his hand before the bartender noticed.

Logan nodded over at Pete Ambrose, who had just arrived and was standing next to them, waiting for a drink. "He'll drink it, right, Pete? Just get something you'll actually like. We finally got you out. I'd hate to ruin it so soon."

"I'd never turn down a drink from Dr. Williams." Pete smirked, followed by a wink.

She wasn't sure how to read that wink. Was he referring to her accepting a drink from Logan? She hoped he didn't think they were there together. Pete was attractive—not on the same level as Logan—but he had twinkling brown eyes and a nice smile. She had no intention of dating him, but she just didn't want him getting the wrong impression. She was definitely *not* one of Logan's ladies.

The bartender stood in front of them, waiting for her order. Julianne quickly ordered a glass of wine. Her cheeks flushed in embarrassment when he handed it over.

Pete was already walking over to the table where Neil and a few others were congregating, so she followed him over before Logan could say anything else. She needed to drink her glass of wine before gathering up the courage to ask about his brother. It felt sort of dumb now that she was here. Julianne had nothing concrete to go off of regarding Lucy missing. But she was already here, so she'd try to make the most of it.

"Julianne! You made it!" Emily said loudly, sounding as though she'd somehow already had a few drinks.

Pete slung his arm around Julianne's shoulders, pushing her up closer to the group. "I believe this girl's first night at Ernie's deserves to be celebrated."

Julianne rolled her eyes. Logan cleared his throat behind them, and Pete dropped his arm, stepping aside so that Logan could squeeze in between them. Julianne wondered if he'd done that to stand closer to her, or if he'd just wanted to get into the circle. She leaned toward the latter.

"I'm totally to blame." Emily grinned, raising her hand. "So don't try to take any credit, Pete."

Pete raised up his hands up. "I'm sure if anyone would try to take credit, it's this one. He's already buying her drinks."

Julianne noticed Emily look curiously at Logan, but he didn't return her gaze.

Logan seemed unfazed by Pete's comment, turning his attention toward Julianne. "Regret showing up yet?"

"Only a little," she replied.

Everyone seemed to have broken off into separate conversations. Julianne thought about trying to get over to Emily, but Logan had her blocked.

Logan gazed at her while taking a drink of her beer. "So what's your deal?"

"My deal?"

"Yeah, none of us really know anything about you. Does your boyfriend keep you locked in a cave, maybe? That was Neil's guess."

Julianne let out a small snort. "No, no cave."

"Handcuffed to a bed then?"

"No cave, no handcuffs, no boyfriend," she said, looking down and taking a long sip of her wine.

A smile danced on his lips. "Good to know. So basically you run, work, and sleep?"

"No. Like I told you before, I go out, just not with people from work."

He was mostly right, though. She did run, work, and sleep. She occasionally found time to go out with friends. Lucy had gotten her out more recently than she'd been out in years. Although it was questionable if that was a good thing or not. Julianne much preferred a quiet night in than the horrible hangover she'd gotten the last time she went out with Lucy.

"So what changed your mind?" he asked, glancing over at Emily who was chatting with Neil.

Julianne's wine was close to gone, but she hadn't made up her mind yet on if she wanted to say anything to Logan about Lucy. Before she had a chance to answer, Pete had once again hoisted his arm around her shoulders, sloshing his beer so that it splashed on the floor. "You guys down for a good old game of shuffleboard?"

Emily threw her hand up and walked over. "I'm in. Logan, you on my team?"

He nodded. "You in, Julianne?"

"I call Julianne on my side," Emily said, grabbing her hand.

"Em, you know we love you, but you're a terrible teacher. And we already know Pete's a lousy player, so I think we should give their team a fair shot," Logan said.

Emily gave Logan a frosty look. Julianne knew this time she hadn't missed it. Emily had a thing for Logan. Julianne wished she could make it clear to Emily she herself had zero interest in Logan. And honestly, she had a hard time believing Logan would really have any interest in her that way. Julianne knew she was decent looking—she had thick, long blonde hair. If she let it dry naturally, it had a wave, but she typically kept it blow-dried straight. She was five-foot-six and had a slim hourglass figure. But unlike Emily, she didn't wear much makeup, and while her clothes were nice, they weren't sexy. Her classic socializing outfit, which she had thrown on tonight, consisted of black leggings, a light blue Madewell chambray shirt, and some plain black flats from J. Crew. Emily, on the other hand, was fully made up and had on some cute skinny black jeans, black pumps, and a skintight, cleavage-revealing red top.

"Fine," Emily muttered, her mouth pressed in a hard line as Pete walked over to stand on the other end of the shuffle-board next to her.

Julianne had no clue how to play, but it was apparent you didn't stand next to your actual partner. She wondered if Logan was trying to avoid Emily.

"So, have you ever played this?" he asked as they reached the end of the shuffleboard.

Julianne shook her head.

"These are weights," he said, picking up a disk. "You need to slide these all over to the other end of the board, trying to get into the highest scoring area. Whichever team has the most points at the end of each round gets the points. We play to twenty-one."

Logan grabbed one of the red weights and slid it down the table.

"Now," he said, handing her one, his hand brushing hers. "You want to either try to knock mine off, or get your disk in a higher-scoring place on the board."

Her blue disk slid down the table before knocking into his, sending into falling off the scoreboard.

Pete threw his arm up across the table and gave a small holler.

"And now that's what we call beginner's luck." A corner of Logan's mouth lifted. He slid another disk down, landing in a two-point area.

Julianne followed suit, landing her disk further in the three-point area. "We'll see about that."

Logan's eyes lit up. He threw an arm around her waist, pulling her in closer to him before whispering, "You're cute when you're competitive."

Julianne concentrated on the game. She didn't want to flirt with him, and even if she did, she really didn't know how. At the hospital she could take on any male; she wasn't intimidated. After all, she was used to dealing with Richard Davis, but she was rusty at interacting with the opposite sex when it came to dating. Not that she didn't enjoy sex—she did—but it was the game that came before sex that she didn't like. Meeting guys in college had been so easy. Once medical school started, not so much. The fact she was a doctor intimi-

dated most men, and those who weren't were doctors themselves. Like Logan. Exactly who she *wasn't* looking for.

When they finished their round, Pete and Emily began.
Pete turned out to be great, and they won the game in just
four rounds. Pete and Emily walked over to their end as they
all headed back to the bar to get refills.

"Nice job, teammate," Pete said, walking in stride with her
so that Logan and Emily had to fall behind. It had become
even more crowded than when Julianne had first gotten
there, and there wasn't much space to approach the bar any
longer.

"Thanks." She smiled at him.

Pete grabbed her hand, pulling her up to a clearing at the
bar where a couple had just left. "You were drinking wine,
right?"

She nodded, although she was feeling uncomfortable
with having all of her drinks bought for her. She had the urge
to turn around and see if Logan and Emily were there, but
she didn't. She started down the bar, trying to refocus on
everything. She had a sudden pang of guilt that she was out
having actual fun when Lucy was missing, possibly abducted.
This wasn't what she had come here for, but that one wine
hadn't given her the courage to ask Logan anything. It was
simply making her forget. She tentatively accepted the glass
of white wine Pete handed to her as he helped guide her out
of the mass of people behind them, waiting to steal their spot.

"I'm glad you came out tonight," Pete said, taking a sip of
his beer. "You don't seem so uptight. I mean, shit, sorry, that
wasn't a good way to phrase it. I just meant that you seem
pretty cool outside of the hospital."

Julianne rolled her eyes. It wasn't the first time someone

had referred to her as uptight. She pointed toward Emily and Logan, who were chatting at the bar.

"Are those two a thing?" Julianne asked.

"If you mean, do they screw? Yes," Pete replied. "But they're not like boyfriend-girlfriend. Logan doesn't really do relationships."

"Ah," she replied, nodding her head like she totally understood. But honestly, she always thought it was such a cop-out when people claimed they didn't do relationships. She didn't really do relationships because she hadn't found the right person yet. But that didn't mean she didn't want one.

"Any other juicy gossip you can give me about anyone else?" she asked Pete.

He laughed, filling her in on who else was sleeping with whom, or dating whom, or who had previously slept with whom. She took a few more sips of her wine, staring over at Logan and Emily, who were walking over toward them.

Julianne jolted upright—a girl with short brown hair caught her eye. She spun to look at her, but it wasn't Lucy. She suddenly found herself barely able to breathe; her face felt hot and her hands clammy.

"I think I need to go," Julianne said, handing her glass to Pete. "Sorry, I . . ."

She ran out of the bar, letting the cool air rush over her. She relaxed her head against the rough cement exterior. The cold against her cheeks felt so good though that she didn't care.

"Julianne?"

Julianne's body tensed before she opened her eyes. Logan stood in front of her, a line etched between his brows. "Are you okay? Did Pete say something? He can be an asshole sometimes."

She shook her head. "No, of course not. Honestly, go back inside. I'm fine."

He raised an eyebrow. "Most fine people don't run out of a bar."

She sighed, raising her arms up in defeat. "Here's the truth, Logan. I came here tonight to talk to you, but I realized it was a stupid idea, and just . . . please go back inside."

His expression remained puzzled.

"Emily told me your brother's a cop, and I just need some help, so I thought . . ."

His jaw clenched. "Are you in some kind of trouble?"

She shook her head. "No, it was dumb. I'm sorry, I need to go."

Logan turned around to walk back inside, but spun around, burying his hands in his hair. "My brother's bad news. You'd be better off finding help elsewhere."

Before she could ask what he meant, he turned around again, this time going back into the bar. Julianne stood alone, shivering, baffled at Logan's words. She couldn't imagine why Emily would have told her to ask about his brother if he was, in Logan's words, bad news.

Julianne took a deep breath. She would go home, get some rest, and head back to Lucy's apartment tomorrow and see if there was information there she could find to contact her parents. She didn't need Logan or anyone's help.

4

Julianne woke up Saturday morning with her pillow damp. She wiped at her mouth, embarrassed at her drool. She always drooled at night when she was stressed about something. She sat up, pushing her hair back away from her face. A lot of her natural wave had returned through the night, so she tied it in a ponytail before throwing her blanket off.

She was nervous about going back to Lucy's today. Even though she was worried someone might have taken her while she was running, there was also a chance Lucy was involved in something else that had nothing to do with that. And what if someone else showed up looking for Lucy while Julianne was there? They might think she was to blame. Regardless, Julianne knew she had to find Lucy's parents, and the only way to do that was to go through Lucy's things.

She rubbed her eyes and stared at herself in the mirror. Apparently *tired* would be her look today. There was a knock on her door before she even had time to put a pod in her Keurig machine. She opened the door, naively hoping to see Lucy there. She wasn't prepared to see *him* there instead, and her mouth felt dry when she tried to say his name.

"Logan."

He was wearing a pair of faded denim jeans and a sky-blue Henley shirt that somehow made his already blue eyes bluer. His sandy brown hair looked slightly damp. There was a smirk on his handsome face that made her all too aware of the fact she wasn't wearing a bra under her shirt yet.

"Hi," he said, holding out a small paper bag and a coffee. "Emily knew your address. Can I come in?"

"Can you give me a minute?" she asked, shutting her door part way.

Julianne rushed to her bedroom and replaced her pajamas with her bra, a pair of neatly folded jeans, and a soft gray sweater. She quickly brushed her teeth before walking back to the door and opening it to find Logan leaning against the wall.

"What are you doing here, Logan?"

"You said you needed help," he replied. "And I brought breakfast."

"I don't need help," she said, picking a piece of lint from her sleeve. "Also, I'm not hungry."

A smile tugged at Logan's mouth.

She *was* hungry, but she hoped that if she kept this up, he would go away. Talking about this with him in the light of day was even worse than it had been last night.

"Emily said your friend is missing," he said, his expression soft. "And that it might be connected to that other missing girl?"

She really wished Emily would keep her mouth shut.

"Yes, maybe," she said, folding her arms across her chest. "But you really don't have to worry. I have it figured out."

He nodded, but he appeared to still be holding back a smile.

"So you can go, okay?" Julianne said.

"Listen, I'm not sure why you think you need to put up your defenses against me," he said. "I'm not a bad guy. I promise. I really am here to help."

Julianne paused. She knew she was being unnecessarily standoffish. She reached out and took the white bag he was holding.

"It's a donut from Jack's bakery on Lake," he said. "You'd be crazy to pass it up. I already ate two."

She looked inside. It did look good. She grabbed it out of the bag and took a bite of the white pastry.

She swallowed her bite. "I'm heading to my friend's Lucy's apartment."

"Alright." He rubbed his hands together. "Let's go."

"Are you sure you really have nothing better to do with your time?" she asked wearily, licking some stray powdered sugar from her finger.

Lord knew she didn't want to be doing this on a Saturday. But Lucy was her friend. Julianne wasn't even sure if *she* was Logan's friend.

"I'm sure."

Julianne insisted on driving, so they walked to her car, parked in the attached parking garage. It was underground and heated.

Logan fidgeted with her radio until he landed on a classic rock station. "So about my brother . . . Sorry, I just—well, we don't talk, to be honest."

"Why would Emily tell me to bring him up to you?" she asked.

He grimaced. "Probably to piss me off. She was mad at me the other day. And she knows I hate talking about him."

"Oh." She wondered if Emily had just been using her the whole time to just make Logan angry. But, then again, she filled Logan in on what was actually going on last night, so maybe she was trying to right herself. Julianne decided she'd hold out judgment on Emily until later.

"And just so you know, he's not a cop," he said. "He's run some type of security business or something like that. I really don't know what he does, and I don't want to know."

Julianne raised an eyebrow.

"I told you, he's no good," he replied to her questioning look. "I don't trust that everything he does is on the up and up, if you know what I mean."

"He lives in Minneapolis?" she asked, glancing away from the road and over at Logan for a moment.

Logan avoided her gaze. "Yep."

"You didn't grow up in Minnesota though, right?"

"Baton Rouge," he replied. "My brother and I moved here with our grandparents when I was about eight."

"Are your parents . . . ?"

Julianne turned to look at him again. His expression hardened.

"Alive?" he asked. "My dad died of heart failure about ten years ago. I couldn't tell you about my mom."

She felt a pang of guilt for how she felt about her parents sometimes. Yes, her father was an overworking, overachieving, sometimes pompous asshole, but he was alive. And she had never been abandoned. She was actually fairly close with her mother. She'd gotten pregnant with Julianne right after she'd met Julianne's father when they were both in medical school. Her mom had dropped out to raise her. She was happily remarried now, running a nonprofit to support families affected by childhood cancer.

"Please, no pity, Davis," Logan reproached.

Julianne flushed. "I wasn't—"

"You were," he said. "Everyone does. But let's just leave it at that, okay?"

Julianne nodded. She turned her blinker on to take the exit for Lucy's apartment. "So seriously, why do you want to help me with this?"

"Well, I just felt kind of like a dick after you left, or I left, or whatever last night," he said. "And maybe I'm just trying to be your friend. Fair enough?"

"Sure," she said. "Is Emily okay with us being friends?"

"What?"

"I just . . . I feel like she was giving us these looks when we talked last night . . ."

"Okay, well first off," Logan said, his mouth twisted, "Emily is not my girlfriend, so I'm pretty certain she has no jealous tendencies toward anyone I talk to."

"But you're sleeping with her. So, yeah, she kinda could have those feelings."

"Who said I was sleeping with her?" he asked, his eyes narrowing.

"Pete."

He rolled his eyes, muttering something under his breath. "Pete should mind his own damn business. Anyway, what I was saying was I'm pretty sure Emily knows nothing would ever go on between you and me, so whatever looks you saw last night, you must have misread."

Emily knows nothing would ever go on between you and me. What was the hell was that supposed to mean? Julianne, of course, didn't want anything to go on between them, but she wanted to know why Emily and Logan were both certain of this. She felt her irritation rise and prayed she'd be able to calm it down before something spewed out of her mouth that she'd regret.

"Why?" she asked instead, using her best calm voice.

"Huh?"

Julianne pulled into a parking spot and turned off the car. She pinned Logan with her eyes. "Why does Emily know nothing would ever go on between you and me? You guys think I'm that terrible?"

"What?" Logan asked, confused.

"You said . . ."

"Sorry, I didn't mean anything by it."

Julianne sat silently. He didn't really answer the question.

"I don't think you're terrible, Julianne," he added, breaking the silence. "It's just . . . Emily knows you're not really the type I go after."

She looked over at him again. "You're really burying yourself in a grave, you know that, right?"

He groaned, rubbing his palms into his eyes. "I didn't mean, you're not—Can we just move on from this, please?"

Julianne blew out a breath. "Okay, since you're already in my car, we're going to Lucy's apartment. We're trying to find contact information for her parents. Her door was open when I went yesterday, so let's just be quick. I have no idea if she could be involved with something I don't know about. And I don't want to be involved with anything criminal."

Logan smiled cautiously. "Okay. You're not mad, are you? About what I said?"

Julianne avoided his gaze. "Nope."

She was though. He'd basically just said she wasn't his type, and that Emily knew she wasn't his type. *None of this matters,* she reminded herself. She was here to find Lucy.

To their luck, a box perched open the front door of the building. Once they got to her apartment, she knocked—just in case—and then opened the door. The inside of Lucy's apartment looked the same as it had the day before. It didn't appear anyone had been there.

"Do you know her parents' names?" Logan called out over his shoulder as they sorted through her kitchen drawers.

"No, I think maybe her mom's name was . . . Judy?" she said, trying hard to find the memory of Lucy discussing her. "No, Janice . . ."

"Jana Aldridge?" he asked.

Julianne turned around. He was holding out a piece of mail.

"Yes!" she squealed, grabbing it out of his hands.

It was a birthday card from her parents, with their return address right there in front of her.

"Three hours north in Duluth," he said, tapping it in his hand. "Maybe we should try for a phone number. Or maybe we could find them online somewhere."

"I can manage," Julianne said, grabbing the card from him before shoving it into her bag. "Seriously."

Logan lifted his chin. "But . . ."

"No," she stopped him, putting her hand up. "I came to

get your help because I thought maybe your brother could help in some way I didn't have the knowledge or access to. But this I can do on my own."

"Alright," he replied. "Did you need to look around for anything else while we're here? Like, did you want to try to find a key to lock her door for her?"

It irritated Julianne she hadn't already thought of that. She went back to the drawers they'd been digging through minutes earlier. Just as she was about to open the last drawer, she heard voices approaching the front door, and the sound of Lucy's doorknob turning filled the room.

Before she knew what was happening, Logan grabbed her hand, yanking her into a small coat closet and shut the door. Seconds later, the front door opened and shut. She heard two male voices—no Lucy. The closet was tiny, but with three winter coats and a vacuum cleaner inside, any empty space was almost nonexistent. Her breasts were crushed up against Logan's chest, and she could feel every breath he took. She tried to see Logan's face in the dark, but it was almost impossible. All she could think about was the finger he had up to her lips for silence.

"Check the bedroom," one voice ordered.

Feet thudded away, and then more noise came from the living room. The sound of furniture being moved around filled the air. Julianne's heart pounded. She tried to move her hips to get more space, but it caused something behind her to fall, making a clattering sound behind them. Her breath stopped as she waited for someone to come toward them, but no one did.

"Anything?" the man asked.

"No," the other voice replied. "We should go."

After another two minutes there was a click, and the apartment went silent again.

Julianne felt herself breathe for the first time in five minutes. "What the hell?"

Logan pushed the closet open, and they both tumbled out.

"They were looking for her," he said. "It didn't seem like they took anything."

Julianne had been thinking the same thing. She tried to calm down by telling herself that the men weren't necessarily bad; she was here looking for Lucy too, but something about them didn't sit well with her.

"Listen, if you want," Logan began, "I'll call Harrison."

"Your brother?" she asked, surprised.

"My brother might not be the best person, but I have a feeling whatever's going on with your friend . . . well, I think you're better off not doing this alone."

She considered refusing his help. She would have, had those guys not have shown up, but she was still shaky.

"Fine," she said.

"I have something going on tonight, but maybe . . . maybe we could meet up before, like four? If I can get ahold of him, that is."

She nodded.

"Also, I think we leave the doors unlocked," he said. "If those guys come back and the door's locked . . ."

"Agreed."

They waited a few minutes before leaving and walking back to Julianne's car.

"So is it a date tonight?" she asked as they drove back.

He smirked. "A hang out."

Julianne wondered how many hang outs he went on. She assumed it was a lot.

"Listen, about before, I keep thinking about what I said —" he began.

"Please, Logan, I forgot about it. Let's just let it go."

Logan sighed. "When I said you weren't my type, I meant it as a negative thing about me, not you. You're way too good for me, that's all I meant. So please, don't be mad about that."

Julianne inspected her fingernails. "Okay."

She pulled up to where Logan's car sat and waited for him to get out, but he wasn't moving yet. She could have sworn he was going to say something, but instead he got out of her car, tapping on the top before walking off to his car.

When Julianne got inside her condo, she pulled out her laptop and began searching for any Jana Aldridges in Duluth. Nothing came up that gave Julianne any way to reach her. She couldn't find her on Facebook or anywhere else, really. Maybe Logan's brother would have more information. She should have probed more into why he was bad news, but she didn't really care if he had the resources to help her.

She scanned online for any news on the missing runner, Angela. They were bringing in additional volunteers to help search for her. But so far there weren't any new updates and no suspects. She shivered, wondering if Lucy should be added to the missing persons list. She could just go the police now, but she worried she didn't have enough information. At least, not yet.

5

Julianne and Logan had planned to meet Harrison at a dive bar called the Ave Tav. She had put on a pair of dark skinny jeans, a gray fitted long-sleeve T-shirt, and her black flats. She'd found time to run an iron through her hair so her waves were once again smooth and swiped on some bronzer and mascara before running out the door. She was ten minutes early when she walked into the bar.

It was dim inside, which made it hard to tell if Logan and his brother had arrived yet. She scanned the bar and spotted one lone man who appeared to be too old to be Harrison and a few unoccupied pool tables lining the back wall. There were also five people spread out at the actual bar, but none of them were who she was looking for. Although she had no idea what Logan's brother looked like, she had an idea of what to expect.

Except minutes later, when the Williams brothers walked in the door, she quickly realized Harrison Williams was not at all what she had been expecting. He was undeniably gorgeous. He was tall—an inch or two taller than Logan—

with loose, light brown curls. His eyes were dark brown with thick lashes, and there was just a hint of a five o'clock shadow growing on his strong jawbone. As they walked closer, she could see a faint scar above his left eyebrow. Even with the scar and his muscular physique, he looked more like a model than the troublesome man Logan had told her about. He was dressed in a pair of khaki pants and a black hoodie with a gray denim jacket over it. Logan was more dressed up in a button-down plaid shirt and dark jeans. They were both so undeniably attractive that she felt out of place with them together.

"Hi," she said to Logan, her eyes traveling between them both as she waited for an introduction.

"Hi." Logan smiled at her. "Julianne, this is Harrison. Harrison, Julianne."

Harrison stared at her, his lips slightly pursed but open. "Nice to meet you."

His voice was deep and warm. When she met Harrison's gaze, she thought maybe she'd seen him before, but she couldn't quite place him.

"Why don't you grab a table, Julianne, and we'll be right over?" Logan said while his eyes scanned around the bar.

She nodded and walked over to a table that sat against the wall in the back of the room next to the pool tables. She was looking down at her phone when the chair slid out next to her, and Harrison sat down.

"So," he said, "my brother says you need help tracking someone down."

Julianne nodded. Both his tone and face were so serious he made her nervous. He hadn't cracked even a slight smile since he'd walked in.

"Yes, a friend," she replied as Logan walked up carrying two beers and a small cup filled with white wine.

She noticed Harrison eyeing her cup skeptically, but he didn't comment. She suddenly wished Logan had just gotten her a beer. This didn't seem like the kind of place to ask for wine, as evidenced by the apparent wine glass shortage. But it was nice he'd tried.

Julianne tucked her hair behind her ear. She recounted everything that had taken place from the time Lucy hadn't shown up to run up until now. Harrison watched her as she talked, not nodding, not saying anything at all. When she was done, he sat silently. She wondered if he expected her to say more. Maybe he thought this whole thing was ridiculous.

"You've heard about the missing runner, too, right?" she asked, breaking the silence. "I'm just worried is all."

"You mentioned a vacation she went on," he finally said. "When was the last time you saw her before your last run together?"

Julianne bit her lip, looking at Logan. She hadn't mentioned this to him yet. She hadn't even wanted to remind *herself* of it. But she knew if she wanted help from Harrison, he might need all the information.

"Well . . ." Julianne began, remembering the last time all too well.

Lucy sprawled across Julianne's pure white down comforter. She was dressed in gray tights, a black miniskirt, and a white shirt covered by a cropped gray faux-fur vest. Her dark hair made a stark contrast with the color of the bed.

"So show me your choices," Lucy said as Julianne rummaged through her closet.

Lucy had convinced Julianne to go out with her that night, even though there was a new season of the *Great British Baking Show* on Netflix that she'd been looking forward to watching.

She feared everything in her closet would be terribly boring to Lucy. She had decided years ago to go with a simple wardrobe that let her utilize her time better. She never really had to think about what to wear. Jeans, a plain top, flats. Leggings, a plain top, flats. The colors ranged from white, off-white, gray, dark gray, tan, and black. Her wardrobe was a sea of neutrals.

"This?" Julianne asked, holding out a dress she'd bought for a Christmas party last year. It was a gray sweaterdress that fell just above her knees.

"Oh, did your mom lend you that?" Lucy asked. Before Julianne could retort, Lucy burst out laughing.

Lucy jumped off her bed, skipping to her friend's closet. She stared inside for a few minutes before shooing Julianne out. "Let me try something."

Julianne was skeptical but went over to her bed and grabbed her phone. She'd had a date last night with a guy she'd met online. She thought it had gone well, but she had heard nothing from him yet. Julianne had made the mistake of texting him about an hour ago to ask how his day went and still nothing.

Lucy peeked her head out of the closet. "Jules, stop looking at that!"

She sighed. Lucy had already berated her about waiting

by her phone for a message and for texting him first, but she couldn't help it.

"Ta-da!" Lucy said, coming out of the closet, holding up the remnants of what used to be one of Julianne's favorite skirts.

"Lucy, what?!" she exclaimed, grabbing it out of her hands. It wouldn't even cover her butt. "Did you seriously go in my closet with scissors? Why did you have scissors on you?"

"I can't give away all my secrets." Lucy smiled, her eyes gleaming. "But I knew I might need a little help."

The once knee-length royal blue skirt was now cut into a miniskirt, which actually might be more underwear-length than miniskirt.

"And I found these in a bin!" Lucy announced, tossing a pair of glittery black tights at her.

"These were from a Halloween costume! Lucy, I can't go out in this."

Lucy walked up to her, placing her hands on her shoulders. "Yes, you will. It's time for a whole new Julianne Davis."

"I don't need—"

"Listen, Jules," Lucy said as they sat down on her bed. Julianne held the skirt and tights in her lap, desperate to run away and flush them down the nearest toilet. "I don't think anyone should change because someone else wants them to. So please believe me when I say I don't want you to change for me. But I think . . . I just think you need to try changing for you. And you should start by putting this on."

Part of her knew Lucy was right, but Julianne wasn't sure if she was ready to let go of how she'd always been.

"I need a shirt," Julianne replied. "I'm not wearing my bra out."

"I would if I had your boobs," Lucy said with a wink. She ran back to her closet and tossed a shimmery gray tank top at her. Julianne normally wore a blazer with that top, but she had a feeling Lucy would not let her go out in a blazer tonight.

Julianne tugged up the tights, cursing as she fell over once trying to get them on. Once she had the skirt and shirt on, she turned around, throwing her arms open to give her best ta-da stance.

Lucy clapped. "Now this is how you should have dressed for that date last night."

"So what you're say is . . . less uptight doctor and more floozy doctor?" Julianne laughed.

"You're going to learn to loosen up before I'm done with you. And you don't look like a floozy!"

They'd gone to an art crawl that Lucy had promised her would be "the most fun night ever." They arrived at the first gallery. A woman handed them both a small glass of bubbling champagne as soon as they stepped inside. She gave Lucy a quick air-kiss before greeting the throng of people behind them.

The studio's walls were covered in large canvases featuring glued-on magazine clippings that created words and pictures. Lucy seemed to know several people there because she was busy chatting while Julianne looked around, her finger lightly treading across a large piece in front of her.

"What do you think?" a male voice asked behind her.

She turned around, almost falling over in the heels that Lucy had demanded Julianne wear.

"It's beautiful," Julianne said, a breath coming out of her she hadn't realizing she had been holding in. And she really had meant it.

The man standing there was about her age, maybe a few years older. He reminded her of someone Lucy would be friends with. He was dressed in tight dark jeans and a black shirt that had its sleeves rolled up to show off the colorful tattoos beneath. Dark wired glasses framed his face.

"Alex," he said, holding his hand out to her.

"Julianne," she said with a smile.

Alex was just as beautiful as the art beside him. She could feel her body warm as he watched her closely. Before anyone said anything else, Lucy ran over, throwing her arm around Julianne.

"Alex, stay away." Lucy grinned. "This one's with me."

He gave a quiet laugh. "Ah, a friend of Lucy's. I should be careful."

"Looks like you've got quite a turnout already," Lucy said, and then turned to Julianne. "This is Alex's gallery. What do you think?"

"I love it," Julianne answered without hesitation.

"She's usually much more cynical," Lucy said with a smile. "So if the girl says she loves it, you should be impressed. Plus, she's a doctor."

Julianne rolled her eyes. "I'm just a resident."

"A resident *doctor*," Lucy added. "Anyway, Alex, we should keep going. My glass is empty, and I think it's time to find another."

He laughed. "See you later?"

Lucy nodded and grabbed Julianne's arm, rushing her out of the gallery and into the crisp early spring air. Julianne hadn't finished her drink yet, so she quickly swallowed the whole glass before tossing the plastic cup into a trash can nearby.

"He was totally into you," Lucy said as they walked down the block to the next gallery.

Julianne raised her eyebrow.

"He's like a super successful artist. He's hot, and he's a pretty decent guy. I didn't want you to mess this up," she said with a grin. "No offense."

"We only spoke like two words. You have no idea if he was into me. You're crazy, Lucy," she said, laughing.

Thirty seconds later Lucy's phone chimed and she grabbed it out.

Meet up later at Ethan's. Bring your friend.

"I'm basically always right," Lucy said as they walked into the next gallery.

After four more galleries and four more drinks, Julianne was pretty sure she was drunk, or at least very buzzed. Ethan's was apparently the last gallery, and it was huge. He held an after-party for all the artists, and Lucy was on the list to get in.

Julianne's feet were officially killing her, so she slipped out of her heels, holding them with one hand while juggling the new drink Lucy had pressed into her hands in the other. The champagne had made Julianne's brain deem itself an art aficionado. She circled around the room, staring at paintings as insightfully as she knew how in her state.

"Ah, if it isn't the doctor," a voice spoke behind her.

"That's me," she said, smiling without turning around. It was definitely him. She was nervous he'd found her. Nervous because he was ridiculous good-looking, and she didn't trust herself to not make a complete fool of herself in front of him.

He grabbed the drink out of her hand and set it down on a nearby cocktail table. He pulled her close to him, and she felt her entire body heat up.

"We should get out of here," he whispered in her ear.

Julianne itched to tell him no. At least, that was what Julianne would normally do. But Lucy had begged her to consider being someone else tonight. She saw her reflection in a mirror: her blonde hair was in loose waves over her shoulders, her lipstick was halfway worn off from an evening of drinking, and her cheeks were flushed from the man practically draped around her. The reflection was definitely not the Julianne she'd come to know.

So she resisted her instincts and went back to Alex's loft. His loft was as beautiful as he was, and they'd had great, unabashed sex. She'd woken up the next morning with no regrets, but the feelings of self-consciousness had slowly crept in. They'd taken a shower together that morning, and afterward he'd kissed her and invited her to stay for breakfast. This was when she realized she had no clue anymore if she was supposed to keep being the real Julianne or the fake Julianne. She needed Lucy. She didn't how to navigate the fake Julianne without her, completely sober in the bright light of the morning. So instead of accepting the offer of orange liqueur-soaked French toast and mimosas with fresh-squeezed orange juice, she'd lied that she was on call and had to get to the hospital.

She took an Uber back to her place. Her car was parked at home as Lucy had driven the night before. She called Lucy as the driver pulled away from Alex's loft. Her friend picked up on the second ring.

"Julianne Davis, it is way too early for you to be calling me."

Julianne sighed. "Lucy."

Lucy laughed. "Listen, I can't wait to hear about your night, but I'm actually about to check my luggage."

"Huh?" Julianne asked, confused.

"I'm going on little tropical getaway. I'll tell you more about it when I get back! See you at running club on Monday?"

Julianne wished her well before the phone clicked off. She felt disappointed. She wanted Lucy to bring back the Julianne from last night—but she was afraid she would have to set her aside for now. At least until Lucy returned.

Julianne looked up at both Logan and Harrison, who were listening silently to her story. She wanted to crawl under a table. Maybe she'd given too many details. Based on Logan's face, she knew for sure she had. She could tell he was trying to hold back a smile, but he wasn't succeeding too well.

Harrison, on the other hand, was proving to be unreadable. She wished she'd gotten more background information on him.

"So you've been back to talk to Alex to see if he knows anything, I assume?" Harrison asked.

Julianne looked down at the table, her shoulders slumped. She hadn't. The idea had briefly entered her mind, but she'd told herself that Alex would know nothing and to just let that go. But Harrison was right to ask. She was just too embarrassed to go back there. "No."

"Could he have been one of those guys in her apartment?" Logan asked her.

She shook her head. She knew Alex's voice, and neither of those men were him.

Harrison leaned back in his chair. "I'd say you should start by getting ahold of this guy. I'll work on trying to find a number to get in contact with her parents. Stay out of her apartment from now on."

Julianne nodded. "Alright."

Harrison took a long pull from his beer before setting it down on the table. "If anything feels off or dangerous when you question Alex, call me."

He grabbed Julianne's phone off of the table and began putting his number in. She noticed Logan was about to say something, but didn't.

"Maybe she shouldn't go see Alex alone?" Logan asked.

"No, I'm going there alone," she said before Harrison could agree with Logan's suggestion. It would be awkward enough to see Alex on her own.

"She looks like she can handle herself," Harrison said, looking at her intently.

"Yes, I can," Julianne replied, glaring at Logan.

"Well, college boy, anything else you need help with?" Harrison asked after he downed the rest of his beer. He set it down fairly hard on the table as his focus seemed to shift off of her and onto to Logan.

Logan's nostrils flared slightly as he smirked, taking a drink from his beer. "Nope."

"I really appreciate you coming," Julianne said to Harrison, but he seemed to still be watching Logan.

Logan's phone buzzed on the table, and he glanced down, picking it up to reply to a text.

"Late for your date?" Julianne asked.

Logan's cheeks looked slightly pink, and Julianne could swear he was almost embarrassed by her question.

"Yeah, I guess I should get going," Logan said. He slid his phone into his pocket as he stood up. He looked at Harrison, who seemed glued to his seat and hadn't made a move to stand. A gray-haired waitress walked up to the table and grabbed Harrison's empty beer glass.

"Can I get you another beer, honey?" the waitress asked, her voice scratchy.

"Sure," Harrison said, his gaze on Julianne. Her wine was empty. "She'll take one, too. A beer that is."

Julianne almost laughed. She really had no idea how to read this guy, and she wasn't sure if his clear disapproval of her drink should insult her.

Logan paused, looking back over at Julianne. She could tell by the look on his face he'd expected her to say she had to go, but curiosity was getting to her. Harrison clearly had more to say to her without Logan around.

"Don't let us hold you up," Harrison said, his eyes danced with some type of challenge.

"Julianne . . ." Logan said, ignoring Harrison.

"Bye, Logan," Julianne said, giving her best sweet smile.

Logan stared at Harrison, his jaw clenched. "Call me later, Julianne."

Logan walked toward the door but turned back around, stepping close to Harrison. "I'm not sure what you're up to right now, but don't make me regret reaching out to you."

A small smirk crossed Harrison's face. "Turn back around, Logan. It's what you're best at."

Logan flinched at his comment, and she knew she'd entered the middle of something she wished she hadn't. But she didn't really owe anything to Logan. She still wasn't even sure if they were real friends.

Logan left after that, not looking back at either of them. The waitress arrived with two beers as soon as the door shut behind him. Julianne grabbed hers, taking a sip to prove she wasn't some girl who couldn't handle a cheap beer in a dark dive bar.

"So I take it you're not screwing my brother?" Harrison asked as he took a sip of his. Slower than his previous one.

"Excuse me?" Julianne asked, her eyes wide.

"He didn't fill me in on how he knew you," he replied. "I thought maybe you were one of his . . ."

Julianne interrupted him. "No. We're both surgical residents."

He stared at her. He had a way of doing that, as if he were trying to reach inside her brain and pull out something. She wished he'd just say what he was thinking. Well, maybe not about the whole "screwing" comment.

"You're good friends?" he asked.

"Not exactly," she replied. "Why?"

He shrugged. "Just trying to understand why he's helping you."

Julianne was wondering the same thing, but she didn't tell Harrison that.

"We could go to this Alex's gallery now if you want," he said, looking at the time on his phone.

"I just told you guys I was going alone."

There was that deadpan stare again. He grabbed his beer and seemed to swallow the remaining amount in one gulp. "Yeah, but I decided it was probably better I go with you."

Julianne huffed. There was no way in hell she was bringing Harrison with her. He would be worse to bring along than Logan. Logan wouldn't look so out of place, but Harrison would. He was tall, muscular, and had a dark persona. He'd practically look like her bodyguard. Plus, Logan had warned her repeatedly that Harrison was bad news. She wasn't sure if she should go anywhere with him.

"You're staying in the car," she said, trying her best to look stern and return his stare.

The corner of his mouth turned up. It was the first time she'd seen him crack even a hint of a smile. "Deal."

"And maybe I should drive," she said, looking at his second empty beer glass. She'd only taken a sip of hers.

He rolled his eyes. "You see I'm like twice your size, right? I'll drive."

Before she could say anything else, he was already up, throwing a twenty-dollar bill on the table and striding toward the door.

"You're sort of bossy," she muttered as she practically jogged to keep up with him.

She followed Harrison into his all-black Jeep wrangler. After Julianne gave him the directions to Alex's studio, she felt her phone buzz in her pocket. It was a text from Logan.

On your way to home yet?

She debated on texting back, but put it back in her pocket. She had a feeling he wouldn't like that she had left with Harrison.

"Logan?" Harrison asked, watching her out of the corner

of his eye. She hadn't even realized he'd been paying attention.

"No," she lied, staring out the window.

He didn't call her out on it, even though she had a feeling he knew she was lying.

"Do you think he'd have an issue with me taking you somewhere alone?" Harrison asked, watching her again.

"Do you mind keeping your eyes on the road? And yes, I do. He said you were bad news, and I don't exactly know what he meant by that."

Harrison let out a short, small laugh. It startled her because it was the last sound she expected to hear from him.

"So, are you?" she asked.

"Maybe," he said, smirking. He pressed his foot harder on the gas so she jerked forward in her seat and had to steady herself with her hand on the dashboard.

"Why?" Julianne asked. "What did he mean by that?"

Harrison looked in his rearview mirror briefly before changing lanes to take the exit. "My brother's a bit of a snowflake, so it's hard to say."

Julianne rolled her eyes. They pulled up at the studio a few minutes later without any further conversation.

"Okay, just wait here," she said. "Seriously, do not come in."

She looked at herself in the passenger-side mirror. She prayed Alex wasn't there right now. She looked nothing like the woman who had walked into that gallery a couple weeks ago.

"You look fine," he said, watching her. "Just go."

Looking *fine* wasn't exactly what she'd been going for. She took a deep breath before getting out of the car.

6

Julianne shakily opened the door to the gallery. The familiar sight of the canvases flooded her with memories of her night with Alex. He'd had a similar painting in his bedroom.

"Hello," a tall, slender, and beautiful redhead said, walking toward her. "Can I assist you with anything?"

Julianne froze. Her mouth was dry and sticky, and she didn't quite feel like she could form words. When she could finally speak she managed, "Just looking around."

The woman nodded. "Let me know if I can help you at all."

"Actually," Julianne said, staring at the idling black Jeep outside of the gallery. "I was wondering if the owner was here."

She smiled. "I am the owner."

Julianne's eyebrows knit together in confusion. "Oh, I thought . . ."

"Maybe you've met my husband, Alex?" she asked.

Julianne's face went white as shame spiraled through her.

Yes, she'd met him. What the actual hell? Hadn't Lucy said he was a good guy? She had to have known he was married; why in the world would she have let Julianne go home with him? She tried to keep her expression neutral, but it was hard. "Yes, sorry. We discussed a piece I was interested in at the gallery hop."

"Oh wonderful," she said. "I'm Elizabeth, by the way."

"Julianne," she replied.

As she said her name, she saw a familiar shadow coming from the back of the room. Alex appeared seconds later, walking up with his hands in his pockets, smiling at both of them. She couldn't believe how calm he looked as he approached. Julianne plastered on a smile, trying hard to focus on why she'd come to the gallery.

"Ah, the lovely Julianne," Alex said, giving her a quick air-peck on the cheek. "What brings you in?"

"She said you were discussing a piece she was interested in?" Elizabeth said before Julianne could speak.

"Yeah?" Alex asked. His eyes had a bit of humor in them, as if he was daring her to say which piece. Julianne realized he was probably assuming she was there for him, so she needed to come clean fast.

"Actually, I'm sorry, that's not true," Julianne said, looking at Elizabeth. who seemed puzzled. "It's about Lucy."

"Lucy!" Elizabeth exclaimed. "I've been trying to get ahold of her all week. Did she lose her phone or something?"

They both looked at Julianne expectantly, and she was quiet for a moment, trying to decide how much information to divulge. There was a ding from the door opening behind her. Julianne groaned quietly—she knew it was Harrison without having to look.

Elizabeth had instinctively turned around to greet whoever had come in with her large smile, but she seemed to falter upon seeing Harrison. Julianne understood. He was as gorgeous as he was menacing.

Julianne just glared at him before giving an apologetic look to both Elizabeth and Alex. "Excuse me."

Julianne grabbed Harrison's arm; his forearm was taut muscle beneath his shirt. She tried to pull him away so she could talk to him, but she quickly realized she didn't have the physical strength to budge him even an inch.

"You must be Alex," Harrison said, sticking his hand out to Alex.

Alex looked confused, but seemed to try to hide it as he took his hand, looking at Julianne.

"Can I help you?" Alex asked, his voice a bit higher than before. "Is he with you, Julianne?"

Julianne wanted to shake her head no, but Harrison spoke before she could say anymore.

"I was just parking the car," Harrison said, his tone lighter than Julianne had ever heard. "You know Julianne, can't walk a block when it's even just sprinkling outside."

Harrison turned to Julianne and wrapped his arms around her waist before pulling her into him and kissing her. His lips were warm, and he tasted like butterscotch. Her breath caught. What the hell was he doing?

"I'm Harrison," he said after letting Julianne go. He smiled at Alex and Elizabeth. Julianne watched as Harrison's eyes crinkled as he grinned at them. It was clear he'd done this a million times. "Julianne's boyfriend."

Alex's head cocked to the side; his self-assured look he'd had when he had first come out of the back office seemed to fade. Julianne wanted to be annoyed with Harrison, but after finding Alex's gorgeous wife in here, she was glad he'd come inside. She wasn't sure if the kiss was necessary, but it did prove a point.

"Did you ask them yet?" Harrison asked Julianne. "About Lucy?"

"I had just started to," Julianne mumbled. "Elizabeth, you were saying you haven't heard from Lucy all week?"

"Nope! Is something wrong?" Elizabeth asked, looking back and forth between them.

"Lucy was supposed to meet me for a run," Julianne said. "A few days ago, actually. And I think something might be wrong. So I was trying to see if any of her other friends might know anything."

Elizabeth looked at Alex, who seemed unconcerned. "Lucy can be a bit flighty. She might have just forgotten."

"No," Julianne said, shaking her head. "I mean, her phone's been off, and she left her apartment unlocked. There's just something really off about all of this."

Harrison must have noticed her shaky voice because he took over.

"When was the last time either of you saw her?" Harrison asked.

Elizabeth looked up toward the ceiling. "Gosh, I think it was a couple weeks ago. I was out of town on a trip and just got back this week. What about you, Alex?"

Alex zeroed in on Julianne. "The gallery hop I guess."

"Do you really think something might be wrong?" Elizabeth asked Julianne, her voice concerned.

"We're just trying to put together all the information first before we jump to any conclusions," Harrison said.

Alex seemed to be studying Harrison. "Are you a cop or something?"

"Or something," Harrison said, his face serious again. Julianne nudged him.

"Lucy likes to run, right?" Elizabeth said to her. "You don't think . . . ?"

Julianne tried to keep her face from faltering, but she was not a good actor like Harrison.

A yelp came from Elizabeth. Alex wrapped an arm around her waist, pulling her toward him. "That seems like a big leap to make."

"Do you know how I could get in contact with her family?" Julianne asked.

"Her parents visited the gallery once," Elizabeth said and walked over to the front desk. "I believe they might have filled out our guest book. Let me see."

A minute later she handed Julianne a small piece of paper. "Here it is. Please let me know if you hear anything."

Julianne took it from her and tucked it safety in her back pocket.

"Is there anyone else you can think of that might know anything?" Harrison asked them. "Any other friends?"

"Lucy has tons of friends," Elizabeth answered. "But none that I can think of that would probably know more than us. Can you think of anyone, Alex?"

"No. Well . . ." Alex paused. "She had a project she was working on. A photo shoot she was excited and nervous about. It wasn't like Lucy to be nervous about anything."

"Do you know who it was with?" Harrison asked.

"I can't remember offhand," Alex answered. "But I'll see if I can find something, and I'll get back to Julianne."

"Yes, please. Anything you can remember," Julianne said.

She felt a buzz in her pocket that had been consistently going off since she'd walked into the gallery. She grabbed her phone and glanced at the screen. There were three more text messages and two missed calls from Logan.

"We should get going," Harrison said.

Julianne smiled at Elizabeth. "Thanks for your help."

Julianne wanted to say more. She wanted to know more. She wanted to slap Alex. But Harrison grabbed her hand, leading her outside before she could do any of those things. She hopped back into the Jeep, buckling her seatbelt and pushing her hair back from her face. Harrison had gotten in, and she noticed a small smirk on his face.

"Don't say anything," Julianne said, really not wanting to hear what he thought unless it had to do with Lucy. Although he'd saved her some humiliation, she was still angry at him for coming in when she'd been adamant Harrison stay in the car, and even more angry about that kiss.

"Was that his wife?" he asked.

Julianne gritted her teeth. "Just drive, please."

Harrison pulled out of the spot and drove away at what seemed like a snail's pace compared to how fast they'd gotten there.

"I'm going to go out on a limb and say you didn't know he had a wife when you slept with him?"

Julianne glared at him. "I asked you stay in the car."

He shrugged. "I had a feeling you needed help."

Julianne shook her head. "Well, I didn't. Can we just not talk about any of this?"

He nodded, but she was realizing his word didn't always mean much.

A few minutes later they arrived back at Ave Tav. Her car was sitting where she'd left it. She couldn't wait to get home and into some sweats and veg out for the rest of the night. Searching for Lucy was forcing her to be much more social than she preferred.

"Thanks for driving," Julianne said, opening her door.

Harrison's mouth twitched. "See you later, Julianne."

When she got off the elevator for her condo, she spotted Logan sitting on the floor, leaning against the wall opposite her door.

"What are you doing here?" Julianne asked before fishing her key out of her bag and wiggling it into the keyhole.

She wasn't in the mood to talk to Logan. She especially didn't want to tell him about Alex's wife. She walked inside her condo, hesitantly allowing Logan to follow her inside.

"You didn't answer any of my calls or texts," Logan said.

Julianne walked over to her kitchen island counter and set her purse down. "Aren't you supposed to be on a date?"

"I didn't go."

"Okay. Well, you should have," she said. "As you can see, I am fine. So . . ."

"Julianne," Logan said, grabbing her arm gently. "Why are you so damn stubborn?"

Julianne pinched the bridge of her nose. "I've had a long evening, Logan. Can we do this some other time?"

"Were you with Harrison this whole time?" he asked, seeming to not hear her. Apparently both Williams brothers were good at that. "I've been calling him too, and he didn't answer either."

Interesting, Julianne thought. Harrison hadn't mentioned

it. He must have known Logan had been trying to reach both of them.

"Yes. We went to Alex's gallery. And then I came home. Is that all right?"

Julianne knew she was being bitchier than was necessary, but her nerves felt fried. She needed a break from everything and the sooner she could get him out of her condo, the sooner she could just relax.

"I wish you could have let me come with," he said, looking down at his hands. "I know I didn't really explain anything about him to you . . . I just don't really trust him."

"Care to explain why?"

He shook his head. "Not right now."

She couldn't help notice Logan looked like a deflated version of his usual confident, happy self.

"Did you find anything out?" he asked.

Against her better judgment, she told him everything that happened. He listened intently, nodding along as she explained.

"Well, hell," he replied. "Sorry about that."

Julianne shrugged. "It really doesn't matter. I mean, sure, I feel like shit that he had a wife when I had sex with him. But I didn't go in there hoping to rekindle anything between us, so I'm not heartbroken. Let's just change the subject."

He gave her one of his perfect Logan Williams smiles— the kind that showed off his dimples and would make most women swoon. "Well, I was thinking, since I canceled my date, maybe you could watch a movie with me to make up for it?"

Julianne raised an eyebrow at him. He couldn't be serious.

Logan laughed softly, giving her a playful nudge with his arm. "Would I be that awful to watch a movie with?"

She debated carefully before answering. "No. But you know *this* isn't a date, right?"

"Yes, Davis, I know you wouldn't be caught dead dating me. Don't worry."

She rolled her eyes, following him over to her soft taupe sectional sofa. Logan slumped down and rested his feet on the nearby ottoman before pulling her neatly folded throw blanket on top of him. She sat down on the opposite side, leaning back before throwing the remote at him. "Pick something out."

Julianne watched him scroll through Netflix. She hated doing it, so she was glad to pawn the remote off on him.

They decided on a new action movie neither of them had seen yet that was supposed to be good. Julianne stared at the screen, waiting for the movie to start, when a blue fringed throw pillow came flying at her. "Hey!"

"I promise I don't bite," Logan said, smirking at her before patting the spot next to him. "Come sit by me."

Julianne knew that smile. Maybe he didn't bite, but she knew it was a bad idea. She didn't budge, so he moved over instead, close enough that their thighs were touching.

"Why did you cancel your date?" Julianne asked.

A man with a gun on the screen was inching slowly against a wall. He was trying to hide from some thugs looking for him. Logan turned to look at her.

His expression softened. "I was thinking about someone else."

"Do you normally worry about your *friends* this much?" she asked, emphasizing the word friends.

Logan blew out a breath, letting his head rest against the coach cushion. "No, I do not."

She smiled at him, resting her hand on his leg for just a brief second. "Well, thanks for worrying about me, but you don't need to next time. I don't want to piss off your girlfriend."

"I don't have a girlfriend. And I can't promise I won't worry about you again."

Julianne sighed. "So now that you can see I'm just fine, are you regretting canceling your date?"

"Nope," Logan said before he threw an arm around her shoulder, pulling her in closer to him.

Julianne felt his lips brush just slightly over her cheek as he turned back to the movie. She wasn't sure if it was accidental or on purpose, but her body didn't know the difference, because she suddenly became all too aware of him next to her.

She wanted to get up and put as much distance between them as possible. She'd spent so long trying to keep her work life and private life separate. But her brain was being hijacked by her body at the moment. And her body didn't want to avoid him at all—the opposite, actually.

Julianne tried hard to concentrate on the movie and not on Logan. The man who had been hiding behind the wall had been captured and was now in a dark room, his arms and ankles both shackled.

Halfway through the movie she must have fallen asleep because she woke up as the credits rolled on the screen. She also realized her head was now on Logan's shoulder. She quickly sat up straight, having no idea how long she'd been that way. She reached up to make sure she didn't have any drool running down her face. Thankfully, she was dry.

"Sorry," she mumbled, but then realized Logan was sleeping too. His eyes opened slowly, and he smiled lazily at her before closing his eyes again.

"Tired," he said, not making any attempt to get up.

Julianne stood up, grabbed his hands, and attempted to pull him to his feet. He finally gave in, and for a second she thought he was going to pull her into a hug, but he put his hands in his pockets instead. "Fine, Davis. Force me out. You make a terrible hostess."

She gave a small laugh. "Well, you did invite yourself over."

"Are you studying tomorrow?" he asked. "Or still on the Lucy hunt?"

They had their yearly residency exam coming up. Julianne normally would have been ahead in terms of studying, but her schedule had been hectic at work lately.

She sighed. "I need to send her parents an e-mail, and then until I hear any more from Alex, I guess I'm at a standstill. And I'm way behind on studying. So yeah, studying."

"You can come over to study at my place if you want."

"Wouldn't you rather have Emily or someone over?" she asked, regretting her words coming out as juvenile and jealous.

But Logan just smiled. "You really make a guy work to be your friend, huh?"

"Sorry," she said, hiding her face with her hands. She dropped them and met his eyes. "I'm really not great at friendships, relationships, you name it."

"Well, if I say I want to hang out with you, I want to hang

out with you." He never looked away from her, and it gave her a few butterflies in her stomach she tried hard to ignore.

"I get that," she said. "I just don't get why."

"Stop asking so many questions."

"Fine, I'll be over," she said, not even sure why she was agreeing to it.

Julianne shut the door after he left and closed her eyes. Even if she was just spending time with him as a friend, she didn't know how long it would stay that way. Not when he looked at her the way he did, or when he sat so close to her, she could feel his breathing syncing with her own. She'd go over to his place tomorrow, but she was determined to keep her distance. Her body was getting too confused, and there was just too much going on right now to let herself get lost in a guy like Logan Williams.

She grabbed her MacBook after he left and quickly drafted an e-mail to send to Lucy's mom before she went to sleep. She did her best to not scare her completely while still trying to communicate the urgency of the situation. She included all of her contact information and hit *send*. Now all she had to do was wait.

7

Julianne went over to her mom's house on Sunday morning. They always got together for breakfast on Sunday mornings—it had been a tradition since Julianne left home for college. Her mom was drinking a cup of coffee and typing on her computer when Julianne walked into the house. Her soft blonde hair, trimmed to bob at her shoulders, was perfectly styled. She was dressed in slim-fitting pants and a lavender sweater.

"Hey, Jules!" She beamed at her daughter.

"Hey," Julianne said, giving her a quick hug. "Working on a Sunday?"

Her mom nodded. "I know I shouldn't, but a few things came up. I'm meeting with a potential donor this afternoon, so I wanted to be fully prepared. I'm all yours this morning, but I should warn you, breakfast might consist of cold pizza from last night."

Julianne raised an eyebrow at her. Her mom was the epitome of the perfect hostess-slash-homemaker, and she didn't think she'd once seen her mom serve cold pizza for anything, let alone breakfast.

"Or maybe an orange?" her mom said, pointing toward the sad-looking fruit bowl on the counter.

Julianne looked at her cautiously. "Mom, is everything okay?"

"Yes, of course," she said, but looked down at her hands. "I just need to talk with you about something."

"Is everything okay? Is it Pierce?"

Pierce was her mom's husband. Her stepfather. She felt odd even thinking the word because they'd gotten married when Julianne was in college. He was a great guy and a partner at a busy law firm in the city, but he just wasn't her father.

"No. Everything is fine, sweetheart. This is about your dad," she said, "and actually has nothing to do with my lack of breakfast food. That's honestly because I've been working my butt off for the nonprofit lately, and Pierce and I practically live on takeout. I haven't been to the grocery store in weeks."

Julianne sighed. Her mom was terrible at getting to the point. She grabbed a slightly wrinkled orange and began unpeeling it. "What about Dad?"

"Please don't be upset . . ."

"Oh, you know!" Julianne exclaimed. She felt relieved that something new wasn't about to be sprung on her and also relieved that she would not have to be the one to break it to her mom.

"About him leaving his job?"

Julianne nodded.

Her mom's eyebrows raised. "I didn't know you knew! Oh

god, Julianne. I was so worried about telling you. I thought—"

"That I'd be pissed?" Julianne asked. "I was. I left Dad's house when he told me. You're not?"

Her mom shrugged. "I've been mad at your father so many times in my life. What's one more thing? And honestly, I'm not truly angry. It's the first decision he's probably ever made that isn't just for himself. And yeah, it isn't for us, but I think we've moved past that now. So thank you for being mad at him for me, Jules, but you don't need to be."

Julianne wasn't sure if she bought her mom's answer completely, but she didn't push it. She got up and poured herself a cup of coffee, adding a splash of almond milk creamer before stirring it around slowly with a spoon. Julianne set the spoon down in the sink before sitting down next to her.

"What do you have going on the rest of the day?" her mom asked. "You look a bit nicer than your usual Sunday morning roll-out-of-bed look."

Julianne looked down at her jeans and plain long-sleeve gray shirt. Maybe she'd put more time into her hair and makeup this morning.

"I'm going over to a friend's place after this. We're going to study for our residency training exam."

"A male friend?" her mom asked, waggling her eyebrows.

Julianne groaned. Her mom was like a dog with a bone with pushing Julianne to date. Julianne was glad she kept it at dating and wasn't begging for any grandkids yet. Her mom had tried to set her up countless times with every young, single guy she came across. She'd never agreed with

Julianne's decision to not consider anyone in medical school or her residency program.

"Yeah, I know. It totally goes against everything I've ever said . . ."

Her mom waved her hand to stop her. "Julianne, I think it's wonderful."

"But really, he's just a friend. Don't get any ideas."

Her mom held up her palms. "Okay."

Julianne sipped on her coffee, her mind moving from Logan back to her father.

"What was Dad like when you met him?" she asked.

Her mom took a sip of from her own cup and smiled at her. "He was charming. Handsome. The smartest guy I'd ever met."

Those things all definitely sounded like Logan.

"Did you know right away? Were you friends first?"

"He definitely pursued me," she replied. "I was much more reserved than him, so I turned him down the first few times. But it didn't take long for him to wear me down. We were very much in love when I found out I was pregnant with you. I was terrified of what his parents would say, but he never cared. He made certain I knew he'd take care of us."

Julianne nodded. "But he didn't exactly push you to stay in school?"

Her mom shrugged. "I think in his mind he wanted to be a provider more than anything. Do I look back now and think that maybe he was secretly glad he would be the high achiever in our relationship? Yeah. But at the time, it never even occurred to me—I was just so glad my life wasn't going to fall apart. And again, I was more in love with this guy than I'd ever been with anyone. Before you and Ella, of course."

Julianne smiled, giving her a mom a hug.

"Are you asking about this because of this . . . friend?" her mom said.

Julianne sighed. "Well, he's definitely charming, good-looking, and smart. Which is why I'm determined to stay his friend."

Her mom laughed. "Julianne, those qualities are actually all good things, as long as he isn't also conceited, selfish, and a pompous asshole. Not saying I know anyone like that."

Julianne laughed gently. Her mom hadn't always confided in her how she felt about her father. She used to keep things much more neutral so her daughter could make up her own mind up about him. And Julianne definitely had found out about her father on her own. All too well.

Julianne finished her orange and coffee, along with a few bites of the cold pizza, as they caught up on more about each other's week. Afterward, Julianne took off straight for Logan's.

Julianne parked in the visitor parking area, slung her backpack over her shoulder, and went inside the brown brick building. It wasn't the fanciest building, but it was clean. Maybe slightly outdated. She took the elevator up to the third floor and knocked on his door. He didn't answer the first time, so she knocked again. She hoped he hadn't forgotten she was coming. Sudden nerves hit her—she'd feel so foolish if he wasn't expecting her.

His door opened up seconds later. Logan was dressed in a pair of worn gray sweatpants and a crisp white T-shirt. He grinned at her as he pushed back his sandy brown hair with his hand, a sliver of his toned abs peeking from under his shirt. His other hand motioned her into his apartment. She wasn't sure how Logan seemed to look better in his sweatpants than his regular clothes, but he did. When she wore sweats, she was sure she just looked like an actual bum, not a sweatpants model. She mentally slapped herself and instead tried to focus on his apartment.

It was bigger than she'd expected. And cleaner, too. His kitchen was to the right when she walked in, a dining room to the left. His living room was in front of her. He had an older brown leather sofa in the living room with a large TV mounted on the wall. An acoustic guitar sat against the couch, and his books and laptop were stacked on a plain wooden coffee table.

"Welcome," he said, shutting the door behind her.

"Thanks," she said. "So this is your place, huh?"

He smirked. "Would you like a grand tour?"

He opened a closed door that contained a queen-size bed and a dresser.

"And the bathroom," he said, opening another door.

Julianne nodded along as she followed him back to the living room. She pointed to the door on the other side of the room. "Another bedroom?"

He nodded. "So how are you?"

"Good," Julianne said, taking a seat on his couch. There was that nervous feeling again. She couldn't believe she was letting Logan make her feel this way—*focus, focus.*

"I had fun last night," Logan said to her, the corner of his mouth creeping up.

"Oh, yeah?" she asked.

He nodded and walked close to her. His eyes gleamed. "Yeah, but I must have been lousy company because my date fell asleep on my shoulder."

Julianne's mouth dropped open. "That wasn't a date."

"Says you," he said, his smile both mischievous and too handsome.

Julianne stared up at him. She thought he might kiss her suddenly, and she wasn't sure which she wanted more—for him to do it or not. He sat down next to her instead. Not.

Julianne sat up, brushing her hair back as she looked at him. She was sure her cheeks were crimson. She quickly said something to avoid sitting there looking like an idiot. "So are you on the review book?"

Logan sighed. "Alright, confession: I've been studying all morning and am in need of a major break."

"What did you have in mind for a break then?" she asked cautiously. She hoped it didn't involve something in his bed. Had she completely misread him asking her over?

"How about a walk?" he asked. "I just need some fresh air, I think."

She nodded, feeling relieved. A walk she could do. Logan grabbed his phone and jacket before they went outside. He lived close to St. Anthony Main, so they walked in that direction. It was one of her favorite areas in the city to grab a drink. Cobblestone bricks lined the street that overlooked the Mississippi River. There was a beautiful view of downtown from across the river.

Julianne rubbed her hands together. It was sunny out, but a cold day. It was hard to keep up with the weather in Minnesota, and she definitely wished she'd opted for something warmer. She knew it was her nervousness of going over to Logan's this morning that had made her forget.

"Are you cold?" Logan asked, studying her.

She laughed lightly. "Yes, I'm pretty much always cold. So don't ask me why I didn't grab something warmer to wear."

"Here. Take my jacket," he said, taking it off before she could stop him.

"Thanks," she said while he draped it over her shoulders. "Are you sure you won't be cold?"

He shook his head, throwing an arm over her shoulder and pulling her in for a moment. "I'm just fine. Plus, it looks good on you."

She smiled. "You know, you're not half bad, Logan Williams."

He raised an eyebrow at her. "That's pretty high praise from you. I guess I'll have to work up to 'damn good'?"

Julianne laughed. "I guess so."

"So really, why do you avoid hanging out with any of us from the hospital?" he asked, kicking a few rocks with his toes as they walked.

Julianne sighed. "It's complicated."

"My favorite kind of explanation," he said with a wink.

She felt nervous opening up to Logan about this. It was personal, and she knew the more she told him, the more she was letting him into her life.

"I don't want to turn into my father," she said. "I love medicine, but it became his whole life. I feel like we can't even have a conversation if it's not about work. I'm sure it's why my parents' marriage didn't work. I just want a part of my life that isn't about it, you know?"

"But you know you're not your dad, right?" Logan asked, his voice soft. "You can be friends with other doctors and still have other interests. I do. I think most of us do."

"I know," she said, playing with the button on the cuff of her oversized jacket. "I just see a lot of him in me sometimes, so I'm just trying to be extra cautious."

He gazed at her. "Tell me more about your friend, Lucy. Are you two pretty close?"

She was glad for a change of subject, even if it was one that still didn't put her at ease. "We've only known each other for a few months, but at the moment she's probably the closest friend I have."

"It seems like you're going through a lot of work to find someone you haven't known very long."

She nodded. "I can see where you're coming from. But my friendship with Lucy is important to me. I'm not great at opening up to people, but it's always been easy with her. She . . . she reminds me a lot of my sister, Ella."

Logan was quiet for a moment, his toe once again moving some rocks along the side of the road. "She passed away from cancer, right? I heard people talking before."

Her throat tightened. "Yes, she was twelve. It was a neuroblastoma. There was no one who understood me better than Ella. I think it's because we both had our dad as our dad, you know?"

A tear escaped that she hadn't been expecting. She quickly looked away so he wouldn't see, but it was too late, because he reached out to her face and wiped at her cheek with his thumb.

"I'm sorry, I didn't mean to get so emotional," Julianne said. She hated that he'd seen her cry, even a single tear. It wasn't something she let anyone see.

"Don't be sorry," he said. "I'm glad you felt comfortable enough to tell me."

Logan pulled her into a hug, taking her by surprise. Her first thought betrayed her—she couldn't believe how good he smelled close up. Her second thought wasn't any better when she realized how good he felt.

"This feels good though, doesn't it?" he asked.

Her face flushed. Had he read her mind? "Hmm?"

He let her go, but he was still just inches away as he spoke. "You and I. Friends. Hanging out."

She laughed. Yes, of course that's what he meant. But she wondered if he was feeling what she was.

Julianne smiled softly. "I think we should get back and try to study for a bit for real. I'm seriously behind."

"Of course," he said.

He was right after all; their friendship felt good. She honestly hadn't even come to terms with calling him that until now. She'd been so adamant to swear off being friends with anyone in medicine, but she knew she wouldn't be able to do that to Logan. Not anymore. He'd proven himself a friend at the very least. And being here with Logan, over-looking the Mississippi River with the sun reflecting brightly off the tall skyscrapers behind it, was just what she needed.

She knew though that just because it was what she wanted or needed didn't necessarily mean it would work out. She had a history of having her friendships fall apart, and she had zero experience with making a relationship work. Every relationship she'd had so far had been short and fleeting. It was easy to blame it on her partner not being the right person, but secretly Julianne feared she pushed people away.

"Julianne?"

She shook her head. He was staring at her, waiting for an answer to a question she hadn't even heard. "Yeah?"

Logan held up his phone toward her. "I just got a breaking

news update on my phone. They found a body of a woman off of Highway 62."

Her blood went cold. "Does . . . does it say anymore?"

He shook his head. "They said she looked between the ages of twenty and thirty. We can try to see if we can find out more . . ."

His voice drifted off as Julianne faded off into unconsciousness.

8

Julianne recognized the familiar sound of the hospital around her. It was comforting. The hospital was something she'd known since she'd been a kid visiting her father. If there was anything familiar in life, this would be it. She listened to the steady heart monitor and wondered which patient she was looking after. Except it didn't make any sense. Wasn't it Sunday? She wasn't on call. She was supposed to be studying. Why was she sleeping?

Her eyes flashed open. Her mom was sitting in the chair next to her bed. Julianne blinked a few times, desperately trying to remember how in the hell she'd ended up here. The back of her head ached. She reached up to feel a giant welt and some caked-on blood clumped in her hair. "Mom?"

Her mom's eyes opened up, and she rushed over to her bed. "Jules, you're awake!"

"Mom, what happened?" she groaned, sitting up. "I was with Logan, and . . . I just can't seem to remember how I got here."

Before her mom could answer, Logan stepped in the

room. He was still in his sweatpants and T-shirt from earlier. Spots of blood now stained his bright white shirt. Their walk flooded her mind, and then the memory of him telling her about the body being discovered rushed back to her. Concern was etched over his face as he walked over to the bed.

"Are you feeling okay?" Logan asked, resting his hand on her arm. "I'll go get the attending. They were just here."

She shook her head. "I'm fine . . . w-what happened?"

"You fainted," he said, his face solemn. "It happened before I could react and you hit your head against a railing on the way down."

"Yeah, it does hurt," she muttered.

A nurse walked into the room and began taking her vitals and asking her questions before Logan or her mom could say anymore. Julianne seemed fine, and now she felt embarrassed for having fainted. She literally had never fainted in her life. Then, as if things couldn't get any worse, there was a knock on the doorframe and her father walked in.

"Julianne. I was visiting a colleague when I heard from your mom." He looked at the nurse standing in his way. "You can go."

"Dad," Julianne scolded, embarrassed. "You can't boss people around here."

"Sorry," he said, looking at the nurse. "You can go, *please*."

The nurse eyed him warily before finishing up her notes on the computer and walking out of the room.

"And who's he?" her dad said, jutting his thumb toward Logan.

"I'll check in with you later," Logan said, tapping his fingers on her legs before leaving the room. Julianne was grateful for his quick departure. She didn't want Logan to have to deal with her father, and Logan would surely run away from her if he stayed for five more minutes in a room with him.

"Dad, I just *fainted*," she said, exasperated. "It's not a big deal. You do not need to be here."

"People don't just faint," he said, looking over at her mom. "Sandra?"

Her mom shook her head. "What, Richard? You think I made her faint?"

Her parents still fought like cats and dogs when in a room together. She couldn't believe her mom had bothered to tell her father about this. She clearly thought it had been more serious than it was, or she would never have bothered.

"I'm fine," Julianne repeated. "Can you please go, Dad?"

"I think I'll find your attending and have a look at your chart first."

"Oh my god, Dad." She tried to rein in her emotions as well as she could. "I'm not a minor. You can't just pull my chart and look at it. So go. There isn't anything you're going to see on it, anyway. I'm not pregnant; I'm not anemic. I'm eating. It was just a freak accident, all right?"

She didn't want to go into detail about the body that had been discovered, even if it could be her friend. Her parents would just be annoyed with her for not remaining focused on her work.

She must have been speaking louder than she realized because now a doctor was waiting at her door. "Sir, she needs rest. I think maybe you need to leave for a bit," he said. He must have been the attending on staff. She hadn't met him before, and he obviously hadn't met her father before.

"Excuse me?" her father asked. Julianne knew what was

coming next, and she mouthed the words along with him. "Do you know who I am?"

"Frankly, I don't care if you're the president of the United States. In this hospital, she's my patient," the attending said, his arms crossed, staring her father down.

Her father gave his usual menacing stare before stomping out of the room. Her mom gave her an apologetic look before following him out, which left Julianne now alone with her doctor.

"How are you feeling?" he asked. He approached the computer and pulled up her chart.

"Fine, which I've had to tell ten people in just the last five minutes," she said.

He laughed. "Welcome to being the patient."

"Can I get discharged soon?" she asked, trying to get a peek at the screen.

He gave her a finger to signal *one moment* before turning toward her. "Everything looks good. Just give me a minute, and we'll get you out of here. I want to have someone clean up your head dressing first though."

She nodded. She couldn't wait to get out of there. Once the doctor left, she shut her eyes. She'd need to ask for some Ibuprofen for her head once someone came back. She heard the door click open and feared opening her eyes. She really didn't want to deal with father any more today.

"Hey there."

She opened her eyes. It was Logan. He was surprisingly the only person she was glad to see standing there.

"Hi." Julianne smiled. "Sorry about my dad. He's—"

"It's alright," Logan said, walking over and sitting on the bed next to her. "How's the head?"

She scrunched her nose. "Sore."

"I feel like such a jerk for not being able to grab you before you fell."

"Don't," she said. "Did you seriously carry me back to your car to get me here? I hate not remembering things."

He laughed. "You're not that heavy. Don't worry."

She gave him a playful punch in the arm. "Well, thanks for not leaving me crumpled on the ground. Did you tell anyone about . . . why I fainted?"

He shook his head. "I thought I'd let you tell them if you wanted to."

"Is there any more information? Did you contact Harrison to see if maybe he knows someone who might know more about the body?"

Logan shook his head, looking down at his hands. "Julianne, I think you just need to rest. Maybe you need a break from your searching. We could go the police once you get out of here, and then you can be done with this. Okay?"

She looked at him confused. "Why? I thought you wanted to help me with this."

"Yeah, but that was before you fainted. Maybe the stress of all of this is getting to you more than you even realize."

"It's not. I'm fine," she said, irritated.

"Hey," he whispered, his hand reaching forward and gently tucking her hair behind her ear. "I'm just worried about you is all."

Julianne looked into his eyes and felt that unfortunate flutter again. She looked away quickly. She could not fall for Logan. Yes, he'd proved himself to be a decent human being and not just a man-whore like she'd originally thought, but if she let herself develop feelings for him, it would not end well.

He'd been clear multiple times about how this was a friend-ship, and she needed to get her little belly butterflies to understand that.

"I had a feeling you would be pretty adamant about wanting to know more though," he said, interrupting her thoughts. "So here."

He handed her his cell phone, which had a text from Harrison. Apparently Harrison knew someone at the city morgue and had got a better description of the body. *Cause of death appears suspicious, possible blunt-force trauma. The victim looks about five-foot-five, female, approximately twenty-five years old, long blonde hair—*

"It's not her!" Julianne exclaimed. She felt elated, but then felt a pang of guilt. This poor girl was still dead. She wondered if it was the missing runner, Angela, or someone else.

"You missed a call while you were out. It looks like it might have been Lucy's mom."

Her eyes lit up. "You really should have prefaced every-thing with that."

Logan smiled. "I knew if I fed your habit you'd never give up. I had to at least try."

She had grabbed her phone and was looking for the voicemail when he spoke again.

"So Julianne, I was ..."

Before he could finish, the door opened and Emily walked in. She was dressed in scrubs and as usual had a little too much makeup on.

"There you are!" Emily said to Logan, grabbing his arm and pulling him up off the bed. "I heard someone saw you. You were a little tricky to track down though."

Emily looked at Julianne and gave her the smallest hint of a smile before planting her plump, too-red lips right on Logan's mouth. Logan pulled back slightly, causing Emily to try again.

"Em, wait. Not at the hospital" he said, watching Julianne out of the corners of his eyes. Before Julianne looked away, she could swear she saw a look of apology in his eyes. Not that he had to; they were friends, and she already knew something was going on with Logan and Emily. She'd been in a bubble of just the two of them for a couple days now, and she'd forgotten that this was the norm—Emily and Logan, *not* Julianne and Logan.

"What?" Emily asked, her voice whiny. "Julianne doesn't care, since when did you get to be such a rule-follower?"

He whispered in her ear, and Emily let out an annoying giggle.

"Just come over after I get off tonight, okay?" Emily said to him. "Like nine?"

"Okay," he said before she tried to kiss him once more. Julianne didn't turn to see if Emily was more successful this time. She kept staring at her phone until Emily left the room and hoped Logan had followed her out because the air in the room suddenly felt tense.

When Julianne looked up, Logan was still there, but seconds later Pete walked in.

"I hear someone needs their head fixed up," Pete said smiling, unaware of the silence.

"Jul—" Logan began.

"Alright, see you later, Logan," she said before he could speak. She didn't want to hear whatever he was going to say.

He seemed to linger for a moment before looking at Pete. "I can do this. You can go."

Pete raised his eyebrow at him. "You're not even working right now. Just go home, Logan."

There appeared to be a stare down between them that Logan somehow won because Pete handed him the supplies he'd brought in and gave Julianne a nod before leaving.

"You should have just let Pete do it," she said once he left the room. "You've taken care of me enough. You really can go home, Logan."

He moved her forward, dabbing at the back of her head with a warm, wet cloth.

"I just wanted . . . are we okay?" he asked.

She stared back at him. "Yes, why wouldn't we be?"

Logan shook his head, his attention back to her head. "I don't know. Sorry I said that."

She let him finish in silence. Once he was done, he set the supplies on a tray. He stood in front of her with his hands in his pockets. "So, we're good?"

"Yes. If this is about Emily, I don't care. Do you think I care?"

Logan blew out his breath. "Nope. You clearly don't care."

"Okay," she said. "So, I'll see you tomorrow, okay? I'm going to call Lucy's mom back, but you really just should go."

He once again hesitated, but finally left the room without another word.

Julianne took a minute to regroup and then pressed the number to call Lucy's mom.

9

"Hello?"

"Hi, is this Mrs. Aldridge?" Julianne asked.

"Yes. Julianne, I assume?"

"Yes, thanks so much for calling."

"Of course, dear," she said. "Listen, I got your e-mail. I'm sorry I didn't get back to you sooner. But you don't need to worry about Lucy."

Relief flooded her body. "Oh! You've heard from her? Is she all right?"

"Well, no, I haven't heard from her in several weeks, but that's my point. Lucy is a bit of a free spirit. Sometimes Dave, my husband, and I don't hear from her for months, to be honest. But that's just our Lucy."

Julianne paused for a moment. "Mrs. Aldridge . . ."

"Please call me Jana, dear."

"Jana, with all due respect, I understand you know your daughter, but something just really seems off. I really was hoping you might consider opening a missing person report on her."

Jane laughed. "Missing person! Oh goodness gracious, I did that one time when she was sixteen. She showed back up two weeks later telling me she had gotten married in Vegas. That was just the first of many times I learned that I couldn't control my daughter. You sound like a really sweet girl, and I'm glad you're such a good friend to worry about her, but trust me, when Lucy wants to be found, she will."

Julianne closed her eyes. She didn't know what else to say. "Thank . . . thank you, Jana."

"Anytime, dear," she said. "When you do hear from her, please tell her that her aunt Susan isn't doing too well, and she might consider stopping home one of these days."

"Yes, will do," she said before hanging up. She wanted to believe this woman. Lucy was her daughter, after all. But her gut was telling her something was just not right. There was too much to the story to let Julianne just give up.

Her only lead was on what Alex found out. She felt frustrated he hadn't called yet, and even more frustrated she didn't have a number to reach him. She looked down at her phone, scrolling until she got to Harrison's number. She felt slightly guilty calling him without telling Logan, but she needed a break from Logan right now. She hadn't liked seeing him kiss Emily, and that bugged her more than the actual kiss. He'd made it clear so many times he wanted to be her friend, but she was having a hard time being alone with him and not feeling something more than that. But based on what she'd just seen, it was just her feeling that way.

Harrison picked up on the second ring. "Julianne."

"Um, yes. Hi, Harrison," Julianne said nervously. He somehow had a way of intimidating her even over the phone.

"Did Logan get you the information you needed?"

"Oh, yes, thank you!" she said, remembering the text about the girl's description. "I actually need another favor."

"Why don't you come to my office?" he asked. "I can be there in thirty."

"Sure, just text me the address," Julianne replied.

After she was officially discharged, she had her mom drop her off at Logan's apartment so she could get her car. Another fifteen minutes later she pulled up to what looked like an abandoned strip mall. There was an Italian grocery store on one end that appeared to still be functioning, along with a small barber shop in the middle. The other store fronts were all closed up or had *For Rent* signs on them. She looked at the number of the building he'd given her. It appeared to be one of those that were closed up but didn't have a *For Rent* sign on it.

Julianne wished she would have told someone she was going here, but she trusted Harrison, even though she really didn't know him. She needed to talk to Logan more to find out why he didn't trust his brother, but that would have to wait.

She walked up to the door and pulled on the handle, but it was locked. It looked dark inside, but she knocked on the glass, trying to peer through the windows. There were what appeared to be dozens of boxes stacked around the room, so it was hard to see much else. When no one came to the door, she knocked harder. Finally, after another minute, she heard footsteps and Harrison twisted the deadbolt, pulling the door open for her.

He had on black jeans and a tight black T-shirt, giving her a glimpse of even more muscles than she'd realized he had last time. He had on a black beanie, covering up some of his curls. His usual frown was across his face as he let her in and locked the door back behind her.

"Interesting office," she said, looking around. Beyond the stacked boxes, there was an array of mannequins in the back of the room besides what appeared to be equipment from a restaurant and several arcade games.

"I share it with a few people."

Harrison led her past the menagerie of items to another room. She followed him into what must have been his actual working space. It was dimly lit from a small green desk lamp that sat on top of an old wooden desk. Next the desk was a chair and a small floral-patterned loveseat that reminded her of her grandmother's furniture. It was apparent the office décor must have come with the office too, because she couldn't imagine him picking out any of it.

Harrison sat down behind the desk and motioned for her to sit on the couch. She eyed it nervously. It was dark, and she was leery who and what had been on it before, but sat down anyway.

"So, Julianne, what can I help you with?" Harrison asked, folding his hands in front of him.

She noticed a silver band on his left ring finger. Her jaw dropped. "Are you married?"

Harrison looked at her, confused, but then glanced at his hand and quickly pulled off the silver band and slid it into the upper desk drawer. "Work."

She nodded as if she understood, but she had no idea what he was talking about.

"So?" he asked.

"Well, Lucy's parents were a dead end. They claim they're not worried."

Harrison stared at her quietly. She really hated that. It made her feel like she needed to fill the silence or, worse, that he thought she was some kind of idiot.

"I need to get Alex to tell us more about that photo shoot he thought Lucy was involved in, or at least find some way on my own to learn more. It's the last lead I can think of to find her."

Stare.

"Oh my god, please say something!"

Harrison looked down at his desk and then back at her. "Don't you think if her own parents aren't worried, that maybe you're being a bit . . . excessive?"

Julianne glared at him. "No, I don't think so. I know something happened, and I think she needs help."

"Alright. So you want my advice, or what?"

She thought for a moment. What exactly did she want from Harrison?

"Well, I was hoping maybe you could go to Lucy's apartment with me and you'll see something that Logan and I didn't. She had a calendar with all sorts of notes. I think there might be something there."

"Okay. Anything else?"

"If you could find me a phone number for Alex, that would be great. A cell phone number. I don't want to go back to that gallery."

"Okay. Any more?"

"That's it for now."

He nodded once, his dark, striking eyes staring into her. "Does Logan know you're here?"

She paused, debating on whether to be honest. She looked down. "Yes."

When she looked back at him, his lips were slightly pursed. She made the mistake of looking at them too long and it reminded her of the kiss at the gallery and sent warm sensations rushing through her.

"Hmm." Harrison rubbed at the stubble across his jaw. "I guess he's changed his attitude since yesterday then."

Julianne's eyes zeroed in back on his. "What do you mean?"

"He called me late last night and told me I wasn't to be alone with you anymore."

Julianne's mouth dropped, but she quickly composed herself. "I don't think Logan gets to decide about who I spend my time with."

She couldn't believe Logan had said that to him. She could handle herself, and so far Harrison hadn't proven himself to be anything but helpful. If he was so terrible, why had Logan even bothered to get him involved in the first place? And if it wasn't for her safety he was concerned about, she couldn't believe he would tell him to stay away because he was jealous. After all, Logan seemed very interested in Emily.

"So he doesn't know you're here?" he asked, ignoring her comment.

"Does it matter?"

Harrison smirked. "No."

"Is there a reason I shouldn't be alone with you?" she asked, slightly nervous about his answer. She knew him being ridiculously good-looking was definitely one of them.

"Does it matter?" he echoed.

"I guess not." She didn't have the time or resources to do

this on her own. "Okay then. Do I need to . . . pay you? I'm not really sure how this works."

She watched Harrison's face closely. She could swear he almost looked like he was going to laugh, but his smirk remained. "I'll bill you."

She thought for a moment. He sounded like he was half-joking and half-serious.

"Did you want to go tonight?" he asked. "To her apartment?"

Julianne pictured Emily's stupid lips on Logan and nodded. "Yes."

She followed Harrison out of the office building, watching his long, tall strides as he walked.

They drove Harrison's Jeep to the apartment. It was about 7:00 p.m., so it was dark when they pulled up. She kept picturing those two men entering the apartment last time she and Logan were there, and she felt the hairs on her arms sticking up even though she had a feeling Harrison could handle intruders.

"Do you have protection?" she asked as they got out of the car.

"Excuse me?"

Her face turned bright red. Maybe she'd phrased that wrong. "Like, a gun?"

"Oh," he replied. "If it's your safety you're concerned about, we're fine."

That definitely didn't answer her question or make her feel any safer, but she continued to lead him toward Lucy's apartment. Someone was exiting the building as they entered, so they were able to get in quickly. When they got to her apartment, Julianne hesitantly twisted the doorknob. It surprised her when it didn't twist open.

Harrison looked at her. "What?"

"It's locked," she said. "It was open the last time we were here."

"Move."

She debated on correcting his rudeness but refrained and stepped aside while he pulled out his keys, opening up what must have been a lock pick. Within seconds, the door was unlocked and they were walking inside.

"Not your first time," she muttered as they entered the dark apartment. She reached for the light switch, but he grabbed her hand, pushing it away. Instead, he pulled out a small flashlight and shined it around.

"Anything look different?" he asked.

She looked around. It was hard to tell in the dim light, but she thought it all looked about the same. She was so surprised about the door being locked. Could Lucy have been back and locked it herself? What if her mom was right and she was literally chasing nothing? She grabbed her own phone and turned it into a flashlight, heading toward Lucy's room. Everything still appeared to be how it was before. If Lucy had returned, she hadn't bothered taking anything else with her.

"Where was the calendar you were talking about?" Harrison asked.

"The fridge."

"Not anymore."

Julianne hurried into the kitchen and saw he was right. The calendar was missing.

"Shit." She could have easily taken a picture before, but hadn't thought about it, and now it was too late.

She watched as Harrison went through Lucy's drawers systematically, pulling out random things and examining them before returning them to their rightful places. He went to her living room next, moving cushions and looking behind her television. She couldn't understand what he expected to find, but there was something undeniably sexy about the way he searched around the apartment. He obviously knew what he was doing.

He moved to her bedroom next, and Julianne followed behind him. He looked around the bed and then pulled open the closet. Lucy had large bins of shoes at the bottom of the closet with more pair of heels than Julianne had ever seen outside of a department store. She watched as Harrison dug through them, pulling up a pair of pink sneakers. Julianne remembered Lucy wearing those during their first run together. She wasn't sure why, but he seemed interested in that pair in particular. He tipped one sneaker upside down, and she watched as a small handgun fell out into his palm.

"How did you—"

"It's not my first rodeo, sweetheart," Harrison said, pocketing the gun in his back pocket. "Hot pink would be the easiest for her to find in a hurry, and as soon as I grabbed it the weight was off."

"Why would Lucy have a gun?" she asked. It made no sense. Lucy was not the type of girl to carry a weapon. Julianne was fairly sure she was fearless.

Harrison sat down on Lucy's bed, and Julianne sat next to him. He seemed to be thinking about something, so Julianne waited to let him speak. She was gradually learning Harrison's way of communicating.

"What are the chances Lucy didn't join your running club just to run?"

"Huh?" Julianne asked.

"Let me show you something," he said. He hurried toward the kitchen and pulled open one drawer he'd been looking in earlier.

Inside was a stack of manila files. Julianne flipped through them, unsure of what she was even looking at. "I don't get it? What does this have to do with Lucy missing?"

"It looks like she'd been doing research on people. Some of these people are pretty well known, including Senator Burnhill," Harrison said. "You said she's a photographer? I'm not sure what your friend is, but I feel like she's more than a photographer, which most likely means we're definitely not the only ones looking for her."

"So you believe that she's missing?" Julianne asked.

"I don't think she would have left her gun behind unless she left in a hurry."

"What about that photo project Alex mentioned?" Julianne asked.

"I'll find you a phone number later tonight."

"Alright."

"Don't come back here unless you're with me," he said as they walked toward the door.

When they got into his car, she buckled her seatbelt as they pulled away. She looked over at Harrison as he drove. His jaw was set, and his expression was unreadable.

"Why are you helping me?" she asked.

He looked over at her, his eyes softening, and sighed. "My brother hasn't asked me for a favor in a long time."

She thought for a moment. "So this is for Logan. Were you guys ever close?"

"When we were kids."

"How old were you when you moved to Minnesota?"

"Twelve."

"Are your grandparents still alive?" she asked.

"No, they both passed away."

Julianne wanted to tread lightly, but she was also so curious to know more about Logan and Harrison's past. "Did you ever consider going back to Louisiana?"

Harrison turned to look at her. A scowl had replaced the softness in his expression. It was a signal their conversation had ended.

Julianne looked out her window. "I have running club tomorrow, so I'll try to talk to some other people and see if they know anything about Lucy that I'm missing."

Her phone buzzed, and she looked down at it. It was another news update on the body. She blinked rapidly, staring at the picture of the girl in the article. It took only seconds for Julianne to recognize the blonde in the photo.

It was Katie from her running club.

"Oh my god," Julianne said, her voice cracking. Harrison had just pulled up to the office parking lot.

Harrison grabbed her phone and looked at the news alert. "You know her?"

"Yes. She . . . she's a friend in my running club," Julianne stuttered. It terrified her she might faint again, so she laid her head back against the seat.

"Are you okay?" Harrison asked.

When Julianne opened up her eyes, she found him watching her intently.

"Yes, I . . ." She reached for the door. It felt like the car was closing in on her. This didn't make any sense. She'd just seen Katie. And what about Lucy? Surely this meant something terrible had happened. Tears burned in her eyes, but she held them in. She hadn't realized Harrison had also gotten out of the car until she sensed him behind her.

"Maybe I should give you a ride home," he said, studying her. "You don't seem like you should drive right now."

She shook her head, wiping her sleeve over her eyes to hide any tears that might have escaped. "No, I'm fine. I swear. Please, just go."

Harrison stood watching her. There was concern on his face she hadn't seen before, and it brought a sliver of comfort. He reached forward, his thumb gently tipping her face up so she was looking at him. They stood that way for a moment before he stepped back.

"Be safe, Julianne."

She looked out of her rearview mirror as she drove off. Harrison was still standing by his car, watching her drive off.

10

Monday morning was the first time in Julianne's entire career she thought about taking a sick day. Honestly, she had never even stayed home during undergrad for a hangover. But this morning felt far worse than a hangover.

She was sure she hadn't gotten more than an hour sleep in total. Katie's face played repeatedly in her head. It didn't make any sense; she had just seen Katie on Friday at running club. She tried to call Molly but didn't get an answer, only a text that Molly was horrified and wanted to meet up after Julianne got off that day. Julianne knew that Molly and Katie hung out together outside of running club, so she could only imagine how devastated Molly must be. But with Lucy missing, and now Katie, there was no coincidence anymore. Somehow they were connected, and Julianne wondered if the missing runner, Angela, was part of it too.

Julianne had come close to texting Logan last night when she got home, but didn't. She knew there was a good chance Emily was with him, and god only knew what they were doing. So here she was, walking into the cafeteria before anyone else. She'd given up on sleep at about 3:00 a.m. and had gotten up for a cool shower, trying to force herself to feel normal.

They were only just starting to fill the cases with food, so she grabbed a cup of coffee before finding a table to sit down at. Her hair was still damp from her shower, and it had left wet marks on the shoulders of her scrubs. She threw it into a messy bun, breaking her rule of ever putting up wet hair. A few other people had trickled into the cafeteria and the food was now out, but she couldn't muster up the energy or hunger to get up. The coffee would have to do this morning.

She caught sight of herself in the reflection of a cooler filled with waters and cold coffee drinks and grimaced. Maybe she really should go home. At the very least, she would head to their workroom so she could avoid an unnecessary morning gossip. As she stood up, Emily and Logan walked into the cafeteria, talking and laughing together.

Logan's eyes immediately met Julianne's. She quickly averted her gaze and walked past them. She rushed down the corridor that lead to their workroom.

"Julianne."

His voice was distant, but it grew closer even though she tried to keep up her pace without running.

"Julianne!"

Logan's hand grabbed her arm lightly. She didn't have the energy to fight him off, so she stopped, looking up at his perfectly rested, shimmering blue eyes.

"What?" she asked finally, as if she hadn't been almost literally running away from him.

"Are you okay?"

"Yes, of course I'm okay," Julianne replied. "I was just out late last night."

"You were?" he asked, his voice skeptical.

"Yes," she said. "So . . ."

Logan paused before grabbing her hand and pulling her into an empty exam room nearby. She tried to leave, but he blocked the exit.

"What the hell, Logan?" she muttered, looking past him. "Just go get breakfast."

"You're being ridiculous. Is this about Emily?"

Julianne's nostrils flared. Her voice was louder than she knew it should be. "Are you freaking kidding me, Logan? I don't care who you screw."

"It just seems like things were good between us, but since yesterday—"

She cut him off. "Honestly, Logan, if either of us is being weird, it's you. You keep acting like things shouldn't be okay between us after Emily kissed you in front of me, but since we're just friends, why wouldn't they be?"

He stood quietly, rubbing at his eyes with the palms of his hands. "I guess you're right."

"So, can I go now?"

"Were you really out late last night?" Logan asked, his head cocked to the side as he watched her.

Julianne sighed. "Yep. Now can I go?"

Logan looked like he might step aside, but he stopped and looked at her. He seemed to still be assessing her, but she wasn't sure which part. Maybe how awful she looked, or maybe he was still trying to see if she was lying or not.

"The girl," she mumbled, looking at the ground. "The body they found yesterday . . . she was my friend."

He moved closer to her. "What are you talking about? You

said it wasn't Lucy."

She shook her head. "It wasn't. It was my friend Katie, another girl in our running club."

His brow furrowed. "I don't understand."

Julianne sat down on the exam table "Yeah, welcome to the club."

"So, let me get this straight," Logan said, sitting next to her. "This Katie wasn't even missing, but she shows up dead on the side of the road?"

"There's sort of more."

"Okay?" he asked.

Ugh. She knew she had to tell him about going to the apartment with Harrison last night, but she dreaded it. She knew he'd be mad, but lying just didn't seem like a viable option here.

She took a deep breath, remembering he had no real right to be angry about it before she began. She told him about her phone call with Lucy's mom, and then how to she called Harrison and what they'd found in Lucy's apartment. She tried to watch his expression for what he was thinking, but he had a poker face. It reminded her of Harrison.

"I know you're probably not happy about me going to Harrison—"

Logan slammed his fist into the exam table, still not saying anything. His perfect features were twisted in anger.

"He told me what you said to him about staying away from me," she added.

"Of course he did," he muttered under his breath.

Another minute passed before he spoke. "Why didn't you just ask me?"

Julianne sighed. "You were busy. And breaking into apartments . . . you don't need to be involved in this."

"I wasn't busy."

She raised an eyebrow.

"Do you know you sort of drive me nuts?" Logan asked, jumping up off the exam table.

Julianne glared at him. "What is that supposed to mean?"

He glowered. "I just feel like you say one thing, but then your actions say another."

"Okay, like?"

"You claim you're not jealous of Emily, but I feel like you have these remarks. I can't read your mind, but I swear I'm trying to, and it's just a mess."

Her eyes narrowed. "Gee, thanks. And why do you even care?"

Logan groaned. He jumped back up onto the exam table and grabbed her face, covering his mouth with hers. Julianne sat frozen, but her body responded for her seconds later, and she kissed him back. His lips were hot and he tasted like coffee and cinnamon. He pushed her down so he was leaning over her, his tongue moving between her parted lips before his mouth traveled down her neck. She could feel his warm hands on her cool skin, his fingers inching toward her waistband.

She grabbed his arm, stopping him. He sat up, and they both remained inches away from each other, heavy breathing filling the silent air. She reached up to her swollen lips; they felt suddenly cold with his absence.

"Why—" she began, but he cut her off.

"You asked why I cared. And the truth is, I can't seem to get you out of my damn mind lately. But I had zero idea if you were feeling the same thing."

Honestly, she hadn't really known she felt that way either. She'd kept lying to herself, saying she wanted to be friends with him. But she was attracted to him. It took everything in her to stop him a moment ago. Logan was addictive. She thoroughly enjoyed making out with him, and she would have even more thoroughly enjoyed letting it go even further, but that wasn't her. She didn't do things like this. Logan didn't want to date her; he wanted to have sex with her. After all, he didn't do relationships. And she wouldn't be another Emily to him.

"Stop," he said, grabbing her hand. "You're thinking right now, and I need you stop."

"But, Logan . . ." His expression was both soft and yearning, and it brought those damn butterflies back. She had to bring him back to reality. "I'm not looking to be . . . I can't just do casual. I'm not looking for that."

"I think we could have a lot of fun," he said, his lips grazing her neck again.

Her body throbbed, but she pushed him back. "But I'm not the only girl you have fun with?" She asked this as both a question and a statement.

Logan didn't answer, so she sighed. "I want to be friends with you, Logan. But I can't do friends with benefits. I'm sorry."

He nodded, putting an actual space in between them as he moved back from her. "That's fair."

She worried he would put up walls against her for rejecting him. Honestly, she expected it. But he looked at her and his eyes were still soft.

"I want to be friends with you, Julianne," he said. The

corners of his mouth curved up in a smile. "But I want you to know the offer is always on the table."

Her cheeks flushed. She wondered how many other women he'd said this to.

"We should go," she said, reaching for the doorknob. Logan grabbed her hand before she could reach it.

"About your friend, and what you told me," he said. "Did you want to get together after we get off today? I could go with you to talk to your other friend who knew her if you want."

Julianne swallowed. "Um, well, Harrison is sorta already coming."

"I'm coming too then," he said, his tone clipped.

"Logan," Julianne groaned. "Just tell me what the hell you're so worried about with him."

He sighed. "It's complicated."

"You have to give me something," she said. "You can't just keep telling me he's dangerous when I've seen zero proof and you've given no reasons."

"Fine. Harrison didn't follow the normal path after high school. He didn't go to college; he didn't even get a job. Instead, he had a friend who convinced him to move away to South America when he was nineteen to join some type of secret militia."

Julianne raised an eyebrow. She could definitely picture Harrison doing something like that.

"He came back after a couple of years, refusing to talk about his time there. Between you and me, I think he was probably forced into some bad shit. And then when he moved back he started up whatever business it is he runs now. I don't even know what it is truly. He doesn't tell me anything, but he's done things that aren't exactly law-abiding to get the job done on many occasions. I don't doubt he knows his shit, but do I trust him? No way in hell."

"Alright." She wouldn't push anymore, but she didn't feel any more scared of Harrison. Maybe she should, but she knew he would not hurt her and most likely had ways to keep her much safer while finding Lucy than she would be on her own, or even with Logan.

"So I'll meet you after we get off," he repeated.

"Yes, that's fine," she said. "Now seriously, we need to get going."

Pete and Emily were walking by when they opened the door. Julianne could have sworn Emily was trying to shoot daggers at her with her eyes, but she looked away, pretending not to notice.

The day seemed to go by slowly. They had grand rounds, so it was about 5:00 p.m. when they finished. Julianne had told Harrison and Molly to meet her at Ernie's. She thought about ditching Logan and running off to her car before he could catch up with her, but he seemed to know what she was thinking and followed her out of the hospital.

"I'll drive," Logan said, somehow beating her pace she'd been keeping up. "Don't even think about ditching me."

Julianne rolled her eyes, waiting for him to unlock the passenger door. When she got in, he was smiling at her.

"You were thinking that, weren't you?" he asked.

Julianne looked down. "No."

"I hate that my handsome charm doesn't seem to work on you," Logan said as he started the car, still smiling at her.

Logan smiled so much; she really did like that about him. He was literally the exact opposite of his brother. It was hard to believe they were related. And Logan was wrong, of course. His handsome charm, as he called it, worked on her. If it didn't, she surely wouldn't have made out with him in an exam room earlier. And she wouldn't have gotten in his car either.

"I'm joking," he said when she didn't answer.

Julianne laughed. "Not completely, you weren't. But it's okay."

"I don't call myself handsome."

"You can. You are."

His eyes widened and his grin grew bigger. "You're just messing with me now."

"Maybe." She smiled at him.

"Although," Logan said, looking out his side mirror before merging into traffic. "You didn't exactly complain about earlier."

"Logan," she scolded. "You need to forget that happened. Please."

He just smirked at her as they drove to Ernie's. As they walked toward the entrance, he seemed to stiffen a bit. She knew it was because they were meeting Harrison. Julianne really wished there wasn't this animosity between the two of them. Without overthinking it, she reached out and grabbed his hand, giving it a quick squeeze.

Logan stopped and looked at her, his face both surprised and confused.

"I just . . . I feel like I need to say thank you," she said as they neared the door. "For helping me, and for letting Harrison help too."

Logan stared at her, his expression still blank for a moment.

"Logan?"

"I feel like . . ." he said, finally, "I might be in trouble with you."

"What's that supposed to mean?".

"You're just not like any of the girls I hang around with," he replied.

She realized she still hadn't let go of his hand, and she felt him holding onto hers, not attempting to let go. She felt a sudden, odd desire for this to be something—that holding Logan's hand out on the street was just her normal. Their normal. *But he wouldn't ever be that guy*, she had to remind herself.

"Not like Emily?" she asked.

She knew the question would make the air sour, but she said it anyway.

"Julianne . . ." he began, just as they both looked up to see Harrison walking toward them.

Harrison was wearing sunglasses, worn out jeans, a black long-sleeve shirt, and black combat boots. As usual, he looked too cool to be hanging out with them. He looked like he belonged in another city, or at least not walking into a neighborhood bar.

"Hey," Harrison said, giving them a single nod.

Julianne quickly let go of Logan's hand, realizing they hadn't yet disconnected. It was impossible to see behind Harrison's sunglasses if he'd noticed. She didn't want him thinking that she was just one of the girls who went after Logan. She didn't know when she started caring about Harrison's opinion of her, but somehow part of her did.

"You two look like you just walked off the set of *Grey's Anatomy*," Harrison said, a hint of a smirk on his face. "It's embarrassing."

Logan cleared his throat. "Think Molly is here yet?"

They walked inside, and Julianne spotted Molly right away. She was at a cocktail table near the front of the bar. She looked how Julianne felt: unrested, stressed out, and, frankly, a bit ragged.

"Oh, thank god you're here!" Molly said, jumping up and throwing her arms around Julianne. "I just can't believe any of this."

Julianne wasn't a big hugger, unless it was her family. While she knew Molly, she didn't feel they were at the hugging level. But then again, maybe when a mutual acquaintance was found dead, hugging was deemed acceptable. She hugged Molly back.

After Molly broke their embrace, she looked at Logan and then at Harrison. She stiffened, taking her seat again.

"Molly, this is Logan and Harrison. Harrison has been trying to help me find Lucy."

"Okay." Molly nodded, eyeing Logan inquisitively.

"He's Harrison's brother," Julianne added. "He introduced me to Harrison."

"He doesn't trust me alone with Julianne, so he followed her," Harrison added.

Logan glared at him before standing up. "I'll get us some drinks."

Molly now looked completely uncomfortable, and Julianne wanted to smack Harrison for not keeping his mouth shut, but she tried to give Molly an apologetic smile.

"When did you talk to her last?" Julianne asked her.

Molly sighed. "Friday at running club. We got together sometimes outside of our runs, but not too much. It's just all so freaky. I honestly can't even stay that long; my husband is really freaking out. I mean, first that one runner goes missing, and then Lucy goes missing, and now this? We could be next, Julianne. We're really not safe out there alone right now."

Julianne swallowed. Normally Molly was overdramatic, but she had to admit she was a little worried herself.

"You don't know any of them are even connected," Harrison said in response to her.

Molly shot him a look. "They are. Doesn't it seem like a weird coincidence to you? Young girls, runners, all just vanish?"

"To be technical, your friend Katie didn't vanish," Harrison replied.

Molly let out a harsh breath before looking away. Julianne could tell Molly wasn't a fan of Harrison. She seemed close to getting up when Logan came back with a tray of drinks: two beers and two glasses of wine.

Molly smiled at him, grabbed a glass of wine, and took a long sip. "I like your boyfriend's taste."

Julianne shook her head, refusing to make eye contact with Logan after the comment. "Oh, he's not my boyfriend."

"Well, whatever. Thanks for the wine," Molly said to Logan. "Anyway, Julianne, I don't know about you, but I'm quitting running club. Things . . . well, you know."

Julianne hadn't thought about it yet, but she wouldn't be going back either—at least not until she could find Lucy. Unless Lucy was in a ditch somewhere, like Katie. Maybe like the other runner, Angela, too. Julianne let out a small shudder.

"You're going to the police about Lucy, right?" Molly asked. "I mean, they're going to need to know. Especially if it could be connected to what happened to Katie."

"I guess, yeah, I should," Julianne said. She hadn't planned on it, but with what had happened to Katie, she had to. "Has anyone talked to you? Like, are the cops questioning people she knows? They haven't said much on the news about anything yet."

Molly shook her head. "I thought about going down to the station, but my husband told me to stay out of it. But I wouldn't be surprised if they want to talk to us. Right?"

Molly directed the last question at Harrison.

Harrison shrugged. "It sounds like you didn't know her too well. And we don't know what the police already know about who did it and what happened."

Molly took another large sip of her wine. "I should get going. My husband is picking up Toby from daycare, so I should get home before he worries."

Julianne gave her another quick hug before she left. They'd learned nothing new from Molly, but she shouldn't have expected too much.

"I think she's right that I should go to the police," Julianne said to Harrison. "Right?"

Harrison said nothing, so Logan replied. "Yeah, I think so. It's been enough time. And if she isn't missing, it won't hurt."

Harrison slid his phone over to the two of them. There was a new article about Katie stating that she'd been the victim of a hit and run. And apparently whoever had hit her had come forward.

"I thought your contact said she died from blunt-force trauma?" Julianne asked.

"I don't know about you, but if I got hit by a car, it would be pretty forceful," Harrison replied, his dark brow darting up.

"Why didn't you show this to Molly?" Julianne asked.

"I just got it now. So while it sure seems like a weird coincidence that Katie was killed, I think you may have to tap this one up to bad luck."

"Does it say who hit her? The person who confessed?" she asked.

Harrison scanned the article further. He showed her the photo of the man who had come forward. "Barrett Kennedy. A thirty-four-year-old art dealer."

She thought for a moment. The name sounded familiar. Maybe she'd heard it with Lucy at the gallery hop. "Did you ever find me a number for Alex?"

"Even better," Harrison said. "I got us an address."

"To his home?" she questioned. "Why?"

Truthfully, Julianne had a brief idea of where he lived after her night there, but probably couldn't pinpoint it exactly.

"No, not his condo," Harrison said. "He has another home in Miami, Florida."

Julianne's eyebrows scrunched. "Well, I don't think we really need to go to those measures. Let's just see what he knows about Lucy's last shoot."

"Alright," Harrison said. "But I've got a feeling that he was hiding something."

"More than a wife?" she asked, laughing about it to make herself feel better.

"Yes," Harrison replied. He slid a piece of paper over to her. "Here's a number for him."

She grabbed it, sliding it into her bag. "Thanks. I'll give him a call later."

"I guess we don't need anything else from you," Logan said, looking at Harrison.

Julianne tried to give Logan a scolding look, but he didn't look at her. She wished he wouldn't be so rude to his brother. Harrison really was trying to help them, and for no other reason than because he was doing his brother a favor. She honestly didn't quite understand their dynamic. It seemed like Logan had much more of a beef with Harrison than the other way around. And with what Logan had told her, it made little sense why he would feel this way. Sure, Logan didn't trust his brother's job, but what had Harrison ever done to prove he was dangerous to Logan? Maybe she would find out eventually, but it would definitely take more time and digging.

"I guess not," Harrison said, staring at Julianne.

"I'll let you know if I need anything after I talk to Alex," she said to him.

Logan seemed like he wanted to comment but kept quiet.

She thought about calling Alex right away but wondered if he would bring up their night together, and she felt weird discussing that in front of either of the two men with her. After she finished her wine, she and Logan left the bar. Harrison left at the same time, giving her a nod before taking off.

Logan was unusually quiet on the drive back to the hospital. When they got there, she thought about asking him what was up but decided against it. If it somehow involved him and her, she didn't want to get into that discussion again. She had enough on her mind right now with having to call Alex.

11

A lex answered on the third ring.

"Hello?"

"Alex, hi. It's Julianne. From the gallery," she said, already feeling stupid.

"Oh, okay. One minute."

She heard some shuffling and then the sound of a door closing.

"Julianne, I have to say, I was pretty surprised to see you the other day." His tone reminded her of the guy she'd met that first night. It sounded slightly flirtatious. Much different from the man who had been standing next to his wife.

"Ah, yes," she said. "Sorry, I really had no idea—"

"That's okay," he said, humor in his voice. "Although I should mention Elizabeth and I have an open relationship. So don't feel like you need to be worried about coming in."

Open relationship. She still didn't feel good about it. And she really had no way of knowing if he was being honest.

"So, darling Julianne," he said. "What can I do for you?"

She cleared her throat, trying to sound confident as she

spoke. "I was wondering if you had any more information on Lucy for me? You said there was a photo shoot you were going to look into?"

"Yes," he said. The phone was silent for a moment. "It was with a guy named Theo Goldberg."

Theo. Could that be the Theo from her running club? It seemed like a coincidence—and wouldn't Lucy have mentioned this to her?

"Do you know why she was nervous?" Julianne asked him.

"He was hiring her to do a series of shots for his fiancée. I think maybe a boudoir-type shoot. I don't think Lucy had ever done anything like it before, so she was feeling nervous. Theo's fiancée is the daughter of some politician. I can't remember his name. Anyway, she's apparently a big deal, so Luce was pretty hyped up."

Julianne shook her head as she took it all in. Lucy's nervousness was easily explained by what Alex had just told her, but none of it really seemed like a reason for Lucy to disappear. But him mentioning Theo really made her worry. She had to look up Theo Goldberg right away and see if it was the same guy in their group.

"Do you know if the photo shoot happened?" she asked.

"No idea," he said. "I guess I'd say you could talk to Theo."

Right. Yes, that was what she would do. She had some online stalking to do once she got home.

"Anything else you can think of at all?" Julianne asked.

She heard a click on the end of his line before the phone went dead. She let out a growl. Maybe he'd gotten disconnected. She didn't really know, but she decided not to call back. She'd have to follow this Theo lead. She dialed Harrison; she didn't want to waste any time.

"Hello, Julianne," he answered.

Julianne quickly explained what Alex had told her. She left out the part about the phone call being disconnected. It might have meant nothing. Maybe it was just his wife coming into the room. That made much more sense than him knowing something about Lucy that he didn't want to tell her.

"I'll look into it and see what I can find," he said. "The name sounds familiar."

Alex had said the fiancée was the daughter of a politician, so it made sense that this Theo might be someone important as well.

"Great. Thanks, Harrison."

The phone was quiet for a moment. She wondered if he too had ended their call abruptly, but then he spoke again. "So you and Logan . . . is there a you and Logan?"

She had not been expecting this question. "What?"

"You were holding hands," he said. "I'm just wondering if there's something going on."

So he *had* seen. She wanted to ask why he cared. Maybe he was going to stop helping her if there was something going on between them., Logan had directly asked him to stay away from her, and Harrison seemed to want to do right by his brother.

"No, there isn't anything going on." And there wasn't, right? Yes, they'd kissed. But Logan had kissed a lot of girls. And she knew for a fact he was doing something with Emily. Yes, she could feel fine about her answer.

"Alright, I'll let you know what I find on Theo," he said before hanging up.

After she parked in her garage, she walked to her condo, fully prepared for a good night's sleep. But she knew as soon as she stepped out of her elevator to walk to her door that something was wrong. Alarms rang in her mind; the shadow wasn't right. Her door was cracked open just enough that light shone into the hall. She never forgot to lock her door, let alone shut it.

She slowly approached toward it. The only person who had a spare key to her apartment was her mom. She pushed the door lightly and it swung open. The entirety of her condo had been turned upside down. It was definitely not her mom —she'd been robbed.

Julianne found herself dialing Harrison without thinking about it. Part of her knew 911 was the better option, but her gut told her something about this had to do with her search for Lucy, and she had yet to involve the police in that. She'd let Harrison tell her when it was time.

"Julianne," he said.

"Hi, um, I just got home, and I think someone was in my condo," she said. Her voice was shaky, and she realized her hands were shaking as she held onto her phone.

"Are you still in there?" he asked, his voice strangely urgent.

"Yeah . . . yes, I just walked in."

"Get outside. Get in your car and lock the doors. We don't know if anyone is still in there. I'll come now."

Julianne agreed and slid her phone into her back pocket. She looked around before going back outside. Drawers had been thrown open, chairs were pushed out of their intended locations, and a few of her wine glasses lay shattered on the floor. She felt a single tear fall down her cheek, followed soon by more.

Somehow minutes must have passed because Harrison was walking through her front door, and she hadn't moved yet.

"I told you to wait in your car," Harrison said, his voice angry.

She looked up, almost surprised to see him there. She had meant to go to her car too, but somehow she'd zoned out and was still standing near her front door with her keys and purse still in her hands.

He seemed to notice her condition and walked forward, moving her to a bench near the front door. "Just sit here, and I'll go make sure it's safe."

After five minutes he came back to where she was sitting. "Whoever was here is gone."

"Did other things seem to be messed up?" she asked, dreading what else had been taken or destroyed.

He nodded. "The whole place looks turned over, almost too much though. Do you see anything missing from first glance?"

She walked around, frustrated by what a mess it was. She'd be cleaning this up for a week. She spotted her laptop in its usual resting place on her desk; it hadn't been touched. Same with her TV. In her room she found her jewelry scattered around, but not missing.

"No, I don't think anything's missing at all," she said, confused and grateful at the same time. "Do you think—"

"My best guess is someone broke in to scare you off."

She nodded. "But who?"

"Well, we know Alex knows you're searching," he said. "And Molly. Anyone else you can think of?"

"I think that's it. Besides Logan, of course. I didn't mention it to you earlier, but on the phone Alex seemed to have maybe hung up on me when I was questioning him about Lucy. But if he's trying to scare me off, does that mean he would know more?"

He shrugged. "I don't know yet, but we'll figure this out. Do you need a place to stay tonight?"

She hadn't thought about it yet, but she guessed staying here was probably not a great idea. She didn't want to go to her mom's house because she'd have to explain what had happened. Her dad's place was definitely off limits. She could get a hotel room, but she was feeling nervous about being alone. She wished Lucy was still around.

"You can stay at might place if you need," Harrison said.

Julianne wasn't sure she felt comfortable with that. She knew for sure Logan would say it was a terrible idea. "Logan has a spare room."

He nodded. "Alright. I have a buddy at the precinct. I'll let him know about the break-in and give him your number if he has questions."

She sighed and almost hugged him. She was exhausted, and the last thing she wanted to do was have to talk to the police tonight. Instead she said, "Thank you."

She went to her room and packed a bag with some clothes and her bathroom things. Harrison waited for her and walked her out to her car.

"Thanks." She smiled.

He leaned against her car as they both stood quietly.

"Are you holding up okay?" he asked. He looked down at the ground.

"Yes, I'm okay."

"You got caught in the middle of some shit," he said, looking up at her. "I know that sucks. I feel like I should have warned you before you started digging."

She shook her head. "I still would have dug. It's not your fault."

Julianne got into her car and drove over to Logan's. She thought about texting him before she left, but didn't feel like explaining everything over the phone. She knocked on his door, suddenly feeling like if she could see Logan things might just be okay.

Logan's door opened, and Emily stared back at her.

Julianne's mouth went dry, and suddenly she couldn't remember what she'd been about to say.

"Oh, hey, Julianne," Emily said.

Julianne looked beyond her but didn't see Logan. She noticed now that Emily was in a large T-shirt that was most likely Logan's and wasn't wearing pants. She wanted to make herself disappear. Her brain raced to think of a way of out this situation, but she came up empty.

"Emily?" she heard Logan call from his bedroom.

"It's Julianne," she called back.

Julianne heard shuffling behind Emily, and her stomach dropped. She had to go. She couldn't deal with him trying to talk to her right now. He had a major thing going on with Emily. Why the hell did he even bother with Julianne?

"Sorry, you guys are clearly busy," Julianne muttered to Emily, turning around and rushing down the hall. This time she refused to let Logan catch up to her, so she took the steps down the stairs quickly, rushed to her car, and sped out of the parking lot. She'd feel like an idiot tomorrow at the hospital in front of them both, but she was so focused on the current moment she didn't care.

She texted Harrison for his address and he sent it back almost immediately.

Julianne's phone buzzed. She looked down—Logan. She swiped ignore. Another buzz. This time she turned it over so she didn't have to see it keep ringing.

Harrison lived in a small blue house in a neighborhood she'd never been to before. It seemed like possibly a sketchy area, but she wasn't worried about her safety. Harrison seemed like someone nobody would mess with.

Harrison opened the door for her as she walked up the steps, dragging her bag with her.

"I'm so sorry," she said. "You really didn't have to take me in. I can still go find a hotel."

Harrison shook his head. "It's no problem."

"Okay," she said, setting her bag on the floor.

"My brother is going to kill me though," he said with a smirk.

Julianne sighed. "He doesn't know I'm here, so don't worry."

Harrison walked toward her; he was so close that she froze. He lifted a hand and placed it on her cheek. His hand was both strong and smooth. For a second she worried he would kiss her, and then she worried that maybe she wanted him to. But he didn't either way. He just stood there for a second, staring into her eyes.

"I'm not sure what's going on between you two," he said, his voice softer than she'd heard it before. "But my brother's an idiot for letting you go tonight."

She blinked a few times. She couldn't tear her eyes away from his. Finally, he did and she felt a breath release from her lungs. She took a step back to put some space between them.

Truthfully, any woman would be crazy to not be physically attracted to Harrison. He was gorgeous, tall, built, and had this mysteriousness that added to his intrigue. The problem was, there was so much wrong with her being attracted to him. For one, he was Logan's brother. And since she was already attracted to Logan, feeling the same way about his brother just seemed terrible on so many levels. And two, he was probably, most definitely, not good for her.

But here she was, in his house, ready to spend the night. She was really starting to wonder what happened to the old Julianne. This new one felt unfamiliar—she felt like she was almost shedding herself gradually each day. She didn't exactly miss her old self, but she worried her priorities were getting blurred. If it wasn't Lucy, it was one of the Williams brothers. And that really wasn't the Julianne Davis she knew.

"Why don't you go relax, and I'll grab you a drink?" Harrison asked, pointing toward his living room.

She sat down on the black leather couch and ran her fingers over the small crack on the front of it. She looked around the room. He didn't have any décor up; this house was definitely all-bachelor. She looked around for any photos, but there were none.

He returned shortly with two cups holding a brown liquid.

"Whiskey," he said, handing it to her.

She scrunched her nose. "I don't think I like whiskey."

He sighed, sitting down next to her and forcing the glass into her hand. "When you've had a day like you had today, you like whiskey."

She took a small sip of the liquid, letting it sit on her tongue for only a second before it burned down the back of her throat. She resisted coughing. She really didn't like the taste, but it quickly warmed her stomach, and she swallowed down more.

Harrison drank his whole glass in a few sips, resting the cup on the table next to the couch. He rested his head back on the couch and sighed. She thought he would say something, but he didn't.

"What was it like in Louisiana?" Julianne asked. She wasn't sure where her question came from. Maybe the whiskey was making her brave. She expected him to not respond, but he sat up, looking at the wall in front of him.

"We had a pretty good childhood when we were little," he said. "Our old man owned a restaurant. Logan and I loved going in and helping. Our mom helped him take care of the books. She'd gone to school for something like that."

Julianne nodded, trying to picture a young Logan and Harrison in her head.

"When I was around nine, Logan was just five, the restaurant went under. It really sucked," Harrison said, glancing down at his empty cup. "It was our only income, and my folks had invested all of their money into it. Dad was down about it for a while, but eventually he started preparing for his next project. He was always ready to try anything to make something work for his family. But my mom, I don't know, it was right around that time that she started getting depressed."

"About a year or so after this happened, our mom had reached a low and my dad kicked her out of the house. At the time, I remember Logan and I both being shocked. I think as kids my dad had really kept a lot from us. We didn't know how bad she was. She was drinking a lot. He'd find her passed out frequently when she was supposed to be taking care of us. I think he thought if he kicked her out, gave her a wake-up call, that she'd shape up. But instead she just took off."

"You . . . you never saw her after that?" Julianne asked, shocked.

He shook his head. "Nope."

Julianne couldn't understand what kind of mother would just abandon her family.

"Did your dad ever try to get her help?" she asked.

"Yeah. But they didn't have a lot of money. And no health insurance because no one had a job. Whatever he'd tried didn't work. I don't know what was worse, her depression or her drinking. I also don't know which caused which."

"So, you were about ten then when she left? But you didn't come to stay with your grandparents here until two years later, correct?"

Harrison looked at her and sat quietly. She wondered if she was asking too much. He'd already given her more than she'd expected.

"Let me get us refills," he said, grabbing both of their glasses. He was back after another minute and handed hers back. This time the liquid didn't burn going down, but it still wasn't her favorite taste.

"Apparently Dad started gambling to get ahead," Harrison said. "I reckon he'd probably had a problem with that for a while. Anyway, he got a job from a guy who used to work at his restaurant—he owned an oyster-fishing boat. Dad seemed to like the work enough, said he was fixin' to save up all his money to try again with a new business. This time he wanted to try something in New Orleans. Logan and I were excited to move there too. But apparently all the money he was putting away he'd actually been trying to double, and soon he had nothing to pay the mortgage and our house was being foreclosed on."

Julianne noticed how his southern drawl seemed to come out more when he spoke about his past.

"Dad's parents lived in Minnesota. He'd moved down to Louisiana after he graduated high school—him and friend rafted down the Mississippi and never went home. He wasn't close with his parents, so we'd only met them once or twice. He didn't tell us until the day before that they were coming to take us back to Minnesota with them. I was pretty pissed at him. I had friends I didn't want to leave. And Logan, I just remember him crying. Sometimes that's all I can remember Logan doing after our mom left, until . . . god, I don't even know how long."

Julianne looked down at her cup. She hadn't even realized she'd finished it. She was definitely feeling its effects and found herself leaning in closer to Harrison as he spoke. She noticed a few curls were hanging down on Harrison's forehead and she had to hold back from brushing them aside.

"Your grandparents, did you enjoy living with them?" she asked.

He shrugged. "It probably wasn't as I bad I thought it was when I was twelve. I hated it. I was mad at the world, really. I think Logan looked to me to see if everything was all right, and when I couldn't give him that, we started to grow apart. He threw himself into school. I threw myself into no good most of the time."

Harrison looked over at her bag. "That thing's been buzzing. Did you want to get it?"

She shook her head. It was clear he was done talking about his past, but she'd gotten more information from him than she'd ever thought she would.

"What did he do?" Harrison asked.

Julianne rolled her eyes. "Nothing. It's just this girl Emily was at his apartment when I showed up, so I just left. End of story."

"Emily," he said, tapping his fingers against this cup. "I met her once."

"They sleep together," she said. "I mean, I think that's all it is. She's another resident. I don't really know Logan as well as you think. We only became friends recently. So I'm still trying to navigate him."

"But you like him?" he asked, gazing at her.

She knew what he meant. She didn't know how to answer. "Maybe."

"I don't know a ton of about my brother's love life," Harrison said. "But I know he's never had a real relationship. So I don't doubt that he's sleeping with this Emily. But I know it might be hard to believe that sometimes sleeping with someone is just, well, that. No emotions, no . . . love."

"Yeah, I don't—" Julianne began and stopped herself. "I mean, I know you know about what happened with Alex and I, but that's literally the only time in my life I've ever done something like that. I'm not saying I'm looking for something serious, but—"

Harrison interrupted her. "What I'm trying to say is, don't discount what his feelings for you might be because of what you think he has going on."

Julianne rolled her eyes. "Just drop it, okay?"

"Okay," he answered, his eyes meeting hers again. "It's just I've seen the way he looks at you, and I can promise you that if he knew you were here right now, I would be a dead man. And I just want you to know . . ." Harrison paused to look down at the floor, his long lashes against his cheeks. Julianne realized they were so close that their thighs were touching. Her pulse quickened when he looked back up at her.

"I want you to know the only reason I haven't done this, was because I was trying to give him a chance with you."

Julianne opened her mouth to ask what he was taking about when his lips crashed down on hers.

Julianne let out a small moan as she leaned into him. Her head spun. He'd been wanting to do this. He'd been wanting her. His tongue was warm as he caressed her lower lip. This kiss felt different from the one at the gallery. More urgent, full of longing.

His mouth began working down her neck and she felt her entire body buzz from the sensation of his kisses.

"Harrison." Her voice was quiet, and she wasn't sure if she was asking him to stop or to keep going.

He glanced up at her, his eyes looking both eager and lustful. She wanted to keep kissing him. She wanted to let him do whatever he wanted with her. But it worried her she might regret it. Maybe she was just mad at Logan because of Emily. There was too much on her mind to let this go any further.

"I'm not going to say I'm sorry for doing that," Harrison said. "I've thought about it since the day I first saw you."

Julianne blushed. "I . . . I should really get to bed," she said. She didn't know what else to say, but she hoped rest would help her sort through everything. At the very least, if she was locked in a bedroom she wouldn't be tempted to do that again.

Harrison led her up the stairs of his small house. The wooden stairs creaked as she followed behind him. Upstairs there were two bedrooms and a small bathroom. She was hoping maybe he'd have his own bathroom so they wouldn't accidentally bump into each other in the middle of the night, but that didn't seem like it would be the case.

"Thanks," she said, standing in the doorway to the room he'd led to her to. It had a small twin bed and nightstand. "For everything."

He nodded. "Goodnight, Julianne."

She shut the door behind her and leaned back against it. Her heart was still thudding from downstairs. She felt like she should have said more about it, commented on it, but it seemed simpler to ignore it. She considered going to the bathroom to get ready for bed, but instead collapsed on the small bed and quickly fell asleep.

Julianne's phone alarm didn't go off the next morning, and she woke up much later than she was supposed to.

"Shit," she mumbled, fumbling to pull her scrubs out of her bag and then on her legs. She couldn't believe she'd slept so well in this small bed. It honestly hadn't been that comfortable, but she was dead tired after the day she'd had. She yanked on her top and then ran to the bathroom to brush her teeth and wash her face. She'd brought her travel makeup bag with her that had some tinted moisturizer and mascara in it, so she put both on and fluffed her hair out with her fingers. It would have to do.

She quickly packed her things into her bag and slung it over her shoulder. She would go home after the hospital and start working on cleaning up the mess—and then she'd sleep there. She couldn't keep sleeping at Harrison's; it just didn't feel right. And well, Logan . . . the picture of Emily in just his T-shirt replayed in her mind.

Logan was the least of her concerns, though. Somehow, with everything that had happened yesterday, she'd forgotten to look into what Alex had told her about Theo Goldberg. As thoughts raced through her head about Lucy's disappearance and her own impending safety, Harrison walked out of his room. He was dressed in only a pair of navy blue running shorts. No shirt. Her eyes locked onto his six-pack.

"Hi." She smiled and forced words out of her mouth so she wasn't just standing there, staring like an idiot.

"Hi," he replied, a smile playing on his lips. "Did you sleep okay?"

She nodded. "Too well. I'm late, and I'm never late."

He smirked. "Guess I'm already a bad influence on you."

Julianne smiled at him. "Guess so."

"After you went to bed last night, I did some digging for you. Do you recognize this guy?" He held out his phone and she looked down. Bingo. That was definitely Theo.

Julianne nodded. "Yep, that's the guy from our running club."

"You meet on Fridays?"

"Yes."

"Do you think you could go and bump into him?" he asked. "I think with someone breaking into your place last night, you might need to be a little less transparent in your search."

"Yes, that sounds good."

"I'll send someone over to your house today to clean things up and see if they can get any prints so we could get an idea of who was there. I already contacted someone at the station about the break-in, and of course they have their thumbs up their asses so we won't expect too much from them."

Julianne just nodded along as he spoke. She wanted to

hug him. Seriously hug him. She felt like a hundred pounds had been taken off of her shoulders since she'd woke up that morning.

"Oh wow, thank you," she said instead. "Seriously, thank you, Harrison."

He nodded, his eyes traveling to her bag. "Are you going home tonight?"

"I think so. Do you think it would be safe?"

"No," he said. "But I can have someone—"

She held a hand up. "No, you've done enough. I don't need personal security too."

"Just consider staying with someone for a few days."

"Alright," she replied. "Well, I really should go."

Harrison walked over to a drawer nearby and pulled out a small black canister and tossed it to her. "Maybe keep this on you too."

"Pepper spray?"

"It's a pretty lethal dose," he said. "Go easy on Logan with it."

She rolled her eyes before smiling softly at him. "Thanks."

He nodded. "Listen, about last night . . ."

She shook her head, her cheeks noticeably pink. "It's okay."

"So it'd be okay if I did it again?" he asked, raising an eyebrow curiously at her.

Her pink cheeks had turned to red. "I . . ."

"Bye, Julianne," he said.

She could swear she saw him wink before she shut the door.

. . .

When Julianne got to the hospital, she had no time to even grab a coffee, so she ran straight to the workroom where Emily, Logan, Pete, and another resident, Sarah, were sitting around a computer talking. They all looked up when they heard the door open. Everyone looked back at the computer when they saw it was just Julianne. Well, everyone except Logan. He looked angry. For a moment she wondered if he knew about the kiss with Harrison, but she realized that was stupid. Of course he didn't. He was most likely angry about the zillion missed calls she hadn't ever bothered to return.

"See Logan? She's alive. Now can you focus your patients who might not be soon?" Sarah said.

Logan turned back to what they were working on as Julianne sat in the only open seat—right next to him. When they finished looking over last night's patients, they broke up to go round on them. Julianne tried to saunter back so Logan would have to go ahead of her, but he held back as the rest of the group disappeared out of sight.

"Lose your phone?" Logan asked.

Julianne looked over at him. "No. Can we just talk about this later?"

Logan grabbed her wrist, stopping her. "No, we're talking about this now."

Julianne looked away from him. "Logan, I just didn't want to talk to you. Okay? Just drop it."

"You didn't want to talk to me, but you came to my apartment? That's weird."

"Seriously, we have patients to see," she said. "Yeah, I came to your apartment. I needed a place to stay last night. But you were busy, so I left and found somewhere else. End of story."

Logan followed along with her quietly as they went to Alice Florez's room. She was an elderly woman who'd been hit in the pedestrian crosswalk and suffered several internal injuries. Julianne checked her heart and blood pressure while Logan reviewed her chart. Her condition was the same as the night before.

"How are you feeling today, Alice?" Julianne asked.

"Oh, not so wonderful, sweetheart," Alice said to her, her eyes squinting up in the corners.

"It might take some time, but you will," Julianne said, resting a hand on Alice's arm. "Your surgeries went well, so now we just need you to heal properly."

Alice reminded her a bit of her own grandmother. She was sweet, and her voice was soft. Julianne always wanted to spend as much time with the elderly patients as she could. She knew how much it meant to them just to have someone to talk with. Which meant it frustrated her that Logan was breathing down her neck.

"I'll have Nurse Riley check in on you again soon, okay, Alice?" Julianne said.

Alice nodded before Julianne and Logan walked out of the room. Logan was already talking before they'd even made it into the hallway.

"Why did you need to stay somewhere?"

"Someone broke into my house," she stated as a matter of fact.

"What?" he gasped. "Is everything okay?"

"They just made a mess," she said. He looked concerned, but right now she just wanted him to forget about her. He would ask more questions, and she knew which one would be next.

"Where did you stay?"

She chewed on her bottom lip. "With a friend."

"You shouldn't have left," Logan said. "Or you could have just answered the phone."

She stared at him as if he had grown two heads. "Um, Emily was standing in your apartment with no pants on, Logan. I was not going to stay there!"

He rolled her eyes as if what she was saying was so trivial. "Emily and I—"

Julianne held up her hand toward him. "I really don't want to know."

"Just please hear me out."

Julianne looked around to see if anyone was watching or listening to them. It appeared they were alone, so she let him continue.

"We've been sleeping together for a while, but there really are zero feelings between us. It should have ended a long time ago," he said. "We were actually talking about that before you came over. We didn't sleep together last night; we were only talking. We almost did, but it's something I've been wanting to end for a little while now."

"Okay . . . ?"

"I feel like we were heading in a different direction, our friendship I mean," Logan said. "I just want you to know my friendships are important to me. And I would never have turned you away last night."

"And that's what you want? A friendship?" she asked, thinking of their make out session. "Because I can't be what Emily is to you."

"I know," he said, his eyes earnest. "And yes, friends. Let's just put everything from yesterday behind us. Please?"

Julianne smiled cautiously at him. "Yes, we can do that." She also wanted to put everything from yesterday behind her. For some reason she felt guilty for what had happened with Harrison.

"Are you going home tonight?" he asked.

She nodded. "Yes, I think so. Har—" She stopped and then cursed at herself. Why had she brought up his name?

"Harrison knows about all of this?" he asked. "Wait, did you . . . was he the friend you stayed with last night?"

She could see a flare of anger in his eyes and but she couldn't lie again.

"Yes, he was helping me figure out this mess, so I just . . . I didn't know where else to go."

"Your mom's?" he asked.

"No, she knows me too well. She would have wanted to know why I needed to come over, and if I told her the truth, she'd lose it."

"Okay, well, maybe your dad's then," he said.

Julianne glared at him. She couldn't believe he'd think her father would be a better choice than Harrison. She felt hurt that he couldn't see past whatever his beef was with his brother to see he was helping Julianne.

"No, thank you. Harrison is being really helpful in finding Lucy. He's also helping to figure out who broke into my house and clean up the mess. I know you have issues with him, but he's doing this for me because of you. Because I'm your friend. Can you just give him a break?"

His jaw tightened. "You don't know him like I do, Julianne. I just wish . . . I wish you'd trust me with this."

"I know," she said. "But you're going to have to trust that I know what I'm doing too."

Logan groaned. "Fine. But I'm coming over to your place tonight. You can sleep there, and I'll stay over if you're worried about being safe."

"You don't need to do that," Julianne said.

"I want to," he said. "I'll even bring over dinner."

"Fine," she muttered.

Later, before she left to go home, she ran into Logan, who said he'd be over around seven with dinner. Julianne thought about telling him no again, but she was seriously hungry. She'd been skipping way too many meals lately, and she was still nervous about being alone. She had no intention of going to Harrison's, so Logan coming to her definitely seemed like the lesser evil.

When Julianne walked into her condo, it surprised her to see it back to normal. Maybe even cleaner than before. She slipped her shoes off and left her bag on a bench near the door.

There was a knock on her door shortly after seven. She checked the privacy hole first, making sure it wasn't someone unexpected. She opened her door, and Logan stood there, smiling at her. Her heart skipped a bit as it normally did when he gave her that look.

"Hi." She smiled back, opening her door for him to walk in.

He was holding a paper bag filled to the top with groceries. In his other hand was another paper bag with what looked like a bottle of wine.

"I come with reinforcements," he said. "I hope you like chicken parmesan. Or eggplant. I brought both."

She almost drooled. "Oh my gosh, I haven't eaten a real meal in days. They both sound sounds amazing."

"Good. I've been told I'm an okay cook, so I hope I don't disappoint."

She watched as he unpacked the bag. He had some chicken breasts, a purple eggplant, bread crumbs, eggs, tomato sauce, noodles, and a few other things. He pulled a bottle of red wine out of the other small paper bag. Julianne grabbed two glasses and the bottle, opening it and pouring a glass for both of them as he began slicing the eggplant.

"Do you cook a lot?" she asked, now curious as she watched him. He seemed to know what he was doing without looking at any recipe. She had to follow recipes to the T in order to come up with anything palatable. Even when she cooked mac and cheese, she always had to read the box to remember how many tablespoons of butter and milk to add.

He let out a small laugh, looking up at her. "Yeah, I figure eating healthy is important, and I've never had a ton of money, so going out to eat isn't really an option, you know?"

She nodded. Except she didn't exactly know. She'd never not had money, or a cooked meal. She found it admirable that he'd learned this.

"You don't cook much?" he asked, grabbing the glass of wine she handed him.

She shook her head.

"Did you want to help?"

"I . . . I mean, sure. I can help. Just don't expect too much."

He laughed again, handing her the carton of eggs. "You can start by cracking a few of these eggs in a bowl."

She took out one of the brown eggs and tapped it on the counter in front of her. Logan grabbed her hand and pointed her toward the bowl. "Try it on the side of that."

It cracked easier, and she let it slide into the bowl in front of her.

"Now mix them together," he said, handing her a fork.

Her hand grazed his as she took it, and their eyes met for a moment. She took a sip of her wine. He was still standing close to her. She hadn't done this with anyone before—cook, that is. Well, her mom, maybe. But her mom really hadn't included her much. She couldn't help but think this was what it would be like to have a boyfriend. And then she wanted to kick herself for the thought. Logan was *not* her boyfriend, nor did he want to be. If she let herself have those thoughts, she would only be disappointed.

"Earth to Julianne," he said, waving his hand in front of her.

"Sorry," she said, realizing she still had another egg to crack. "I'm already slacking on my job."

"It's all right. You can sit down and just enjoy your wine too."

She shook her head. "No, honestly, I was just thinking about how I like doing this with . . . someone."

She almost said *with you*, but stopped herself.

He smiled at her, nudging her playfully with his hip. "So does me cooking for you move me up past the not-bad category yet?"

Julianne grinned at him. "Maybe."

After she finished mixing the eggs, Logan had her dip the chicken breasts he had just pounded out into a flour mixture, then into the eggs, and then he followed by placing them in a bowl of the bread crumbs. She repeated the same steps with the eggplant slices. Her fingers were a pasty mess when they were done.

"Now, we fry," he said, smiling at her.

Julianne went to the sink and washed her hands.

"So you really taught yourself?" she asked as she dried off her hands. "Did you learn from your dad at all? Harrison said he owned a restaurant."

Logan nodded slowly. "Yeah, I guess I learned from him early on. But my grandma taught me most of what I know about cooking. This is one of her famous recipes."

"Harrison told me, about your parents and how you ended up here," she said quietly, worried about looking up at him. She thought about not mentioning it, but it felt like she was keeping something by not telling him.

When she looked up, she wondered if he'd heard her for a second because he was just still busy frying up the pieces of chicken, and his facial expression hadn't seemed to change. But then he looked over at her. "Okay."

"That must have been hard."

"I don't really like to talk about this," he said, his expression hardening.

She felt herself involuntarily moving back, and she wanted to kick herself. She needed to keep mouth shut. She understood more than anyone what it was like to not want to open up to someone.

He walked over to her, grabbing her by the waist and pulling her into him. She let her body melt into his, even if her brain was telling her to push back against him.

"Please don't feel bad," he said. "But just understand that really is a part of my life I want in my past."

"I get it." She took a moment to soak in his smell: piney and warm. "So, now what?"

He looked down at her. "Um . . ."

She hadn't seen Logan at a loss for words before, and she realized now that maybe he hadn't realized she was referring to the next step for dinner.

He took a step back, sliding his hands into his pockets and looking at the food. "I lied earlier."

"Oh?" she asked.

Her phone rang, and she looked at the screen. It was Harrison.

Logan had seen it and looked away at the food.

"I should grab this," she said, hitting answer before walking toward the dining room to talk. It was still within Logan's hearing, but it also gave her a little privacy.

"Hey," she answered.

"Hi," Harrison said. "Your place look okay?"

"Yes, thanks so much. It's hard to tell anyone was even here."

"Did you find a place to stay tonight?" Harrison asked.

She paused before answering. "Yes, I'm at my condo, but Logan's here with me."

His end was quiet for a moment. She could swear Logan had also stopped working in the kitchen to hear the phone call. She felt nervous, wanting to flee the entire situation she'd gotten herself into. How had she gotten caught between two brothers?

"Good. Good for him."

Julianne swallowed. She couldn't tell if he meant that. She honestly didn't know how Harrison felt toward her. She knew he was attracted to her, but she didn't think he wanted any more than that. He couldn't have actual feelings for her.

"Yes, well, I should go," she said, hoping he didn't feel rebuffed by her ending the phone call quickly. He'd been doing so much for her, and his help with trying to find Lucy was invaluable.

"Wait," Harrison said before she hung up. "I called because my guy was able to get some prints off of a few areas that were turned over at your place."

She felt her pulse quicken. "Yes?"

"They came back as Lucy Aldridge's."

Julianne's eyebrows scrunched in confusion. Logan must have sensed her change because he'd set his spoon down and walked over toward her.

"Well, I mean, Lucy's been over here before," she said. "That must be why, right?"

"Maybe," Harrison said. "But they took prints from several areas that were disturbed. I have a theory."

"Okay . . . ?"

Logan was now next to her. He signaled for her to put the phone on speaker.

"I think maybe Lucy broke into your house," Harrison said, "and I think she wants to scare you off from looking for her anymore."

13

Julianne stared at Logan after she ended her phone call with Harrison.

"Do you think he's right?" she asked. "Why would Lucy not just reach out to me and tell me to stop looking for her?"

Logan was about to answer when they both smelled smoke and looked toward the kitchen.

"Shit," he muttered, rushing over to the stove where smoke was billowing.

She followed him over and helped him move the pan.

"It's not ruined, is it?" she asked. She felt bad that her phone call had possibly ruined the food he'd been working on.

"No, it's okay," he said, turning on the stove vent so that a low hum filled the room. "And about Lucy . . . I don't know, Julianne. I guess it's possible. Maybe it really is time to stop looking."

That was the same thing Harrison had told her before

they ended their call. She wanted to consider the possibility, but it was hard to wrap her head around.

Logan was finishing up their plates, so Julianne brought their glasses and the rest of the wine over to the table. He followed shortly with their food. Despite the smoke, it smelled delicious.

"This looks great." She smiled at him before taking a bite.

Logan reached over to her lip with his thumb and dabbed. "Sorry, you have some sauce . . ."

She looked up at him and saw that same expression she'd seen when he kissed her. She clearly had gone crazy because she wanted him to do it again, but he didn't. He just sat back and returned to his plate.

She tested the waters. "Why did you say you lied?"

He sighed, setting down his fork. "Because I said I wanted to be friends with you."

"You don't?"

Logan rolled his eyes. "No, Julianne. I do not."

She sat quietly for a moment. She was confused. "What do you want then?"

"Honesty?"

"Always."

He studied her before taking a sip from his glass. "You. All of you. *Not* as a friend."

She swallowed. "Logan . . ."

"I know," he said. "I was just hoping things could be different with you. Because I like you. Like, I really like you, Julianne. And I was just hoping if we could do this, *this* being friends, it would enough for me."

"And is it?"

"God, no." He laughed softly. "But I'm trying."

She knew her options. The first was to let him keep being her friend. But she had a feeling it wouldn't work, not for long. Not when he looked at her the way he did. But her other option was to just become another friend with benefits like Emily. She didn't want to be that girl. But the last option was to just cut him out of her life, and she felt was in too deep to do that.

Looming over all of this was her kiss with Harrison. She wished she could push the guilt away. It was ridiculous. She and Logan were just friends. More or less. She felt the confession rushing to the tip of her tongue. "Logan, I need to tell you something, but I'm worried you won't want to even be my friend after."

He tilted his head, concern in his eyes. "I don't understand."

"Harrison kissed me last night," she blurted out. She felt like the world froze around her as she waited for his reaction. "I kissed him back too. I don't like him, I mean I don't think I like him, but you're being honest with me, and I feel like me keeping this a secret is not giving you the chance to see I'm not really that great, anyway. I'm actually kind of a mess lately."

He let out a harsh breath, staring off into the distance. "Can I have a minute?"

"Yes," she replied. She grabbed her glass and walked to the back patio. She sat down in a chair and looked out at the night sky.

Her patio overlooked downtown, so she could see all the skyscrapers lit up. It was her favorite place to go in the evenings to free her mind. And right now her mind was a wreck. She was sure she'd just ended any connection she had with Logan.

Moments later she heard the screen door open. She didn't look up, but felt Logan sit down next to her. She looked over to see him staring out at the twinkling lights.

"When anyone has compared Harrison and I, it always seems like at first look he's the one who would be unattached, would never have any personal relationships," Logan said. "But it's not true. He's always been the one to be closer—with our grandparents, with friends, with anyone really. Once he's close with someone in his life, he's able to open up with them. I'm sure our mom leaving when I was only five screwed me up."

Julianne looked over at him. Logan was still looking up at the sky.

"I wouldn't blame you for liking him," he said, finally looking at her. "I mean, I don't think he has the best moral decisions, but he can care for people in a way I've never been able to."

Julianne met his eyes. "I don't like him, Logan. I mean, I hardly know him. And I don't think you're screwed up."

He looked back at the sky. "I've never been in a real relationship. I've slept with, well, countless of women, but I've literally never felt emotionally attached to a single one. Wouldn't you call that screwed up?"

Maybe, but at the same time—while she wasn't an expert in psychology by any means—she could see how being abandoned as a child could have an effect on him. She didn't think relationships were easy either.

"No," she replied. "You're just human."

He looked over at her and kicked her foot lightly. "Thanks."

She brightened. "It's pretty out here, isn't it? I mean, I know you can't see any actual stars, but I'm a sucker for city lights."

"Yes, very," he replied.

"When did you decide you wanted to be a doctor?" she asked.

"I was about twelve," he replied. "Our dad visited us up here once or twice a year, and he told us something was wrong with his heart. I started researching and found out I really loved the human anatomy. I used to think it was because I wanted to save him, but I think maybe it was always the science that really drew me in."

"I'm sure it also had to do with wanting to save him," she said.

He didn't respond for a moment. "Maybe, but if it was, it was stupid. He abandoned us too."

She hadn't realized this was a sore subject with him, so she quickly let it go.

"What about you?" he asked. "When did you decide?"

"I guess I just always knew I'd do it," she said. "I used to look up to my dad when I was a kid. I thought he was basically god. But it was after Ella got sick that I decided I wanted to go into pediatric oncology. She had a surgical oncologist I idolized, maybe even more than my father. I knew I wanted to be her someday, so here I am."

"Sitting next to me," he said with a soft laugh.

"Yep," she replied. "You're not mad at me, are you?"

"No," he said quickly. "Of course not."

"Good. With Lucy gone, you're kind of my closest friend at the moment."

"Have you decided what you're going to do?" he asked. "About Lucy?"

"I've been thinking about it all day actually," she said. "I feel like I've gotten involved in something I shouldn't have. Maybe I never knew Lucy as well as I thought. Maybe I let my baggage with Ella cloud my judgment. But I don't want to quit, not now. Not if there is a chance she really does need help. Is that crazy?"

"No, Julianne, I think you're being a good friend. We'll figure it all out."

"I need to at least talk to Theo," she said. "I guess if it doesn't feel like he's involved at all, I'll just let it all go. I won't have any more leads, anyway."

"Did you look him up at all? You said his fiancée was someone sort of famous?"

They sat up as he pulled out his phone, searching "Theo Goldberg and fiancée."

Photos of the two of them in the City Pages of the local newspaper came up. She was tall and pretty with long brown hair. Ashley Burnhill. When they clicked on her picture, it said she was the daughter of Paul Burnhill, a senator from Minnesota. She and Theo were apparently well-known. Their faces were plastered in photos from various dinners and events, and now their engagement photos.

"Senator Burnhill," she said slowly.

"Yeah?"

"It sounds so familiar." She tapped on her chair, and

sudden recognition hit her. "Oh my god, Lucy had been researching him. I remember Harrison found files on people in her apartment, and one was full of research on him. Do you think this is related?"

"I'd say without a doubt," he replied. "Let's see if we can find anything on Theo and Ashley on social media."

Julianne searched for her on Instagram and found her profile that was public. Her last photo was from just yesterday. She was posing with a friend.

"Alive and well," she said.

They scanned for pictures of Ashley and Theo, and they seemed scattered around. Her eyes zeroed in on a photo about three rows down. The man she was with in the picture looked familiar. She touched the photo, following the link to the guy who was tagged. He hadn't uploaded anything before. He only had others he followed. She looked at the name: Barrett Kennedy.

She looked over at Logan. "That's the guy who hit Katie."

He grabbed her phone and glanced at the screen. "Are you sure?"

"Yes," she said. "It's too weird to be a coincidence, right?"

She went back to Ashley's account and looked at the photo. It wasn't a coincidence.

"So we know that Lucy was friends with Theo, and maybe subsequently Ashley. And Ashley clearly knew Barrett . . . who apparently hit Katie. And there is also the fact that Lucy had a file on Ashley's father."

"What if it wasn't on accident?" she asked. "Him hitting Katie."

"Why would he turn himself in then?" Logan asked.

Julianne paused. "It just seems—"

"Weird," he said. "I agree. Hey, this picture here was from tonight."

A new picture had just been posted of Ashley and Theo. It was captioned: *Getting ready for a silent auction for Arts for the Allies here at Aria.*

"We could go," Julianne said, looking at him. "We could pretend we're a couple attending the event, and I could try to talk to Ashley, and you could try for Theo."

She expected him to turn her down, but he nodded. "Sure."

"Really?"

Logan smirked. "Yes, but I'm afraid I can't show up there in my jeans. So we might need to stop by my apartment first."

She nodded. "Okay. I'm hoping Theo doesn't recognize me, so maybe we can find out more. I might . . . amp it up a little. Just hang out while I get ready. I'll try to go as fast I can."

Julianne went to her closet. She needed something between gala and cocktail. She spotted a shimmery, strapless gold dress with a sweetheart neckline. The skirt fell just to her knees. She hadn't worn it yet—it was one her mom had given her. Julianne hadn't quite been comfortable enough to wear it. The dress was tight in the chest area, showing off her breasts more than she was usually comfortable with. She pulled off her jeans and top and shimmied into the dress. She would normally wear a cardigan over something like this, but tonight she needed to look less like the usual Julianne.

She went to the bathroom to figure out her hair and makeup. Since she didn't have time to do too much with her hair, she ran a straightening iron through it. She went for a more exaggerated side part and pinned the right side back behind her ear. Afterward, she applied foundation, powder, bronzer, some dark eyeshadow and liner, and mascara. She ended with a pair of dangling diamond earrings she saved for special occasions.

When she walked downstairs, she had forgotten for a moment about her makeover and didn't quite understand the look on Logan's face. And then she remembered, and her face turned red. "Is it too much?" she asked, spinning around.

"No, no, you l-look," he said, his words stuttering together, "well, hell, you look hot, Julianne."

"Thanks," she said, her cheeks flaming red. "Not, like, too much though, right?"

He gave a lopsided grin. "As long as I'm pretending to be your boyfriend tonight, I think you'll be okay."

Logan didn't have a tux, so he'd opted for a dark gray suit that had slim-cut pants, a fitted jacket, and black dress shoes. He had used some gel so his hair was smoothed over. He reminded Julianne of old Hollywood handsome.

They discussed their plan and backstory more as they drove to Aria. Julianne could feel Logan's eyes on her more than usual. She considered scolding him, but secretly enjoyed the attention.

When they arrived, they had the valet park the car to keep up with their roles. Logan laced his fingers through hers as they walked to the main door.

"Relax," he whispered as they walked inside. She tried to

let her tense shoulders drop, but it was hard. She really needed a cocktail to make this all feel easier.

It seemed they were late because people were already done bidding on items and were now just milling around, talking and drinking. She hoped Theo and Ashley hadn't left early.

Julianne scanned the room, not recognizing anyone yet. Someone walked by and bumped into her left arm. When she turned around to apologize, he'd already walked away, but she recognized Theo.

She nudged Logan with her elbow, and he turned to look. He nodded. "You'll be okay alone?"

"Yes," she whispered. She didn't want to waste any time.

After Logan took off, she looked around the room again. Ashley wasn't near Theo, so she would have to keep walking around. She grabbed a glass of champagne from a waiter's tray and quickly swallowed the entire thing.

She spotted Ashley at a cocktail table with a friend Julianne recognized from her Instagram pictures. Julianne debated how she'd break into the conversation. She wasn't exactly great this kind of thing—actually she royally sucked at it. She was about to step forward to talk to her when she felt a hand on her arm.

"Julianne?"

She spun around. There stood Alex and Elizabeth. Well, so much for her cover story.

She had been so close to Ashley's table that Ashley turned to look when Alex called her name. She really, really wished Logan hadn't already left to talk to Theo.

"Oh, hi." She smiled.

"What are you doing here?" Alex asked, giving her cheek an obligatory air-kiss.

Her brain raced to think of a reason for being at the event. "Oh, I'm—"

"Here with me," an all too familiar voice said behind her.

Julianne felt her entire body tense. What the hell?

14

Harrison was behind her. She turned around to look at him, and she was sure her mouth dropped open for a moment. He had a bit of stubble on his jaw and was dressed in a black tuxedo that fit him perfectly. Her heart fluttered for a moment. What was he doing here? She knew Logan hadn't call him. Oh lord, Logan. What if he'd already told Theo that he and Julianne were together? How would they explain that with Harrison here? Alex already had seen her and Harrison together; it would be too weird to say they weren't.

Harrison wrapped his arm around her waist, pulling her close to him. His mouth moved to her neck, and she could swear he was about to kiss her, but he instead whispered harshly into her ear. "What the hell are you doing here?"

She wanted to say the same thing back, but she remembered how he'd told her she needed to stop looking for Lucy. He'd come here to find out more without her. She cursed silently. She wished she had listened to him now. She'd much rather he'd have done this all alone.

She just smiled at him instead of answering, turning her attention back to Alex.

"I see," Alex said. "Nice to see you again, Harry."

"Harrison," he corrected.

"Right," Alex said, nodding. "And how did you get invited again? I can't quite remember what you said you do."

She'd noticed Alex's tone wasn't as friendly as it had been before. Her guess was that he knew something was up, and he wanted to call them out on it. She waited for Harrison's answer. It was an art auction, and she didn't think Harrison really knew a thing about art. His apartment had been devoid of it. So his answer surprised her.

"I'm good friends with Anthony. He's the host of the event. We came to support him, and I'm looking for a new piece for my house. And you don't need to be invited to this auction anyway, Alex."

Alex grimaced. She was glad he'd been put in his place.

She saw Logan across the room. He'd spotted them all, his expression blank. She needed to get to him before he came over.

"Will you excuse me? I see a friend I need to speak with."

She hurried off, knowing all eyes were on her. She walked past Logan so they wouldn't see her stop at him and stood next to a few women admiring a blue and gold painting. Logan approached her after a moment.

"Why is he here?" he asked. He sounded angry. Maybe angrier than Julianne had ever heard him.

She sighed and met his eyes. "I don't know. He must have been following leads and came here like us. I swear I didn't mention it to him. Listen, Harrison was with me at the gallery when I went to talk to Alex, so he thinks

Harrison and I are together. Did you mention me to Theo at all?"

"No," he answered, agitation still in his voice. "I guess it's Harrison to the rescue again then."

She realized now he was hurt because he'd wanted to help her this time. And Julianne wished he could, too. She just didn't know how to change it right now.

"Well, I don't think anyone really saw us come in together," she said. "You might be able to find out more information than us, anyway. Alex was suspicious of us being here. I'm sure he knows it's about Lucy."

Logan took a sip of the drink he was holding without looking at her, setting it on the table. "Meet me out in the hallway in two minutes."

She watched Logan leave and wondered if Harrison was watching her, but didn't turn to look. She idled around for a few minutes and then followed Logan. He was standing in the hall, leaning against the wall with his eyes closed. He must have heard her because he straightened up. She walked toward him, not sure what he'd needed to talk to her about out here in the hallway. No one could have heard them inside the room.

Logan grabbed her suddenly, pinning her with arms so she couldn't get away, not that she planned to. When his lips melted into hers, she quickly understood why he'd chosen the hallway. His hands dug into her hair, messing up the pins she'd placed, but she didn't care. This felt good—way too good.

"What are you doing?" she asked between kisses. Her voice was raspy.

He didn't answer as his hands traveled down her dress.

They were leaning against a door that opened from their pressure. They both fell into a dark closet filled with paper reels and more paintings. She laughed lightly as she tried to get her balance. Logan shut the door behind them. He lifted her up onto a small shelf behind her, her dress was now riding up so high that her bare thighs wrapped around him.

"Logan," she said, her skin flushed. "We . . ."

He paused. His breathing was heavy, and she wished she hadn't said anything because she didn't want this to stop. She wanted this to keep going, even if it was only a one-time thing.

"You look too damn good tonight," he said, then dragged his lips down her neck. "I was hoping I'd get to be close to you all night. But now . . ."

Her eyes narrowed. "You're not jealous of Harrison, are you?"

A flare of anger lit up in his eyes, but it quickly faded. "Yes."

"What are we doing, Logan?" He was still standing between her legs, but the moment felt like it was fizzling out. "Didn't we both just agree we don't want to ruin our friendship?"

He rested his forehead against hers. "I just want it to be different."

"Then be different."

He shook his head. "I don't know if I can be."

"Do you know what I was thinking a moment ago?"

He shook his head again.

"I was thinking how I wanted was you. Even if it was for just right now. I know if I let it happen, I might just be another of the girls you—"

There was a knock on the closet door. Logan backed up and she hopped down, quickly pulling at her dress. She tried to tame her hair with her hands as the door opened.

Harrison smirked at them from the doorway. "Is this the secret meeting room?"

She was sure Logan was firing daggers at Harrison with his eyes, so she grabbed his hand, keeping him from approaching his brother. She didn't know what he'd do.

"You can't give us one fucking minute?" Logan cursed at him.

Harrison raised an eyebrow. "Oh, you told him? Listen, Logan, you can be pissed at me all you want, but the truth is you weren't there and I was."

Logan almost lunged at him, but she grabbed his arm, pulling him back.

"Stop it!" she yelled at both of them. "Please, just stop it. You can't fight, not over me."

They were both still glaring at each other and neither of them said anything.

"We came here to get information, and us all hiding in a closet yelling at each other isn't going to accomplish anything," she said. "Harrison, I'll meet you inside in one minute, okay?"

He nodded and walked away.

After he left, she looked back at Logan. She wasn't sure how to read his expression.

"Ready?" she asked him.

Logan nodded. He seemed so far away from her now.

"Logan, look at me," she said before they left. She didn't want to walk away with how things were between them. She knew she was in deep, that she'd lost all hope of ever just being friends with the man in front of her.

"I want you to know," she said, grabbing his hand as she spoke, "if there was a choice to be made, if you decided you wanted just me, I would choose you."

He wrapped his arms around her and pressed his lips to the crown of her head.

He didn't say anything back, but she didn't really expect him to. She didn't think he'd change because of her, but it seemed futile to not say how she was feeling. For a brief moment her mind flashed to Harrison, who was standing out there waiting for them, and she was ninety-five percent sure what she said was true.

She moved out of Logan's embrace and reached for the door, but in the dim light of the closet she accidentally knocked over a row of paintings that were lined up neatly along the wall. The front painting was pushed down hard by the others behind it and a loud rip was heard from its collision with a coat hanger.

"Shit," Logan muttered, helping Julianne quickly pick up the heavy paintings. Harrison must have heard them because he opened the door back up.

"What are y'all—"

He switched the light on, saw them, and bent down to assist. When they reached the damaged bottom painting, he pushed it up and looked down at the floor. A white substance covered it.

"What is that?" Julianne asked. She looked at the ripped open painting, it was also covered in whatever was on the floor. She began to look inside of the painting when Harrison moved her away, grabbing it and moving it further toward the light.

"Is that—" Logan began.

Harrison ran a finger over the power and rubbed it on this tongue. "Cocaine."

Julianne's eyes opened wide. She'd never been near drugs. Well, maybe some marijuana in college. But not drugs like these. She didn't even want to know how Harrison could know what it was just by taste.

"What is it doing in a painting?" Julianne asked.

Logan and Harrison both looked at each other in alarm. Harrison reached into his pocket, pulling out a small Swiss army knife. He ripped the canvas open further, revealing a torn plastic bag half-full of white powder. He grabbed the painting behind it and this time traced the knife on the outside of the canvas. When he had half of it cut open, he pulled it back to reveal another bag of powder.

"Someone's smuggling drugs in these," Harrison muttered. "We need to get out of here because there is no way these will be left alone long."

"Should we go to the police?" Julianne asked.

Julianne could tell by Logan's face he was nervous. She was, too. She couldn't wrap her brain around what any of this meant.

The three left the closet, and Logan guided Julianne away with his hand on her lower back.

"We need to go try to talk to Ashley and Theo before they leave. It might already be too late," Harrison said to Julianne. "Logan, why don't you talk to Alex? He won't know you. See if you can find out any more about the paintings at the auction.

The guy who's hosting this event, Anthony, he's new to the area. He just moved here from Miami, actually."

Julianne looked up at Harrison. "Didn't you say Alex has a house there?"

Harrison nodded. "I would place bets on them knowing each other. If I had to make an initial guess, I'd say both Anthony and Alex are fully aware, or maybe fully to blame, for those paintings in that closet."

"And Lucy?" she asked.

"I'm not sure yet."

Julianne felt like he was lying. She was sure he thought she was in on this too, but Julianne herself knew Lucy wasn't. Maybe she'd somehow gotten in the middle of it, but Lucy wouldn't be involved in a drug crime like this.

"Fine," Logan said. "I'll take a walk around the room first and just get an idea of the paintings up for auction. And Harrison?"

"Yeah?" he asked.

"Could you do me a favor and keep your hands off of her?"

Julianne's mouth dropped, and she glared at Logan. This wasn't a time to fight, but she didn't say anything, nor did Harrison.

Harrison linked his arm through hers as they approached a cocktail table where Ashley and Theo sat by themselves, both enjoying what looked like the cocktail of the evening. It was in a martini glass—the liquid was white and had bubbles popping up from the dry ice in the drink.

"Hello," Ashley said to them, giving a toothy smile. "Do we know each other?"

"I'm Harrison," he replied, sticking his hand out. "We met actually at one of these a month back."

She nodded as if she knew what he was referring to. "Right, Harrison, sorry. I think I remember. Not sure I remember you though." She was now referring to Julianne, and her smile didn't seem as genuine.

"Julianne," she said.

"Any pieces you were interested tonight?" Ashley asked. "It's such a great charity that Anthony does, isn't it?"

"The Marzatidetto painting caught my eye," Harrison answered. "You?"

It surprised Julianne at how good he was at playing parts.

"That one is wonderful, isn't it? Theo, you mentioned that one as well," Ashley said.

Theo hadn't heard her though because he was staring at Julianne. "I know you from somewhere, don't I?" he asked her.

Julianne pondered. "Hmm, I don't know. I guess you do look familiar."

Theo stood there, his eyebrows pinched together. "Oh, you run!"

Ashley gave him a bemused look. "What?"

"Julianne is in my running club. She's friends with . . ." His voice trailed off. Julianne noticed an expression travel over Theo's face, but it was gone after a moment.

"Lucy," Julianne said. "I'm friends with Lucy. And Katie— I'm sure you've heard, right?"

"Yes, it's so terrible," Ashley said.

"You know Barrett, don't you?" Julianne asked her. She saw Harrison shoot her a look, but Julianne didn't care. She had to see what she'd say.

Ashley nodded. "Yes, and he's just broken up about the whole thing. It's just tragic for everyone involved, if you ask me."

Except Julianne no longer believed any of this was accidental. She just didn't know how to piece it all together yet.

"How did you say you knew Anthony again?" Ashley asked Harrison.

"I manage Club Alredo. Anthony comes in regularly," Harrison answered.

Julianne had to resist raising an eyebrow.

"I love Alredo," Ashley cooed. "Maybe you can help us get a table next weekend. That place is impossible to get into, even for me."

"Sure," he replied, his eyes scanning the room behind her.

Julianne prayed this Anthony didn't decide to come over soon because she was pretty sure he'd have no idea who Harrison was. She wanted to stop all the small chat and quiz them with her real questions—Did Lucy take their photos? Did something happen? Where was she? But she knew it would only make them defensive. She had to think of something else.

"Ashley, baby!" a man said, walking up to them. He was dressed in a baby blue suit, his pants tighter than Julianne's dress. His hair was dyed blond and spiked to a point. "You look gorgeous, as always. How are you?"

She kissed him on the cheek, clearly loving the compliments. Julianne was certain a girl like her lived off of them.

"Great, Yuzi. You?" she asked.

"Wonderful, darling," he replied. "I was hoping I'd run into you here. I had to tell you that I got ahold of one of your naughty pictures, and wow, you looked smoking."

Ashley tilted her head; color drained from her face. "Sorry, I don't think I know what you're talking about."

His mouth dropped open. "You're kidding me, right, baby? The shoot you did with Theo. The stirrups were literally mind-fucking. I mean, you know I like men, but you were really hot in that picture. I would consider maybe changing for you, darling."

She swallowed, looking at Theo. "I thought we got rid of all the photos?"

It appeared they'd forgotten Julianne and Harrison were standing there because they continued their conversation in front of them with no hesitation.

"We did," Theo said, glaring at Yuzi. "Where did you see it?"

He shrugged. "I dunno. I think in my e-mail, maybe. Or maybe on Snapchat. Who knows, baby? All I know is Ashley looked ridic-good. You didn't look too bad either, Theo. But you're not really my type, you know?"

Theo sneered.

Yuzi threw his hand over his mouth. "Oh my god. Was no one supposed to see those? I totally thought you put them up on purpose. I would have."

"Lucy, she shot your photos, right?" Julianne asked.

Another look from Harrison, but she just shrugged at him.

"Who is this?" Yuzi asked, his eyes scanning her from her head to literally her toes.

"Julianne," she said, sticking her hand out. "This is Harrison."

Yuzi gave Harrison the same once-over he'd given to Julianne. "You are hot."

Julianne felt snubbed, but she watched Harrison with amusement. Harrison just stared back at Yuzi, his face blank.

"Yes, Lucy took the photos," Ashley said. "But after I saw the pictures, I decided I didn't like them and told her to delete them all."

"Nothing is ever deleted online," Yuzi said.

"Clearly," Ashley muttered. "Yuzi, can you please remember where you saw it?"

Yuzi grabbed his phone and scanned through different apps. Julianne wasn't sure she'd ever seen someone move their fingers on a phone as fast as he did.

"Here it is," he said, showing the screen to everyone at the table. "I forgot I took a screenshot."

Ashley grabbed it out of his hand roughly and examined it. Theo and Ashley looked at each other again and then back at the photo. Julianne stepped forward to examine the picture herself. Ashley was on display, minus a tiny lace thong panty that barely covered anything. A man, presumably Theo, was leaning over her in the shot. He had on pants but no shirt. It looked like they'd taken the shot on an exam table based on the placement of Ashley's feet in the stirrups.

Julianne looked back at Harrison, who was definitely looking at the picture. She wasn't sure if any man would turn away from it. Ashley didn't seem nearly as embarrassed by the photo as she was irritated.

"Who sent it?" she snapped. "I can't see a name on this."

Yuzi shook his finger. "Tsk tsk. I'm not going to show and tell. Plus, I don't even remember. Don't sweat it, babe."

"You still haven't heard from Lucy?" Ashley asked, looking at Julianne. "Because she and I need to have words."

"No, and I really don't think Lucy would have sent out a photo of you that you didn't want," Julianne said.

"If they were deleted like she said, this wouldn't be on here," she said. "Excuse me, Harrison, Julianne, nice to meet you, but Theo and I need to go."

Ashley grabbed the small bag she had sitting on the table and stomped toward the door. Theo hesitated for a moment before taking a final sip of his drink and then walking after her.

"Later, nobodies," Yuzi said, blowing Julianne and Harrison a kiss as he skipped away from their table.

Julianne could see Harrison was about to comment on him, but she put her hand up. "So, that was interesting."

"Yeah, especially since that man in the pictures was definitely not Theo."

"What?" Julianne exclaimed. "How could you tell? I thought it looked like him. And didn't Theo hire Lucy to take photos of them? Why would it be a different guy?"

Harrison shrugged. "I'm sure it wasn't him. The man's height was off. He was a few inches shorter than Theo. I could tell by how he was, er, leaning over her."

"Alright," Julianne said, tapping the table. "I wish this told us anything."

"Let me process it all for a minute. Your boyfriend looks like he's trying to get your attention over there."

Julianne looked over to see Logan next to a few of the paintings up for auction. He gestured her over.

"He's not my boyfriend," she said to Harrison. "And you know that, so please don't make snide comments."

He chuckled softly. "I wasn't being snide. But you, evidently, have issues making up your mind. And since you kissed me back last night, I think I have the right to call you out on it. Fair?"

Julianne pressed her tongue to the roof of her mouth to hold in any nasty comments that might spew out. He was right, but she didn't want to hear it.

"I'll be right back," she said, beginning to walk away toward Logan, but Harrison grabbed her and planted a hard kiss on her lips. She did her best to push him away without making it obvious to everyone in the room except Logan.

"Why did you do that?" she hissed under her breath. She couldn't look up to see Logan because she feared what she might see on his face.

"Just playing dirty," he said. He glanced away from her. "And because Anthony just walked into the room and was looking at us."

She sighed. He wasn't doing it all to just be a jerk. And honestly, she didn't even know when Harrison had gone from helping her because he owed his brother to helping her and pissing his brother off. There was too much drama between them both for her to keep up with, and she was not making it any better. Maybe after tonight she'd swear off seeing both Williams brothers forever.

"I might make myself scarce for a bit," Harrison said. "Call me if you need me."

Julianne walked over to Logan, who scowled as she approached.

"Hi," she said, trying to offer a peace-making smile.

"Hey," he said. "I found something weird."

"Oh?" she asked, happy he didn't comment on Harrison's recent kiss.

"Look," Logan said, pointing to the painting resting in

front of them. It was the same painting from the closet that had been ripped open.

"It's—"

"It's the same one, right?" Logan asked.

"Yes, definitely," Julianne said, tracing her fingers over it. She reached behind the painting. This one had no back, just the canvas and the frame. "But . . . it's not."

"And look that one," Logan said, pointing to another painting. "I saw that one in there too."

"So people are bidding on these and then most likely . . . ?"

"Receiving the other piece with the drugs," Logan filled in.

"So everyone here must know the truth. I think we need to get out of here. I have a bad feeling about this."

He shook his head. "There's no way everyone could know. Why not just put out the piece with the drugs? Maybe we could look for the highest bidders."

They looked down at the sheet in front of the piece; the name was Alfred Lucile.

Alfred Lucile.

Lucile Aldridge.

Lucy.

Julianne gasped. "That name—I swear it's Lucy. I think she's here, Logan."

15

J ulianne looked around the room, her eyes desperately looking for her friend. The name seemed too unlikely to not be her. Logan didn't seem as convinced.

"We don't know that it's Lucy," he said.

"Just trust me."

Logan grabbed her arm, pulling her away from the painting and toward the bar. "We might have just gotten some attention. I'm going to go outside and find Harrison and tell him what he found. Why don't you do a circle around and see if you see Lucy and then come find us?"

"Alright," she agreed, noticing where Anthony and Alex were talking together, watching her and Logan together.

Julianne wandered around after he left, but she didn't notice anyone who looked like Lucy. After about five minutes, she gave up and headed toward the exit. People were starting to leave the event.

She looked around for Harrison or Logan as she exited through the main doors of the banquet room, but spotted neither of them. She assumed that maybe they'd already made it outside. She prayed they were both still alive as well and hadn't gotten into any fistfights in her absence. Just as she was about to head outside, a woman knocked into her, sending a glass of dark red wine onto her gold dress.

Julianne looked up, and the woman gave her an apologetic look before quickly rushing off. There was a restroom just a few feet away, so she went in to try to clean up. She tried dabbing at the spill with wet paper towels, praying that she'd avoid a stain. Luckily, the sequins had deflected a lot of it. As she finished wiping off the last of it, the lights in the bathroom turned off. At first she assumed that maybe they were automatic and she'd been in there too long.

A hand suddenly flew up over Julianne's mouth, while another hand wrapped around her waist, pulling her toward a bathroom stall. She tried to throw her arms back in protest, but whoever had her was strong, and her movements weren't budging them at all.

"Stop kicking," the voice said. It was male, and she wasn't sure how she remembered, but she knew right away it was one of the guys from Lucy's apartment.

Oh god, she was going to be raped, or killed, or raped *and* killed. Maybe someone else would find her in here? Logan and Harrison couldn't be far away. She tried to keep kicking, her feet now hitting the toilet in the stall she'd been dragged into.

"You couldn't just mind your own business," he said gruffly. He turned on his phone and it let in enough light so she could see his face. She didn't recognize him. He had a scruffy beard and was dressed in black cargo pants and a dark green flannel. Surely he hadn't been at the auction dressed like this, but somehow he'd known where to find her.

"My friend is my business," she replied when he removed his hand for a moment.

He laughed manically and slapped a piece of tape over her lips. Julianne regretting not using her only free moment to scream, and now it was too late.

"Let's just say that after this, you might regret worrying about your friend and not yourself."

Julianne tried to keep screaming, but the tape muted her. She kept slamming her feet onto the ground, but the man had her arms in a firm grasp as he began tying them together with rope.

Julianne heard a knock on the outside of the bathroom. Someone trying to get it, but it must have been locked. She kicked harder.

There was more pounding on the door before it sounded as though it opened. The man tensed up, backing out of the stall. Julianne heard a brief noise and then suddenly he fell to the ground. She waited and heard footsteps approaching her. She looked down at the black boots approaching her stall. They stopped in front of it. Julianne looked up through the darkness. She couldn't see the person's face at all.

They turned on a flashlight and shined it right at her face. Julianne closed her eyes from the bright light and then finally opened them again, looking up.

It was her.

"Lucy!" she exclaimed, though it came out more like "oosy!" through the tape.

Lucy reached forward and slowly peeled the tape off of Julianne's mouth.

"Hi," she said.

Julianne wanted to scream at her. She'd been missing for

a week, Julianne had been through hell trying to find her, and all she could say was "hi"? But her eyes went to the man slumped on the floor.

"Oh, he's out for a while," Lucy said, smiling and holding up something. "Stun gun."

"What the hell?" Julianne said, remembering just now the pepper spray Harrison had given her.

"Listen, I know there's a lot to explain," Lucy said, "but we need to get you out of here."

"Who is he though?" Julianne asked, still staring at him as Lucy helped her out of the ropes he'd tied her arms with.

"Just a thug who's been following me," she said. "I swear I'll explain everything, but seriously, we need to go."

Julianne got to her feet and flung her arms around Lucy. She laughed and hugged her back. "Now, Julianne!"

They rushed to the bathroom door, and Lucy poked her head out, glancing in both directions before grabbing Julianne's hand and running for the doors. It was dark outside, and Julianne worried she might tumble down the steps at the speed Lucy was dragging her.

"I need to find my friends," Julianne said, pushing her feet into the ground to stop Lucy from bringing her any further.

Lucy raised an eyebrow. "You mean those studs you've been running around with? Girl, I leave you for a little over a week, and you've done well for yourself."

Julianne rolled her eyes. "The only reason I've even been with them is because I've needed help to find you."

"Yeah, about that . . ." Lucy began, but her eyes seemed to focus on something as she grabbed Julianne, shoving her behind a large display of trimmed evergreen plants.

"Agh," Julianne mumbled as she spat the end of a plant out of her mouth.

"Shh," Lucy said, holding a finger up to her lips.

A minute passed, and Lucy gave her a nod. "Alright, let's go."

Julianne just realized she hadn't even bothered checking her phone since this whole fiasco had started. She fished it out of her purse; there were numerous missed calls from both Logan and Harrison. She looked around the parking lot and building entrance but didn't see them anywhere.

"Can I get a second?" Julianne said to her.

Lucy shook her head. "Just come to my car and you can then."

They ran quickly to a small black Mazda parked three rows back. Lucy locked the doors and looked around. She'd had on a blonde wig since Julianne had seen her in the bathroom, but she took it off now, revealing her short brown bob.

Julianne quickly dialed Logan, who answered on the first ring.

"Where are you?"

"Sorry, things got a little . . . just, I'm okay. Are you with Harrison?"

"Yes, we're both looking for you inside."

"Just come out. I'll meet you at my place, okay?"

"What?" Logan questioned. "Who are you with? Julianne, I'm sort of lost here."

"I found her."

Logan was quiet for a moment. "I hope she has a good explanation for this all then."

When she hung up the phone, she turned to Lucy, who put the car in reverse. "Yeah, I hope you do too."

"I'm so sorry, Jules," Lucy said. "I never had any idea you'd go to these lengths to find me."

"You're my friend. Of course I would."

Lucy smiled at her. "Yes, I can see that. I can't believe you called my mom!"

"How did you know?" It surprised her she'd been in contact with her mother.

"My mom. She knew the whole time. She didn't know who you were, so she lied."

"What is with all the lying? What is going on, Lucy?" Julianne asked. "Are you into drugs or something? Because we found—"

Lucy interrupted her. "No, I'm not into drugs. I'm an undercover journalist."

"You're what?"

"I'm working on a piece about Senator Burnhill. There were rumors that his daughter was part of this multi-state drug cartel, and that not only did he know about it, he was helping fund it."

Julianne's mouth dropped.

"I joined running club to meet Theo so I could get an in. I hit the mother lode when he and Ashley hired me to take photos of them. Except, things went in a different direction," Lucy said. "Barrett, the guy who killed Katie, was there when I showed up to take the photos of Ashley and Theo. They had another girl with them too. Angela King."

The name fired in Julianne's head. "The other missing runner?"

Lucy nodded. "I was freaked out. She was drugged. She could hardly keep her head up straight. Ashley freaked out, screaming at Barrett for bringing her with him. Apparently

Barrett and Angela had been dating, but they'd broken up. Or she broke up with him. He'd been drugging her afterward to keep her so doped up she didn't know enough to leave him. At the shoot Angela literally passed out in a chair shortly after they got there, so Ashley asked to continue with the photos."

"So this happened right after she was abducted?" Julianne asked her, horrified.

Lucy nodded.

"Apparently Barrett was threatening Ashley that he was going to expose her involvement in the drug trade, so he used that to blackmail her into taking photos with him, I felt so weird about taking them. But then he asked for me to take the photos of him and Angela, and that's when I knew I was in trouble."

Julianne gasped. "Did you go the police?"

"I didn't get a chance right away," Lucy said. "Once the shoot was done, when no one else was looking, Ashley pulled me aside after and begged me to delete all the files. Of course I wanted to do the same thing. But when I went to get in my car, Barrett came up to me and demanded the files, but I refused and left. As I was driving off, I noticed Barrett following me. I drove for over an hour, but he kept going. I know I'm an idiot for not just calling the police right then, but I was desperate for this story, and I felt like I might lose it if I turned this all in."

"Why do you think he wanted the photos taken?" Julianne asked.

Lucy glared. "Because he's a sick fuck. He drove me off the road and tried to attack me. Luckily, I had my stun gun and was able to get him unconscious for a while. Unfortunately, I ran off without my camera, so I had no proof. When I tried to go to the police, it turned out Barrett Kennedy's family is extremely wealthy and well-known here, and they didn't want to even touch what I was saying without any concrete proof. That was also why the police never even questioned him about Angela's disappearance in the first place. I was shocked. I knew then I had to hide until I could get more information to get him turned in."

Julianne listened in silence. She couldn't believe this was what had been going on while she'd been looking for her friend.

"But what happened to Katie?"

Lucy's voice was shaky as she continued on. "Barrett was trying to find me. He wanted me shut up regardless of if he had the camera. He knew from Theo that I was in the running club, so he tracked down my friends and started following people. He was following Katie to get to me but accidentally hit her and just left her there. Can you believe it? He's seriously a monster, Julianne."

"What about Angela?" Julianne asked. "The police must have believed you about that."

"They said they'd ask him about it. But with no proof, they didn't believe me. They said maybe she just looked like Angela. He seriously had, like, police immunity. I think the only reason they were able to arrest him was because he turned himself in for the hit and run."

"But why did he do it?" Julianne asked. "Why turn himself in?"

Lucy sighed. "I have some connections of my own. When I saw on the news about Katie, I just knew, you know? There was no coincidence. So I had to dig deep into what I like to call my you-freaking-owe-me pot. Basically sources or other journalists I've helped in the past. One of them had a lot of dirt of Barrett, including proof of rape that had gone unprosecuted. It was the daughter of a retired navy seal who could have literally snapped his scrawny neck with his pinky finger. So I let him know if he didn't turn himself in about Katie, it was going to be exposed. He decided to do it, pleading that it was a terrible accident."

"That's horrible," Julianne muttered. "But Lucy, you can't keep this information from the police. That poor girl deserves justice, just as much as..."

Lucy held up her hand. "I know. And I didn't owe the prick anything, so I turned over the information to the police as soon as he turned himself in about Katie. He won't be getting out anytime soon."

As they pulled into Julianne's parking lot, Julianne watched as headlights pulled up behind them. She was fairly sure it was Logan on their tail, but she felt nervous until she saw for sure it was him.

"I didn't know who Barrett had on the outside helping him, so I knew you were still at risk, especially since you were searching for me. So I broke in your house to scare you off."

"We thought that might have been the case," Julianne said.

"Yeah, but you did a shitty job of staying away!" Lucy exclaimed.

"I'm sorry," Julianne said. "But honestly, can you blame me?"

"You might not make a bad journalist yourself," Lucy said with a wink.

Julianne laughed. "I think after this week, I'll stick to being a doctor, thank you very much."

They sat in silence for a moment before Julianne spoke again. "Do you have any idea yet, about what happened to Angela?"

"I've been searching, believe me," she said. "But no, not yet."

"We have another thing to talk about," Julianne said. "Specifically, the fact that Alex was married."

Lucy's face turned red. "You needed to loosen up—and I knew their marriage was open. So, yes, I'm sorry about that. But I hope we can maybe just forget about that, especially now that you've got that hunky doctor waiting in the car out there for you."

Julianne sighed. "So, how much do you have left to do?"

"I should be finished up with everything I need in the next couple of days," she said. "I need you to promise to lie low until I'm done. Just be a busy resident, all right? Or get busy with one of those guys. But whatever you do, don't search for anything. And also, maybe don't be alone until this is over. I'd hate for our bathroom buddy to track you down again."

"Sure," she said, nodding. "Be safe, Lucy."

Lucy smiled at her. "Always."

Lucy blew a kiss at her as she got out of the car and drove away.

Logan was waiting now on her front steps of her condo building, his expression torn between curiosity and irritation.

"I'm sorry," she said, sitting next to him. "I don't think you want to know what happened."

"Try me."

She explained everything that had happened and everything she'd learned in the last hour. When she was done he seemed to be at a loss of words.

"And here I thought your friend might just have fled to Mexico."

Julianne smacked him playfully on the arm.

He reached over, brushing her hair behind her ear. "In all seriousness, I'm really glad you're okay. You had us pretty freaked out."

"Harrison was freaked out?" she asked. "I have a hard time envisioning that."

Logan chuckled. "Let's just say finding you was a rather urgent task for both of us."

Julianne was about to invite Logan to come inside when he spoke again. "I think he has real feelings for you."

"What?" she asked.

"I don't really trust him, but that might be my own personal beef. I tend to like to do things by the law, and not by own rules. I've never liked that about him. But I've seen him care for our grandparents in ways I never could. I saw him cry at our father's funeral. I think he has the function to love like a normal human."

Julianne listened to him, his voice despondent. Her own throat tightened. She wanted to stop him, but she also wanted to hear him out to see what he had to say.

"I think we could . . ." He rubbed his face. "I feel like we could have fun, but I think if you're looking for a relationship, looking for someone to love you, he'd be a better guy. So I know you said earlier you would choose me, but I need you to know I don't think I'll ever be able to want something like that."

"Alright," she breathed. He was rejecting her without her even asking for anything. He was rejecting any possibility of what could be.

"Harrison's coming here," Logan said. "I called him and asked if he could stay here tonight. I'm sorry."

Julianne felt a surge of anger—how dare he decide what she wanted. But she said nothing as they both watched Harrison's car pull up and park nearby. Logan walked off without saying anything else. They exchanged brief nods as Logan got into his own car and drove off.

"I'm going to go to bed," Julianne said to him as he walked up. "If you want to know what happened, just talk to Logan."

She felt frustrated at both of them for trying to decide what was best for her. She thought about telling Harrison to go home too, but she was still shaken up from the man attacking her earlier, and Lucy had also asked her to not stay alone. So instead she walked inside with him following silently behind her. When she got inside, she went straight to her room and fell asleep.

16

The next couple of days went by as if life had gone back to normal. Before Lucy. Before Logan and Harrison. She performed some interesting surgeries—a splenic rupture from a car accident where they had to remove the spleen, and a thoracotomy to remove a punctured and necrotic lung that had been impaled with a steel rod.

When Saturday came around, her father asked her to stop by so they could talk. He wasn't happy with how things had gone the last time, so she agreed. She didn't think her attitude would change, but his invitations weren't always optional.

When she knocked on the door, Miss Muffet barked as usual. Her father answered the door this time, giving the dog a soft nudge with his foot. Julianne smirked. She was certain Lauren wouldn't have approved of that.

"Hello, Julianne," he said. "Thanks for coming."

She nodded and followed him inside. She looked at the spread of food on kitchen island: bagels, lox, cream cheese, chocolate croissants, fruit, orange juice, and a whole carved ham. She wondered if she'd misunderstood that this was a solo invitation—there was enough food for twenty people.

"I ordered from Kowalski's," he said, following her gaze. "Lauren's out of town."

She was glad to know she'd been correct before; he definitely didn't cook all the time. She wondered what he'd think if she told him the Sunday before her mom had offered her leftover pizza. While she wanted to overlook the fact that he'd clearly wasted money on the immense amount of food that likely neither of them would touch, she suddenly found she couldn't. She thought of Logan cooking, learning from his father and grandmother. She knew food wasn't ever a luxury to him, not like how it was to her father. And to her.

"It's a little much," she said. "I know you love to impress people, but it doesn't work on me."

He didn't respond at first and instead took a drink of his coffee. "Julianne, we need to find a middle ground," he said after a moment. "I can hear you're angry with me."

She huffed. "Yeah, and you think you can fix it with an Easter feast."

"Ignore the damn food then," he said, anger in his eyes. "Lauren hates how hostile our relationship has become. She doesn't want us to move with you and I in the situation we're in."

Julianne shrugged. "I don't know what to say. I don't think there is anything you could say either."

She watched her father grab a bagel, spread on a thin layer of cream cheese, and pile it with a thick stack of lox. He took a bite, setting it down on the plate in front of him.

"I've done a lot for you, Julianne," he said. "More than you know. When you have kids someday, you'll understand the sacrifices a parent has to make. You have everything you have now because of me. Do you understand that?"

Julianne felt the urge to grab her hair and scream. But she took a deep breath instead, praying the right answer would come to her before she could say something she couldn't take back.

"Then maybe it's time I don't," she said calmly.

"Excuse me?"

"Maybe it's time I don't have everything," she said. "I made it to where I am, at my residency, because of hard work. And when I apply for my fellowship, I don't want to think for a moment that I got it because you pulled any strings. So don't do anything for me; don't give me anything else. Take my car. Stop my rent. I'm done."

She threw her hands up and walked back to the door. She waited to feel regret, but instead she felt relief. She'd been living under her father's will for so long she had never even considered what it would be like to just *not*. But she thought again of Logan, his life. He didn't have someone like her father, and he wasn't any further behind than her. And she was certain he had to feel a hell of a lot better about how he'd gotten there—only from his own from hard work.

"You'll be back," her father said.

She shut the door. Not anytime soon.

When she got out to her car, she saw she had two missed calls from a number she didn't recognize. The number hadn't left a voicemail, so she just called it back.

"We have your friend," the voice said as soon as they picked up on the second ring.

"Excuse me?" she asked, confused. Which friend? She'd found Lucy. She wasn't even searching anymore.

"Show up at 5498 Ellison Street in twenty minutes."

The man hung up before she could say anything else. She stared at her phone in dismay. She thought she was finally done with this, but it turned out that wasn't the case. She tried Lucy's phone, praying she had it on her so she could ask her what to do, but it went to voicemail.

She dreaded having to make the call she was about to make, but she did it anyway.

"Julianne," Harrison said, answering his phone.

"Hi, um, sorry to bother you. I need your help," she said.

"Alright."

She told him the address to meet her at and drove over quickly.

When she got to the address the caller had given her, she saw Harrison parked across the street. She parked and hopped out and into his car. She explained what she'd been told on the phone.

He scowled. "This sounds like a terrible idea."

"What would you do?"

He shrugged. "Well, what I am going to do is go into that building and kick some asses. What you're going to do is stay in this car."

Julianne glared at him. "No way. They're expecting me. If you show up, who knows if we'll get back whoever they have."

"You know this is most likely a trap? Those people at the auction were looking for you, and now you've seen the drugs, so they have even more reason to want you gone."

"I'm still coming with."

He sighed. "No, you're not."

She stared at him. His face was set in a firm scowl that she'd grown used to it.

"You could go without me, but then I'd just follow you."

He rolled his eyes. "Logan will kill me if I get you hurt."

"Logan doesn't care," she replied, maybe a little too quickly.

He didn't reply, but handed her a small black object. A handgun.

"It's Lucy's," he said. "The one we found in her apartment. You need something stronger than that pepper spray I gave you."

"I . . . I don't know how to use this," she said, staring at the gun in her hands.

He smirked. "Just pull the trigger."

She held it apprehensively, terrified of shooting someone —or even herself—accidentally.

"You coming?" he asked.

She nodded, following him out of the car. The address they were given was to a small tan house in a shady-looking part of town. As they walked inside, her phone rang. She looked down to see the number that called her earlier. She hesitantly brought the phone up to her ear.

"Leave the bodyguard," the voice said. "Or there's no deal."

"Hey, asshole," Harrison said, grabbing the phone out of her hands. "No one agreed to any deal. So if you want Julianne inside, I'll be with her."

The call ended before any reply.

"You don't think they're going to kill us, do you?" she asked.

Harrison scoffed. "They should be more worried that we will kill *them*. Especially with your killer aim."

Julianne rolled her eyes. She did not understand how he wasn't terrified, but then again he probably did stuff like this all the time.

She followed behind him. He had his gun up in one hand and his other hand was held out in front of Julianne as they walked inside through the open front door.

Harrison signaled for her to be quiet as he looked around the main floor of the house. It was quiet inside, and there didn't appear to be in anyone in the kitchen, dining room, or small bedroom within their line of sight. Julianne pointed to a door she was sure led to a basement. Going into a basement felt terrifying—she was sure they wouldn't come back up. She debated letting Harrison go on his own, but she knew they wanted her. Plus, she wasn't sure she wanted to be alone upstairs either.

He kept his back against the wall as they went down the stairs. When they got downstairs, there was someone sitting in a chair, their back to them. Julianne rushed over before Harrison could stop her and spun the chair around to face them. The face of the missing girl, Angela, stared back at her.

Her hair was matted down, and tears stained her face. She had tape over her mouth, but she seemed to be pleading with Julianne as she looked at her. Her eyes looked at Harrison and lit up in fear.

"He's with me," Julianne said. She gently took the tape off of her mouth. "Harrison, do you have something we could cut the rope with?"

He pulled out his army knife and bent down to saw at the rope that held Angela to the chair.

"I'm Julianne," she said. "I'm doctor—are you hurt at all?"

Angela shook her head, breaking down in a sob.

"Is there someone here with you?" Harrison asked, inspecting around the room as he searched for anyone else.

She shook her head again.

"He must have seen us from outside," Harrison said. "I'll be right back."

Julianne almost stopped him but let him go. She grabbed Angela and helped her to her feet. "You're going to be okay. We'll get you to the hospital, and you can call your family on the way over. What do you know about what's happened to you?"

"I . . . I remember Barrett grabbing me. And then so much is a blur. I've been here for a few days now. There's been a man keeping me here. I don't know his name."

Julianne nodded as she spoke. "Someone called me to let me know you were here. I have a friend who is trying to find out more about Barrett and his friends. I'm guessing she has something to do with all of this."

Angela's tears had slowed down. "So you're really going to help me?"

Julianne nodded, a tear escaping her own eyes. "Yes."

They got upstairs just as Harrison came back inside.

"I don't see anyone," he said. "I'm just worried this all might be—"

"Hush." Julianne glared at him. She didn't want him scaring Angela. Just as she was about to speak, she got a text message from an unknown number.

Jules—I hope you picked up the trade I arranged for you. Please care for it. I'm taking off until the dust settles on everything. Keep an eye on the news. XOXO.

—L

She grinned at Angela. "We're good. We're good."

Harrison called the police as they drove to the hospital, letting them know what had happened, while Julianne called Angela's family for her. When they got her into the hospital about twenty minutes later, both the police and Angela's mom were already there waiting for her. Angela threw herself into her mom's arms and began sobbing loudly. It saddened Julianne to see someone is so much pain, but there was relief in knowing the worst was over for her. Julianne went to sit with Harrison, who was flipping through a magazine.

"Feeling all right?" he asked.

She nodded. "Yes."

"You were good with her," he said. "Your patients will be lucky."

She smiled at him, appreciating the compliment. "Thanks."

"Check this out," he said, handing her his phone.

It was an article highlighting the drug smuggling that was being trafficked using art. The ring leader, Anthony Lawrence, was brought in, along with socialites Theo Goldberg, Terrance Ripple, Frederick Woods, and Senator Burnhill's daughter, Ashley Burnhill. Already imprisoned Barrett Kennedy, for both the hit and run and rape charges, was also been noted as being involved. New charges against Kennedy are now also pending for the abduction of just now located Angela King.

"She did it," Julianne said, smiling at him.

"Might be some pissed off people," he said. "I'd advise you to keep clear of her for a while."

She sighed. "I'm fine. Don't worry."

"Maybe if we teach you to use that gun," he said.

She'd given him it back in the car. She didn't want to learn to use it. She really hoped to never be involved with something like this ever again. Although, since Lucy was her friend, she knew she should at least consider getting a stun gun. Who knows what she'd come up against in the future?

"Have you talked to him?" Harrison asked.

"Who?"

"I think you know who," he replied.

"Why would I?" she asked. "He said he wasn't interested in me."

"He was trying to be chivalrous."

"He said he thought I'd be better off with you."

Harrison took a deep breath before responding. "He's wrong. Not because I wouldn't want you, but because you're the first person I've ever seen him truly care about. He might still need to do some learning, and I doubt he'd be the perfect boyfriend right away, but I think you'd be good for him."

She shook her head, looking down. "That's not what he said. I don't want to talk about it."

"Alright."

"I feel like you're both telling me I should like the other one, but no one really cares how I feel. And I'm fairly certain if anyone wanted me enough, they wouldn't be giving me away so quickly."

Harrison pinched the bridge of his nose. He didn't respond to her comment, but she didn't really expect him to.

"I should get home," she said.

"Alright, Julianne."

"What?"

He smirked again. "Don't worry yourself about fixing mine and Logan's relationship."

She opened her mouth to speak, but he stopped her.

"I get it. We're really all each other has for family," he said. "But we're very, very different. And Logan is holding things against me I don't think he'll ever forgive me for."

"What things?" she asked. She'd been curious for a while now. Logan kept warning her about him, but he's never really said why or what.

"I have to do things for my job that aren't always . . . legal," he said. "One time, when we were younger, I needed his help. Logan was a freshman in college I believe. We were a little closer then, but he was reluctant because Logan's known forever he wanted to be a doctor, and I think he thought if he broke the law it wasn't going to happen. Well, things didn't go as planned, and Logan and I were both arrested. He was angry at me, saying he'd never get into medical school all because of my fake, bullshit job. He's never really forgiven me. He told me once he'd consider if it I did something else."

"But you haven't," she said.

"I'm not planning to get Logan involved again," he said. "To be honest, him asking for help with you was the first time he's talked with me about my work since then. But I'm not going to change who I am or what I do for him."

"Well, thanks for letting me know your guys' deal," she said. "I really should get going this time."

His expression softened. "You can always call me if you need anything."

She smiled, wrapping her arms around him. She realized he hadn't expected a hug because he was stiff. Honestly, she wondered if anyone ever hugged him. He wasn't the kind of guy you hugged. She felt embarrassed when she let him go.

"Sorry," she muttered.

He laughed softly. "Don't be. But since I'm doing my best trying to resist you, it doesn't help to have your breasts pressed against me."

Her eyes open wide, which made him laugh more.

"See you around, Julianne." He smirked before she took off.

She stopped for food on the way home. She regretted not taking food earlier from her dad's house, but it wouldn't have helped prove her point. She was more sure than ever that she'd made the right decision. Life wasn't going to be easier, but that was okay.

She sat down on her couch with her pizza. She folded the large, thin slice in half before shoving it into her mouth when there was a knock on her door. Her first guess was Lucy. Maybe her father. But when she swung open the door, she saw the handsome face she knew all too well.

"Hey, Logan," she said. She looked down at the piece of pizza she was still holding onto. She debated on shoving the rest of it into her mouth. She was starving, but she set it back down on the box instead.

"Hey."

"What are you doing here?"

"I saw the news," he said. "I just . . . I don't know, I found myself coming to see you before I really thought about it."

She nodded. "Come in."

He slipped off his shoes and walked closer to her. He looked good in his jeans and light blue button-down.

"I've missed you," he said, staring at her from their distance of now only a few feet.

She wanted to tell him the same, except she knew better.

"Okay," she replied. "Listen, I'm fine with us chatting at work, but I don't think we're going to be the kind of friends that like, hang out and stuff. So thanks for coming over, but you should probably go."

He sighed and took a seat on the sofa nearest him. "I see what you're doing."

She threw her arms up, exasperated. "What *I'm* doing? I'm asking you to go, not make yourself at home. We've been over everything, Logan. Nothing has changed since we talked last."

"Just come sit by me."

"I'm hungry," she said, looking back at the pizza waiting for her. Truthfully, she'd lost her appetite, but she'd run out of excuses to avoid him.

He shook his head. "Please, Julianne."

She sat next to him, making sure there was space for at least two more people between them.

"I've been doing a lot of thinking," he said. "The last couple of days."

"Good."

He cracked a smile. "Anyway, I've been thinking I might have been wrong about what I said."

She raised an eyebrow. "Which part?"

"Everything, really," he replied, scooting over closer to her so they were practically touching. Her body became very aware of him, and she cursed herself.

"Well, I still think you might have to be a little more specific," she replied.

"I don't want you to want Harrison. I don't want you to want anyone. Well, I want you to want me."

She stared at him, waiting for him to go further. "And you?"

"I don't want to want anyone else either. I want you to choose me because I want to choose you."

She wanted to reach over and kiss him, but she worried he didn't really mean what he was saying. He was Logan Williams. He didn't do relationships.

"You're skeptical," he said, grabbing her hand. "I get it. I've never done this, wanted this. So I can't promise to be perfect, but I can promise to try. I think we'll be good together. Like, great together."

He kissed her, and she let her lips melt into his. She knew this might not be forever, but that wasn't what she was looking for, anyway. Right now she was looking for this. With him. He helped Julianne let loose into who she really wanted to be. Not the over-the-top Julianne that she was with Lucy. Not the uptight Julianne she was on her own. But the confident Julianne—this Julianne.

"Maybe we should go to your room," he said, his lips tracing down her neck.

Julianne faltered. "I . . . I need more time before I'm ready for that. It's not that I don't want to with you, I do, but I need for us to make sure that isn't just going to be about sex. And—"

He smiled at her, pressing a finger against her lips. "I get it. Don't worry, I can wait."

Julianne kissed him lightly on the lips again. "Thank you."

He looked her over, his hand rubbing gently on her thigh.

"I promise I'll get a 'damn good' out of you someday, Julianne Davis."

They spent the rest of the evening talking and making out. She'd almost forgotten how fun just making out could be, especially with Logan, who turned out to be an excellent kisser. She'd both reluctantly and willingly let him sleep in her bed that night.

Her eyes fluttered open the following morning and landed on the image of Logan lying next to her.

"Good morning."

She swiped at her mouth, thankful to not find any drool. "How long were you watching me?"

"Just a moment," he said, his smile soft. "I promise."

She smiled back, closing her eyes. She'd gotten better rest than she had in the last few weeks. She was almost worried about the contentment she felt—like a hammer was about to fall, but she didn't know from where or who. She shook her head at the feeling, trying to stay in the moment.

"Any plans this morning?" he asked, sitting up. He grabbed his jeans off the floor and tugged them on.

"My mom and I do brunch every Sunday. So I'll be heading over there. You?"

He ruffled his hair with his hand. "I was hoping maybe I could impress you with my cooking skills again."

She thought about what her mom offered for food last Sunday. "I wouldn't be opposed to an early breakfast."

Logan's phone beeped and he glanced at it. His eyebrows furrowed.

"Everything okay?" she asked.

He set his phone down and pulled his shirt over his head.

"It was Harrison. He wanted to know if I could meet with him this morning."

"Oh?" she asked. "Any idea what about?"

She wondered if maybe he was taking her advice and trying to fix things between them. Although getting together at eight in the morning seemed odd.

"Nope," he replied. "Maybe we'll do a rain check on breakfast?"

She nodded. "Of course. Go talk to him."

She gave him a kiss and hug before he took off.

17

She'd texted with Logan Sunday afternoon, but after her last message around three, she never heard anymore. She hated being the one to send the last text. It irritated her more than she rationally knew it should. If she wanted to talk to him, she just had to talk to him. His silence made doubts creep in, though—maybe he'd just said he wanted them together in the hopes she'd sleep with him.

Monday morning came quickly for Julianne. She felt nervous walking into the hospital—she wasn't sure how she was supposed to interact with Logan now that they were technically together.

Logan wasn't the only thing making her feel on edge. She was also frustrated that Lucy still had her phone off. Everything was done. Why was she still not coming forward? Julianne figured maybe she needed a few more days, and she knew enough to just give Lucy the time. She was a doctor, not a detective. That was why Logan was good for her, and why Harrison would definitely not be.

She walked toward the cafeteria and spotted Emily at a

table alone with a steaming cup of a coffee and her breakfast. She was eating a light yogurt with an empty banana peel sitting next to it. If there had been anyone else around, she'd have sat with them, but Emily's eyes met hers, and she knew it was too late to look away.

"Hey, Julianne." Emily smiled sweetly, too sweetly. It was definitely a fake smile.

After grabbing a coffee and a powdered donut, she sat down next to her. It wasn't the healthiest of breakfasts, but she wasn't starving and planned to just nibble on it.

"So," Emily said, tapping her fingers on the table, "I hope this isn't awkward."

"You hope *what* isn't awkward?" Julianne asked.

"Logan was over last night and he said—"

Julianne felt her stomach drop. "What?"

She watched a smile twitch across Emily's face. She had to resist reaching over and scratching it off.

"We've been friends for a long time, Julianne. I hope you don't think we're going to stop being friends because you guys are, like, a thing or whatever."

Anger swelled inside of her. She couldn't believe Logan had gone over to Emily's last night. They'd been sleeping together like, a week ago, and he'd thought it was okay for them to hang out?

"You look upset," Emily said. "Don't worry, nothing happened. I mean, he kissed me, but he was super drunk so I told him to stop."

Julianne stared at her. Unbelievable. She wanted to throw her coffee and donut in Emily's face but tried to remain calm.

Emily kept talking. "I think you should know—this whole thing started that night at the bar."

"Which night?" Julianne asked, confused.

"The night I told you to come out and talk to Logan about helping find your friend."

"Sorry, I'm not following. What *whole thing* started?" Julianne asked.

Emily dipped her spoon into her yogurt, swirling it on the sides to get the last bits of it before sticking it into her mouth. She pulled out the spoon and grinned. "I told Logan I'd find a way to get you the bar, and you basically handed me a way. I bet him if he got you to sleep with him I'd take his call for a whole month. It was why he was helping you find your friend. He was pretty determined right away to win this bet."

Julianne stared at her. She didn't want to believe any of it was true, but part of her brain screamed that it all made sense.

"Anyway," Emily said, now swiping her finger into the empty yogurt carton. "Apparently he actually likes you now, which, whatever, but I just thought you should know."

Seconds later Logan walked up to their table, and Julianne debated on what to do. She wanted to burst into tears and run away. But she knew it would give Emily a good laugh. She could just picture Logan and Emily laughing at her together—silly Julianne. She bit down on her lip. *No tears, no tears, no tears.*

"Hey, ladies," he said with his prize-winning grin, sliding out the chair closest to Julianne and sitting down.

Julianne grabbed her donut and took the biggest bite she could manage. She didn't feel hungry at all, but a full mouth would give her a few seconds to think about what to say.

"Hey, Logan," Emily said, smiling and getting up from her chair. "You look better than I thought you would this morning. Anyway, I need to go catch up on some charts, so I'll see you two later."

He waved her off and looked at Julianne who was now taking a sip of her coffee to wash down the extra-large bite she'd taken. He pulled his chair a little closer to hers and whispered into her ear, "Morning, beautiful."

"Good morning," Julianne managed. "I think I need to go too, actually. Sorry I can't eat with you." She stood up, avoiding eye contact.

"Everything okay?" he asked before she could walk off.

"Yes," she lied. "We'll catch up later."

She took off before he could say anymore. She avoided being alone with him for the rest of the day and got to her car as soon as she was done rounding on her last patient. It was still early, and she had running clothes in the back of her car, so she drove to the lake. She needed to run and free her mind of everything. She'd dropped her guard and now wished she'd never let Logan Williams into her life. She wondered if it was only Emily who knew about the bet she and Logan had made, or maybe everyone had been laughing at Julianne the whole time. Even Emily telling her that Logan liked her now, it didn't matter. Everything had been built on lies, and she couldn't believe what a hypocrite he was being. He claimed he valued honesty above all else. But that wasn't true— because if he had, he would have told her about it.

Her feet hit the pavement, and she ran. And she kept running. She didn't even bother with headphones. She didn't need music. The peaceful sound of nothing let her feel the cathartic rhythm of her steady pace. She kept going until her legs didn't feel like they could go anymore, even when her brain kept trying to push her forward. She'd made up her mind about a few things by the time she slowed down to walk back to her car. She wouldn't cry over Logan. She wouldn't get mad. She would just pretend the last two weeks hadn't happened. She'd be the uptight Julianne they all thought she was, and she was done caring about what anyone thought. She knew she wasn't actually uptight, but it wasn't worth trying to show people who didn't even really bother getting to know her that.

When she got back to her car, she had two missed calls from Logan and another from her neighbor, Serena. Serena had heard about the robbery at Julianne's place and had been diligently watching the rest of the hall now. She cleared the ones from Logan and called Serena back. Julianne prayed her place hadn't been broken into again. She was still finding things in the wrong places from the last time it had all been cleaned up.

"Hey, Julianne," Serena said. "Where are you?"

"Just out running," Julianne said, taking a drink from a bottle of water she'd had in her bag. "What's up?"

"Someone came to your place looking for you. He was knocking like, really hard and really long."

Logan.

"I went out there to ask him what was going on. He didn't give me a name, but he just seemed a little off."

Julianne's eyebrow scrunched together. "I'm sorry, Serena. I'm sure it was just a guy I was seeing."

"That hot one I saw leave your condo Sunday morning?" she said. "Not him. This guy looked a little, well, scary."

She wondered if maybe it had been Harrison. He seemed like the next logical choice. And "scary" seemed about right if he showed up with the menacing expression he sometimes had.

"Did he say who he was? How I should reach him?" she asked, still trying to confirm her suspicion.

"No," Serena replied, pausing. "He said he'd find you."

"Alright." Julianne replied, annoyed. She just wanted to be left alone by all the Williams men. "Thanks for letting me know, I think I have an idea of who came. I'll—"

"You're not in some sort of trouble, are you, Julianne?"

"What?" Julianne asked. "Of course not."

She hoped that was true. She hung up her phone and drove over to Harrison's place. She ran out of her car and buzzed the front doorbell. When he didn't answer, she knocked hard several times.

When he still didn't answer, she went back to her car and grabbed her phone, sending him a quick text to ask if he stopped at her place. She was about to turn on her car when she heard rustling in her back seat. She looked into the rearview mirror and drew in a breath, but everything went dark before the scream left her lips.

Julianne's mouth felt like someone had stuffed it with cotton balls. Vertigo coursed through her head, so much so she could swear her body was no longer on solid ground. Her eyes slowly fluttered open and blinked a few times. She couldn't remember where she'd been last. She thought back to the time she'd fainted with Logan, but she wasn't anywhere close to a hospital right now. She stared out the window at the white clouds ten thousand feet in the air. Yes, she was definitely not on solid ground. But how in the hell did she not remember getting on a plane? She looked around. And when had she started flying private? There was no one else around her on the extravagant-looking jet. At least no one within her sightlines. She wasn't sure she had the physical energy to get up and look around.

"Hello?" she croaked, her throat drier than she expected.

Footsteps approached her and stopped.

"Good morning, sunshine." The beautiful redhead in front of her grinned.

Julianne blinked. "Elizabeth?" Alex's wife was definitely not who she'd been expecting to see.

"My real friends call me Liza," she replied, sitting down in the seat across from Julianne. "But, yes."

"Is Alex here?" Julianne asked, her brain still fuzzy and trying to pull together what was going on.

Elizabeth bit her lower lip, scrunching her eyebrows up as she stared toward the back of the plane. "Sort of."

Julianne stood up and had to grab onto the seat for balance. Alex was in the back of the plane, slumped on the floor with a bullet in the back of his head.

"Poor Alex," Elizabeth said, tapping her manicured fingernail on the table in front of her. "He really didn't deserve that, but he was the means to an end, you know? There was no way I could carry you onto the plane on my own."

Julianne clenched her teeth. She was certain she would vomit any moment. She'd seen dead bodies before, but a cadaver was much different than seeing a person you knew sprawled out in a pool of their own blood.

"Why . . . what . . . ?"

"Just be chill okay, Julianne? Be happy that the other one back there is just drugged like you."

She wondered what Elizabeth meant by "the other one." She didn't see anyone besides Alex. Fear clawed through her, and that gave her enough adrenaline to rush to the back of the plane to see Harrison slumped in another seat. She quickly reached out to take his pulse and found herself grateful for the first time since she'd woken up.

Before she could move back, his eyes flashed open. A confused look quickly replaced pure rage as he registered he was looking at Julianne.

"Oh, good. You're both up now." Elizabeth looked over at them. "Oh, and don't get any ideas, big guy. I have all the weapons you had on you. And as you can see, our friend Alex over there didn't fare too well."

"What do you want with us?" Harrison croaked.

"Good question," Elizabeth said. "It turns out someone we all know—Lucy. You know her, right, Julianne?"

Julianne just stared at her, waiting for her to continue.

"Well anyway, that little bitch took a few things worth more than this plane we're riding on. And you two seem to be so damn good at finding her. So you're going to bring her to me. And if that doesn't happen, well, you'll be looking like him soon enough."

"I'm sure you're wrong," Julianne said. "Lucy's a journalist . . ."

Elizabeth interrupted her with a laugh. "A journalist? She told you that? Her group has been trying to bring Anthony down for years so they could get into the cocaine business. She's a liar and a criminal."

"And what are you?" Julianne asked, glaring at her.

Elizabeth shrugged. "A better liar and criminal. Alex and Lucy had no idea I was involved in any of this. I was just pretty little Elizabeth. In Alex's defense, he didn't know any of this was even going on. But Lucy, you'd think she would have been smart enough to know I was involved."

"Why would Alex help you get us on the plane then?" Julianne questioned.

"A gun to your head will make you do a lot of things," she replied. "I think you'll learn that soon. Basically, Lucy thinks she got everyone in the Anthony Lawrence ring in jail. But she missed me—Anthony's girlfriend."

Harrison stared out the window of the plane as it began its descent. "The Miami condo," he said, looking at Elizabeth. "It wasn't Alex's. It was yours."

Julianne recalled Harrison saying Anthony was from Miami. She'd forgotten all about how Harrison had concluded that Alex and Anthony had to be connected somehow.

"You are good," Elizabeth said, smiling at him. "I'm sure you'll be able to get Lucy for me in no time. I got word she was heading to Miami to meet with Anthony's contact for future business."

Julianne still couldn't register what she was saying about Lucy. Why would Lucy have lied? It seemed like too much. But she knew one thing: even if what Elizabeth was saying was true—Lucy wasn't the bad guy. She'd found Angela and had gotten her help. She'd turned a drug group in to the police. But Elizabeth was accusing her of some major theft. What, exactly, she didn't even know yet. That Lucy Julianne definitely didn't know.

"What did she take?" Julianne asked.

Elizabeth stared at her like she was an idiot. "Cocaine. The group she's involved with has never dealt drugs before because Anthony had almost the entire surrounding area covered. But Lucy helped change that. And, well, you can guess some people aren't too happy. Including myself."

"Jesus," Harrison muttered. Julianne could guess by his tone of voice they were in serious shit. And honestly, even after seeing Alex dead on the ground, it wasn't until now that she realized how much trouble they were really in.

"So when we get to Miami, you will need to find that leach. And if you don't, or you try to let her in on what is going on, it won't just be your lives at stake."

18

"What is that supposed to mean?" Harrison asked before Julianne could herself.

"Remember Johnny? The guy who grabbed you in the bathroom at the auction, Julianne? I'm sure you haven't forgotten that yet. Well, he just so happens to have your mom's address. And your little lover boy, Logan? Johnny has his address, too. So whatever you're thinking, don't. Don't go to the police. Don't try to kill me. Don't try to get out of this. Just get me Lucy and my drugs, and you all can go back to your lives," Elizabeth replied.

"And what will you do to Lucy?" Julianne asked.

Elizabeth sighed in frustration. "I think we've had enough questions. My head hurts, and I have a dirty vodka martini up front that's calling my name."

Harrison gave Julianne a nod, so she waited to say any more until Elizabeth was out of hearing range.

"Are you okay?" Harrison asked her. She was still kneeling on the ground next to his seat, but they were so close to Alex she didn't want to move away to the empty seat nearby.

"Yes. I mean, no. What the hell? How is this happening?"

"I had a bad feeling this wasn't resolved," he said. "I should have trusted my gut. I let my guard down and now . . ."

"Do we just do what she's asking?" Julianne asked. "I mean . . . we don't have a choice, right? They could kill my mom and Logan."

Harrison scowled. "We don't even know we can do what she's asking. She wants us to get Lucy, but I'm certain Lucy knows Anthony's connections to Miami."

"What I don't get," Julianne said, "is that if Lucy has no idea Elizabeth is involved, why doesn't she just try to lure Lucy herself?"

"Lucy is smart, especially to get this far in whatever scheme she is a part of. My best guess is she's already been tipped off that Elizabeth knows she has the stolen cocaine. I don't think she'd be going to these extremes to get Lucy if she hadn't already tried herself," Harrison replied.

"So what do we do?"

"I don't know yet," he replied. "We'll think of something."

Julianne couldn't believe this. And what was she going to use as an excuse for not showing up for work? Maybe she'd say a grandparent died out of town. Honestly, it wasn't even a very good excuse. But she had to say something, especially if this took over one day. And she could not let this mess get in the way of something she'd worked so hard at for so long. Especially now that she didn't want to ask her dad to fix things.

And what would she tell Logan? And did she care? Maybe she would just tell him she'd run off to Miami with his brother. She wanted to. She wanted to hurt him the way it had hurt her to find out the truth. Why couldn't he have just told her? She wouldn't have been happy about hearing it, but hearing from Emily that he'd started their entire friendship on a stupid bet just made her feel so stupid. She wanted to know how long it took until things had become real for him. And then there was the fact that Emily and Logan had kissed —drunk or not—it just wasn't okay. He shouldn't have been at her place. It made her stomach churn. It was a friendship she couldn't approve of, not if her and Logan were a real thing. Maybe it would be selfish of her to ask, but she'd ask it. If she even wanted that anymore. She'd let Logan stew for now.

The plane landed about twenty minutes later. Their pilot, apparently part of Elizabeth's group, was the only other person aboard the plane. Julianne didn't want to know who would take care of the clean-up of Alex's body.

There was a white Rolls Royce waiting at the runway when they exited the plane. They followed Elizabeth into the car. She greeted the driver with a toothy smile as she got into the front seat and handed him an envelope. Harrison and Julianne sat in the back, silently looking out the windows as they took off and soon ended up on a busy Miami freeway.

"Anthony owns the entire building, so you two can stay in the unit next door to mine. It's stocked with clothes for you both."

Julianne looked at her, confused.

"You're not going to be running around Miami dressed like this," Elizabeth said. She gestured to Julianne's running clothes as though she found her repulsive.

The building Anthony owned was at least forty stories high. When Julianne envisioned this building he owned, she'd thought there would be maybe six units; this place had hundreds. She didn't doubt that he was instructing Elizabeth from prison. He clearly had enough money to pay anyone to do anything.

Elizabeth gave a smile and a four-fingered wave to the man at the front desk. Her heels clicked on the marble floors that lead to the elevator.

"Your unit's small. I'm in the penthouse, so the only other unit up there is a studio. Hope that isn't a problem. I'd put you somewhere else, but I can't trust you too much. Here are your phones back. I think you both have a clear under-standing of what you shouldn't do with them with right now. Use them to find her, but know that I'll be tracking all your moves."

As the elevator doors opened up, she flashed a keycard in front of a card reader and held the door open for them. When they reached the studio apartment, Julianne stared inside at the single king-size bed. She looked up at Harri-son. *Great*, she thought to herself, *why not add to this nightmare?*

The door clicked behind them, and Elizabeth was gone.

"What are the chances she has this place bugged?" Julianne asked.

"Likely," he replied.

Julianne slumped down into a large blue chair. Her body sank down into the soft, fluffy material. If she just passed out now, maybe Harrison could find Lucy himself. She really didn't feel like she had it in to her do any more. Not after seeing Alex. After what had happened with Logan. After being drugged by that lunatic next door.

"Logan called my phone three times in the last ten minutes," Harrison said, looking at his phone.

"If he calls you again, please don't mention we're together," she said. "Just say you haven't heard from me."

"And if he calls you?" he asked her.

"Oh, I'm not answering."

He raised an eyebrow. "Do I want to know why?"

"Probably not."

He didn't reply, but walked over to the wall of windows that looked over the ocean. The moon and city lights glowed blue. Julianne tried to see from her chair, but she had to sit up to get a better view. They were in North Miami Beach, the ocean, many floors below, splashed in gentle waves against the sand. She took a moment to take in Harrison's appearance. He had his arms crossed in front of him, which made his muscles even more apparent through his white T-shirt. Her brain betrayed her for a moment, letting her envision what it would be like to just be here on vacation with her boyfriend. As if they weren't being held hostage. As if this was just part of their lives. The moment passed quickly, and she stood up, found the small bathroom, and shut the door behind her. Her face felt hot, so she splashed it with the cold water from the sink.

She grabbed her own phone; she hadn't looked at it yet, but she knew she had to address the missed calls and texts from Logan. Except there was only one missed call and one text. She felt slightly rebuffed. She reread his text a few times, wondering how to take it.

Heard from Emily why you might be upset. Sorry I didn't mention the whole stupid bet thing to you. It really wasn't a big deal. Let's chat later, okay?

So he was sorry he didn't mention it to her, but wasn't sorry he'd taken part in the bet? He knew she was upset about it, but didn't seem to care. He hadn't even mentioned the kiss Emily had told her about; she wondered if Emily had made that whole thing up. She wished she was back at home so they actually could talk about this. She had a few choice words brewing up inside of her that she worried might cause her to explode if they didn't come out soon.

It was 9:00 p.m., which was basically 6:00 p.m. according to the nightlife in Miami. Julianne knew if they wanted to find Lucy, they didn't have time to waste. She took a quick shower, scrubbing off her run and unfortunate recent travel.

With her towel tied securely around her chest, she exited the bathroom, looking for the closet with its promised clothes. She stared at what was in front of her. This was definitely not a Julianne outfit. But she was certain Lucy would approve. *Whatever that meant,* she thought. She wasn't sure how much she should put into their friendship anymore. It was all a lie. Which meant Julianne wasn't sure if she should still embrace the new Julianne that Lucy had brought to life. But Julianne knew in her heart it wasn't just for Lucy.

Julianne came out of the bathroom a half hour later dressed in a short, sparkly silver dress. The sides were cut out and the tops of her breasts were completely exposed. She couldn't believe this was an actual outfit. It felt like someone had literally taken scissors and cut half of it away. She'd taken time to dry and blow out her hair and swipe on some of the makeup Elizabeth had left her, including some bright red lipstick with a pair of fake lashes Julianne tried out of curiosity.

"Well, I'm ready," she said, startling Harrison who had been looking at his phone.

He looked up at her and his eyes darkened.

"Well, damn," he said, walking toward her. "You're still off limits, right?"

Julianne swallowed. "Yes."

He gave her a small smirk before walking by her so close that their hips met as he shut the door to the bathroom. He came out minutes later. She made the mistake of looking at the towel hanging around his hips.

"So, do you know where we're going?" she asked to keep from staring at his still-wet abs.

He was about to reply when there was a knock on the door. Julianne went to answer it, but the door opened, and Elizabeth walked inside.

"Oh, good," she said, looking at Julianne. "I was worried you might have fallen asleep. There is literally no time to waste. I just heard that Lucy arrived at Club Grounded. You two need to get there, stat. Please don't mess this up."

Julianne resisted rolling her eyes. She did not understand how they would get Lucy back here with them. Lucy would obviously know something was up when they just happened to be at the same club as her, a thousand miles away from home.

Elizabeth's eyes zeroed in on Harrison. She walked closer to him so that there were only a few inches between them. She placed one of her red manicured nails on his chest.

"You can stop by my room later," she said before turning around and walking out.

Julianne was sure her own eyes had bugged out of her head. Harrison's expression was unreadable. Truthfully, Elizabeth was gorgeous, and he was gorgeous. She shouldn't even be surprised if something happened there. But could she deny that she felt a burst of jealousy course through her veins? No, definitely not.

"I'll go get dressed," he said before grabbing the outfit he'd been left and disappearing into the bathroom.

Harrison came a few minutes later in tight white dress pants that hit a few inches above the blue espadrilles on his feet. His white button-down shirt looked to be missing a few buttons on the top, showing just a hint of hair on his tanned chest. While he looked good, she knew this wasn't a look Harrison would have ever willingly put on. She bit her lip, trying to a hide a smile at his scowl.

"Don't," he said, glaring at her.

"It's not bad," she said, getting up and walking toward him.

"It's horrible, but let's go."

"I think a lot of girls actually like this look," she said, still smiling at him. "Miami chic."

"More like Miami dweeb."

Julianne walked closer this time, reaching her hand to the collar of his shirt. She'd meant just to see if the buttons were actually missing, but her hand accidentally moved over his bare skin and she saw something flash in his eyes. She tried to ignore the heat inside of her.

"I don't think you could look bad in anything," she said quietly, looking up at him.

He pushed her hand away from him, rushing them both to the door. She couldn't quiet read his expression, and he didn't say anything else as they got off the elevator and walked to the same Rolls Royce that had picked them up earlier.

They arrived at the club twenty minutes later. The line

was about twenty people long, but it was a warm evening, so it felt good to stand outside. She knew once they got inside all feelings of peace would be replaced by the thumping she could hear inside.

"Ready for this?" he asked.

Julianne shook her head. "Not really."

He rested his hand on her lower back as they inched forward.

"Are you sure people won't be able to see I don't belong here?" she whispered to him, tugging on the hem of her dress. "I feel like I'm sticking out like a sore thumb."

She felt his eyes traveling over her, and that heat she'd felt earlier returned.

"I promise," he replied.

The humid air was making their skin dewy. It drew attention to the scar on Harrison's forehead she frequently wondered about.

"What happened there?" she asked, signaling to it, but not making the mistake of physical contact like she had earlier checking his buttons.

He grimaced. "Work."

"Is what you do ever safe?" she asked.

"Yes, now it is, sometimes at least. It wasn't always."

"How often are you around?" she asked. She was curious how he seemed to be tan, when her own skin was pasty from the Minnesota winter.

"My job requires a lot of travel, but I don't mind it," he replied. "There's not really anything that keeps me in one place."

"Or anyone?"

He raised an eyebrow at her. "You're digging."

She smiled softly. "I'm just trying to figure you out."

"No, there's no one." Harrison rubbed his chin. "My life doesn't exactly allow for it. Most women don't love when you're gone for weeks at a time."

"But has there ever been anyone?"

"A long time ago." The corner of his mouth quirked up. "Should I be flattered or concerned you're so curious about my lack of love life?"

Julianne flushed. "Sorry."

"And if you're wondering," he said, "I have no interest in the psychotic woman holding us hostage. I saw your face earlier."

Her mouth fell open. "I didn't . . . "

Before anymore could be said they'd reached the front of the line and the bouncer ushered them inside.

Pulsating lights, along with the scent of strong cologne and perfume, overtook her senses as they walked in doors.

"Oh wow," she muttered, looking around.

She had never seen so many good-looking people all in the same place. Ever. There was a sheen of sweat on everyone that just seemed to enhance their looks. She wondered if she stood out like an impostor.

"You should go to the bar," Harrison said when they got inside. "I'm going to go walk around. I want to see if I can spot her. We need to see her before she sees us. So try to keep a low profile."

"Oh, okay." She pushed her way to the clear, long bar. There were hundreds of bottles of liquor lining the back of the crystal shelves.

"*Hola, mami,*" a voice said next to her.

She turned to see the man who was talking to her. He was

just like everyone else in the club—beautiful. His dark lashes fluttered as he stared down her dress.

"Hi." She smiled, hoping the bartender would come over soon. She needed about twenty drinks. Why the hell had Harrison left her? She literally had no idea how she was supposed to be acting. Did a low profile mean acting like she was meant to be there? Should she try to blend in?

"You from Miami?" he asked. "Haven't seen you around before."

Julianne smiled. "Doesn't everyone look the same in here, anyway?"

He laughed. "Don't fool yourself. You're more beautiful than all the women in here."

"Right," she said with a roll of her eyes. The bartender came over, and the man interrupted her before she could order a drink.

"Grab this pretty lady whatever she wants on me," he said, giving her a wink.

Julianne ordered a vodka soda and tried to sip it as slowly as possible, but she found her glass empty in minutes.

"I like your style," the man said. He had yet to leave the spot next to her at the bar "I'm Ernesto."

"Jules."

"So, Jules, are you here with anyone tonight?"

She looked around to see if she could spot Harrison, or maybe even Lucy, but she couldn't see past the mass of random scantly clad strangers.

"I have a friend somewhere in here," she said. "You?"

He grinned. "Everyone in here is my friend, cariña."

She ordered another drink, this time making sure to only take a small sip. She had to keep her wits about her.

"Come dance with me," he said, staring at her with his deep brown eyes.

It didn't feel like a question, and she hoped it might give her a better chance to find out where Harrison had gone, so she took another sip before abandoning her drink and following out the complete stranger onto the dance floor.

The music thumped around them, and she tried her best to keep the rhythm as she watched for both Harrison and Lucy. She wondered if Lucy would be here in disguise or as herself. There was so much Julianne didn't know about her; it felt like trying to find someone so foreign compared to her friend.

"*Ernesto, has hablado con el nuevo Anthony esta noche?*" said a man said nearby.

The name *Anthony* drew Julianne's attention. She knew enough Spanish from high school and her freshman year of college to understand bits. And she thought he'd just asked him if he'd spoken with the new Anthony. It seemed too weird to be a coincidence. Could Ernesto be who Lucy had come to meet with?

Julianne's eyes suddenly found Harrison, who was standing off to the side, watching Ernesto intently.

She listened to Ernesto reply to the man, but he just gave him a quick shake of the head. She wondered if that meant he hadn't talked to her, or if it wasn't the time to discuss it.

"*Ella está aquí en rojo,*" the man said before walking off.

She's here in red.

19

Yes, it was definitely about Lucy. She could tell by the look on Ernesto's face. He'd become more serious than he'd been minutes before.

"Jules, I have to go handle something. I'll find you later?"

She just smiled at him as he took off. Harrison paced quickly toward her, taking Ernesto's spot on the dance floor. He grabbed her by the waist, keeping her from rushing off.

"You knew, didn't you?" she asked.

"Yes, I got a photo of him and saw him at the bar when we walked in. I knew if I told you it was him, you would over-think it."

He stared down at her, pulling her in closer as the music changed to a slower, but just as rhythmic, song. Everyone on the dance floor reminded her of sex and being this close to Harrison put her entire body on alert.

"What did you find out?" he asked, seemingly oblivious to her thoughts.

"He hasn't spoken with her yet, but she's here, in red. How did you even know he'd talk to me?"

Harrison smirked at her. "I knew."

She shook her head at him, perplexed, and got out of his grasp and off of the dance floor. She hadn't ever finished her second drink and felt she'd earned a new one.

Harrison followed behind her. He ordered a beer, and they found a cocktail table nearby to rest at.

"There are about fifty girls here dressed in red," he replied. "It's so dark, it's hard to know how we'll find her. If you see Ernesto, get up to him again. He could be looking for her too, and he might have gotten some more information."

"And once we find her?" Julianne asked.

"Then we take her."

"Like we pull her out of here against her will?" she asked. "Won't we draw a little of attention? Or are you saying we're going to drug her, or worse?"

He pulled his chair close to her so that her bare thigh now rested up against his pants. He spoke in a hushed tone so that no one could hear him but her.

"Listen, Julianne, if we want to get Lucy to Elizabeth, it's for our own sakes. Nothing about what we're doing is morally right, and you need to come to terms with that if we want to get out of this on her terms."

Julianne nodded. "And if we want to do it on our terms?"

He sighed. "It's dangerous. We don't know who is watching us here right now. But if I know you, I have a feeling there is no way in hell we're doing it on Elizabeth's terms, are we?"

She shook her head. She couldn't just hand over Lucy, not without talking to her first. It wasn't right.

He studied her for a moment. "Well, I'll do my best, Julianne."

"I know," she said, giving him a supportive smile

"What makes you think Lucy is the good guy and Elizabeth is the bad guy?"

"Intuition," Julianne replied. "I feel like I'm a good judge of character."

He raised an eyebrow. "I hope you're right."

"I don't think she would have ever let me find her before if she wasn't really my friend," Julianne said. "And yes, I realize Logan and my mom's lives may very well be on the line with my choice. But I have to trust my gut here."

"She's likely to run away from me sooner than you, so you're going to have to be the one to approach her," he said. "If anything goes in a way you don't like, signal to me. I'll be close by with Plan B."

"I don't want to know what that is, do I?"

He shook his head. "You're stronger than most people, did you know that?"

She rolled her eyes. "Not really."

"Seriously," he said, leaning in closer to her. "Most girls I know, hell, most guys, would have panicked when this whole mess started. But you've been . . . different. You surprised me, is all."

"Should I take that as a compliment?" she asked.

He didn't answer, but tapped his fingers on the table in front of them before looking up at her. "So tell me, how is everything working out with Logan?"

She hadn't expected him to bring his brother up again, and she wasn't sure how she wanted to reply. "I thought they were good. But now . . . I don't know. I found something out, and I think maybe we shouldn't talk about this, okay?"

He narrowed his eyes at her.

"Apparently the only reason he even became friends with me in the first place was some stupid bet he and Emily made," she said, the words falling out of her. She needed to talk to someone about this, and although she knew Harrison was the worst person, he was here and would have to do.

"That's bullshit," he replied.

"Right? I mean, who does that?"

He shook his head. "I mean that's bullshit if you think that's why he became friends with you. Logan would have to be a blind idiot not to see you. And if there's anything I know about my brother, he's not that. If he accepted this bet from Emily, it was only because it finally gave him an excuse to talk to you—one he'd probably been looking awhile for."

She tried to absorb what Harrison was saying. Maybe it was what Logan meant about the whole thing not being a big deal. There was still a piece of her heart that had a hard time accepting any of it.

"Okay," she said, finishing her drink. "Let's just not talk about it anymore."

"Last question," he said, holding up a hand.

She sighed. "Alright."

"You said to me before that if either of us wanted you, we wouldn't be trying so hard to give you away. Is there any part of you that wants me to fight for you? Should I not being trying so hard to give you away?"

Julianne swallowed. She gave a long pause before answering. "Not right now."

She knew she could have just said "no, never," but a small part of her wouldn't let her close the door and throw away the key. It had been that way since she'd met him.

Before he could say anything else, Julianne noticed his eyes locking on something behind her.

"Ernesto just came out of the VIP lounge up there. You better go work some magic."

For someone who had never even been to a real club before, it was humorous to her she thought she'd be able to just walk up to the VIP area and get inside. But luckily for her, the bouncer at the entrance didn't bat an eye as she attempted to enter without pausing. He opened up the rope for her and let her in. Apparently confidence was the key to success.

She looked around for a woman in red. She spotted a U-shaped booth about ten feet away. The girl sitting down was dressed in a red miniskirt and a red blazer. She had long blonde hair with blunt bangs, but Julianne could see it was Lucy behind the expensive wig. There were two other couples at her table she appeared to be with, which Julianne hadn't even considered. Lucy wasn't there alone. If Julianne just walked up now, Lucy would never leave with her. She'd probably get kicked out of the club instead. So she made a quick beeline for the VIP bar and made sure she wasn't in Lucy's line of sight.

As she took a sip of her of her drink, a piece of paper slid in front of Julianne. She spun around to see its sender, but there was no one there.

Meet me behind the club in 5. Come alone. XO.

—L

Julianne looked back to the table Lucy had been at. She was gone. She couldn't believe she'd seen her. And now she had to decide if she would do what the note said. She didn't even know if she could sneak out of this place without Harrison noticing. She quickly looked around to see if anyone was watching, rushed out of the VIP area, and ditched her high heels so she could move faster and be seen less easily from above. She made it out the door and out into the warm Florida air.

She used her phone as a flashlight as she walked, still holding her heels and trying her best not to step on anything on the ground. Lucy was leaning against a dumpster out back, her wig removed and her dark brown hair matted to her head.

"What the actual hell, Julianne?" Lucy said, throwing her arms up. "What are you doing here?"

Julianne paused. She remembered Harrison saying she'd be able to signal him inside. If he didn't see her leave and she needed help, she had no one.

"Lucy, I—"

Lucy's nostrils flared. "You promised you were done following me, Julianne. You don't know how much shit you could get me in tonight by being here. I am fine. Please, please, please go home!"

"I know, Lucy," Julianne said, slowly approaching her.

"You know what?"

"I know about the stolen cocaine."

Lucy raised an eyebrow. "What are you talking about?"

"You're not a journalist. You stole a bunch of cocaine and now you're—"

"Again, what are you talking about? Have you lost it?"

"Elizabeth kidnapped me and has me here trying to track you down, Lucy. She told me what you're really up to."

Lucy huffed. "Of course she did. Where's Alex?"

"Dead," Julianne said.

Lucy was quiet for a moment. "She's wrong," she finally said. "She's lying to you, Jules. I'm sure she very much wants to find me, but not because I stole her cocaine. I am an undercover journalist. The DEA got interested in my work after I busted the most of the Anthony Lawrence ring. They wanted everyone who was left and also who was supplying them. They have all the cocaine, not me."

"But why would she be so certain? Why would she drug and kidnap Harrison and me to come here to get you? Did you know she was involved? That she's Anthony's girlfriend?"

"Not until recently," Lucy replied. "But yes, I found out. She's definitely on my list of people I'll be turning over to the DEA. Naturally, she would not tell you any of this."

"But you came here to pretend to be taking Anthony's place?" Julianne asked.

"Yes," she said. "You can call my contact at the DEA and they'll confirm I'm working for them."

"But Elizabeth could have easily have figured out where you were tonight, so why did she need us to come here and find you?"

She paused, shoving her hair away from her face. "You said Alex was dead? What happened?"

"She killed him on the plane she brought us here in," Julianne said. "She shot him."

"Alex had just found out the truth about her. That she was involved in this. She had both me and Alex to worry about turning her in. She clearly took care of him, but she probably had to make a plan to cover her tracks. And Julianne..."

"Yes?" she asked.

"I'm worried you might be the plan."

"I don't get it."

Lucy looked past Julianne, causing her to turn around to see who she had spotted. Julianne noticed Harrison's silhouette in the dark.

"Could you maybe have brought me with you?" he asked, his jaw clenched.

"I asked her to come alone," Lucy said.

"And?"

"Just relax," Julianne said, grabbing his arm to calm him down. "Lucy was just explaining everything."

"Right," he said, glaring at Lucy. "Hate to tell you, but I believe little out of her mouth anymore."

Julianne sighed. "I know, but I do. She's not who Elizabeth says she is, Harrison."

"And honestly, you don't have to believe me, but I was about to tell Julianne something. She might be setting you guys up for Alex's death."

He scoffed. "That's ridiculous."

"Is it?" Lucy asked. "She could frame you by saying you found out your girlfriend had slept with him. You followed him and his wife down to their Florida condo and killed him. Hell, she might have sent you out tonight just so she could work on setting you up. Like Julianne said, she could come get me herself; she knows where I am. Don't think she won't try. I'm sure she'd love if you delivered me to her—two birds with one stone."

Julianne looked at Harrison to see if he thought there was anything to this. He grabbed his phone and walked off to make a call. Julianne felt sick to her stomach. This was turning into a nightmare of proportions she hadn't imagined.

"Listen, I haven't turned her into the DEA yet because I'm waiting on hooking Ernesto and some others. If what I think is true, you two need to go into hiding until this is over. I can't protect you right now, and if you're wanted for murder—"

Harrison came back before she finished. "There's an APB out on us. We need to go, Julianne."

"I'm going to be sick," Julianne muttered, leaning over to hug her knees. Her job, her everything was going to taken away. This couldn't be happening. She wasn't strong enough, not for this. It was too much. Without warning, her stomach let loose and she vomited between her bare feet.

Harrison rubbed her back gently while Lucy held up her hair. She burned with both fear and humiliation.

"We will fix this, Jules," Lucy said. "Let me get back in there, I swear this will be over soon. Once I'm able to turn Elizabeth in, I'll convince them she did this. You have to have faith in me."

She stood up straight, falling back onto Harrison so she didn't have to stand on her own. She looked at Lucy and prayed she was right.

Lucy took off for the club, leaving them outside on their own.

"We need to go now," Harrison said, grabbing her arms and turning her to face him. "Remember inside when I said you were strong?"

Her heart was pounding. She shook her head, tears streaming down her face. "I can't do this, Harrison. I can't."

"You can," he said, tipping her chin up so she met his eyes. They were surprisingly warm for the situation they'd found themselves in. "I have a friend who will let us stay with her. But we need to go now. They'll be coming here for us; we have minutes at most. We need to ditch our phones. Elizabeth said she put trackers in them, and we can't risk taking them with us."

Julianne wiped her hand over her face, trying to clear some tears away. She handed him her phone, and he stomped on both of them until they were in pieces.

Harrison grabbed her arm and led her to a motorcycle that was parked out back. Without warning, he quickly took the headlight off and did something to the wires inside. Seconds later he had the motorcycle on and handed her the helmet on the back. Julianne thought about arguing that stealing this motorcycle was probably not the best idea, but she saw red and blue lights flashing in the distance, so she quickly hopped on behind him, grabbing his waist as tight as she could. They tore off in the opposite direction of the sirens, soon only surrounded by normal highway noise.

Her mind raced. Would this be on the news? Her parents, Logan, the hospital, everyone would see her wanted for murder with her secret lover. No one would believe it, right? And what would happen if Lucy wasn't able to convince her contacts that Julianne and Harrison had been set up? *No*, she told herself. You have to think positive. *You have to be strong like Harrison said you were.*

Their route got quieter as they continued driving. It looked like they were leaving Miami and possibly going south, based on what she could see. She wished she could ask where they were going, but the noise of the motorcycle made it too hard to hear.

It was over an hour before they finally stopped at a small house in Key Largo, a few miles off the main Florida Keys highway. She took off her helmet and shook out of her hair.

She couldn't believe she was still dressed in this ridiculous dress.

"Are we staying here?" she asked, praying he said yes. She was beyond exhausted and just wanted to fall asleep.

"Yeah, we should be good here."

She followed Harrison to the front door and waited while he knocked.

The door opened up to reveal a stunning woman staring back at them. She had a striking combination of flawless deep brown skin and emerald green eyes.

"Welcome home, husband."

20

Julianne stood in the small kitchen of the woman who had just introduced herself as Harrison's wife. She chugged a glass of water the woman had handed her. Harrison had disappeared to the bathroom, leaving Julianne to her own introductions.

"Thanks for the water," she said, setting her glass back on the counter.

"Of course," the woman said. "I'm Ruby."

"Julianne," she replied.

Ruby was in a pair of light blue pajama pants and a white silk tank top. Her tight spirals of brown hair hit just above her shoulders. She didn't have any makeup on, but she was still gorgeous. Also, she clearly didn't feel the need to put a bra on for them because Julianne could see the outlines of her breasts well. Of course, she was one to talk. She really needed to get out of this dress.

Harrison walked into the kitchen, opened up the fridge, and grabbed a beer.

"Make yourself at home," she said to Julianne. "I'm beat,

so I need to get to sleep. There's a spare room down the hall you can use. I left some clothes in there for you—Harrison mentioned you guys didn't get a chance to bring anything with you."

"Thanks so much," Julianne said.

Ruby stopped to look at Harrison. "We'll catch up tomorrow."

Julianne tried to parse what was going on between them, but she wasn't able to read anything from Harrison.

After she left, Julianne spoke, "I think I'm going to go to bed too. It's almost morning and my body will not hold up much longer."

She was glad to find a pair of worn gray sweatpants and a small blue T-shirt lying on her bed. She put them on before going to the bathroom. She looked horrible. There were black streaks running down her cheeks. Her hair was a mess from the motorcycle ride. She'd shower again if she trusted herself not to fall asleep. Instead, she opted to wash her face, go back into the bedroom, and fall asleep before she could worry about tomorrow.

When she woke up, the sun was already high and bright. She could hear birds outside and the whooshing of waves nearby. She felt rested, so she knew it was probably much later than she should have slept in. She did her best to not let all her thoughts come crashing in at once. It was the first time she was glad she didn't have her phone any longer—her entire world might be falling apart around her, but without being able to see it, she could ignore it.

There was a small knock at the door. She sat up and hurried to put her sweatpants back on before opening it. Harrison stood there, holding out a steaming cup of coffee.

"Good morning," he said.

She gave him a small smile and accepted the cup. "Thank you."

"Ruby made breakfast if you're hungry."

Her stomach rumbled at the smell and mention of food. She couldn't even remember when she'd eaten last. She followed Harrison out to the kitchen where Ruby had set out what looked like an egg dish and lemony smelling pancakes.

"This looks delicious," Julianne said, smiling at her.

"Goat cheese asparagus frittata and lemon poppy seed pancakes with lemon curd," Ruby replied.

"Ruby owns a restaurant," Harrison said.

She smiled at Julianne. "I own four, but Harrison doesn't like to boast."

"Where at?" Julianne asked as Ruby handed her a plate of food.

"Miami, Dallas, New Orleans, and Baton Rouge. I'm actually not around here as often as I'd like, so y'all got lucky I took a getaway when I did."

Julianne sat down at the kitchenette and dug in. "Should we be worried the police might look for us here? I mean . . . did you say last night Harrison was your husband?"

She had to ask; it was eating her inside to know, almost as much as her hunger.

Ruby looked like she was about to reply, but Harrison spoke instead.

"Ruby and I have known each other since we were kids. We started dating when Logan and I visited our dad in Baton Rouge," he said. "We got married when we were seventeen. And then life happened."

"I hated his guts for years after he just up and left," Ruby laughed as she took a sip from a blue tea mug with the little white tea bag tag still dangling from it. "But eventually years passed, and we were able to settle back into a friendship again. We've never had the chance, or the need that is, to formally end the marriage."

"I've escaped here several times over the years when I needed some protection, and I've always been safe," Harrison said. "I wouldn't bring you here if I didn't think you'd be safe too."

Julianne wondered if Ruby had been who he had referred to last night when she asked if there had ever been someone in his life. She hated how this made her feel jealous.

"How's your food?" Ruby asked. "Harrison told me you're dating little Logie bear."

She raised an eyebrow at Harrison. "I don't know if I'd call it that. The food is good though. Thanks so much."

Ruby laughed as she went over to the sink to do a few dishes.

"I'm going surfing this morning a little south of here. You two are welcome to join, but I guess you're probably better off lying low for now. Your faces are all over the news."

"Great," Julianne muttered. Now that she'd gotten enough food in her stomach to squelch the hunger pains, her nerves were killing her appetite.

When Ruby came back from her room she was dressed in a teal long-sleeve cropped rash guard and matching bottoms. She said a quick goodbye before heading out the door.

"How are you feeling this morning?" Harrison asked, sitting across from her as he ate his second helping of food.

Harrison was dressed in a yellow T-shirt and gray shorts. Not a color she was used to seeing him in, but it looked really good on him. The concerned expression on his face made warmth spread through her.

"Like I'm wanted for murder," she said with a smirk. "You?"

He shrugged. "Would you be surprised if this wasn't the first time I was in a situation like this?"

"Not really." She laughed nervously. "Not for actual murder though, right?"

"Oh, Julianne," he said, smiling and shaking his head. "You really need to work on who you trust. No, not any actual murder."

"Do you think I could try to reach out to anyone at home to let them know I'm okay?" she asked. "My poor mom . . ."

"I have someone doing it for you," he said. "They'll go to her house and talk to her. We can't risk using the phones right now. Your mom's could be tapped and someone could trace our location back here."

"Did you . . . is someone reaching out to Logan?" She couldn't even imagine what he was thinking.

"Not yet," he replied. "If you want me to, I can try. But I think Logan will piece together what's going on. I figured your mom might be more clueless to everything."

"Yes. That makes sense." Even though she could just imagine what Emily was trying to convince him of otherwise. "What are they saying on the news, anyway?"

"That you came down to Miami with your secret lover, Alex, and that I followed you and murdered him out of rage. And then you and I tried to cover it up together and took off. Elizabeth claims she showed up because she had a feeling something was going on with you and her husband and found her husband dead in their condo with our belongings and put two and two together."

"Good lord. I feel like we should have gotten a way to contact Lucy so we could know when she was done. Or so we could know if she failed so we can hurry and move to Mexico and never come back," Julianne said, mostly joking.

"My friend who let me know about the APB will let us know if there are any changes with Alex's case. He's high up and can get us the information fast," he said. "I say for now we just try to relax—enjoy a little trip to the Florida Keys. There's a small private beach area right behind the house. We can lay out and get some sun."

Julianne looked skeptically at him. "You don't seem like the type to sunbathe."

"I am if I have a cold beer in my hand and a beautiful girl by my side."

"Well, I'm sure Ruby will be back soon enough."

Harrison smirked. "I didn't mean Ruby."

Julianne smiled at him, and his dark eyes smiled back at her. His normal dark stubble was longer than usual, but it just made him more devilishly handsome, especially when he looked at her that way. She refused to let him see her blush, so she stood up and placed her plate in the sink before leaving to go get ready for the beach.

Julianne found a simple black bikini in the clothing Ruby left her. It fit her fairly well, except her breasts were a little more exposed than she'd prefer. She threw on a large sun hat that was sitting on a side table and stopped in the bathroom to brush her teeth and splash some water on her face. When she came out, Harrison was in sunglasses and a pair of blue swim trunks that hung low on his hips. She'd felt like she'd been seeing a lot of Harrison's abs lately, maybe too much, if there was such a thing.

They walked quietly out the back door and down the small walkway to the beach. There were some seagulls on the beach, along with some washed up seaweed and a few random sticks and rocks. Harrison had grabbed two beach chairs for them on the way down and sat them on the sand so they faced the ocean. He'd also stuck to this word and had a cooler with him that she guessed was full of cold beers.

"So tell me about you and Ruby," Julianne said after they had been sitting down for a few minutes.

Harrison reached into the cooler and handed her a bottle of beer. She accepted it, twisting off the cap before taking a long drink. She'd never found beer to taste as good as it did right at that moment.

"There isn't much to tell," he replied, taking a drink of his own beer. "We were young and stupid when we got married. Now that we're older, it turns out there isn't that same spark we thought was there when we were younger. But she's been a good friend for me the past few years—always a respite when I need to escape or hide."

Julianne nodded. "Maybe if you were living in the same city it would be different? Maybe you'd rekindle something? She seems kind of awesome."

"No, I don't think so," he said. "We're just too similar, if that makes any sense."

It did. She felt that way about Logan sometimes—they were too alike. She wasn't any better at relationships than he was. And there was the obvious thing of both of them being doctors.

"Yes, I get it," she said. "Well, I'm just saying, I like her."

He scoffed. "You hardly know her."

"I told you before, I'm good at judging someone right away."

He sat up, pushing his sunglasses on top of his dark brown hair. "What did you think of me when we first met then?"

Julianne took another drink to buy time to think of her answer.

"You seemed dangerous and intimidatingly good-looking, but something in me still trusted you," she replied, keeping his gaze.

"I thought you looked a bit stuck-up, but somehow I couldn't quite look away from you," he said.

"What?" she asked, her mouth hanging open a bit.

"I saw you before we met the first time, at the—"

Julianne interrupted him before he could finish. "At the medical foundation fundraiser!" she exclaimed. "I knew you looked familiar."

He grinned. She wasn't sure she'd ever seen him grin before. "So you did see me."

She blushed. "Um, yeah, I think any girl would see you, Harrison."

"I don't care about just any girl though," he replied, his eyes looking down so she could only see his long, dark lashes. He finally looked up after a moment, holding out his beer out to her. "I think we should toast."

Julianne raised her eyebrow. "To what?"

"To being here, together, alive. For you trusting me," he replied with a wink.

She clinked her bottle with his; he was right, this could be worse. Much worse.

"Can I ask you something about Logan?"

She sighed. "Yes, I guess."

"Did he mention anything to you recently about our mom?"

Julianne shook her head. "No, how come?"

"It's a bit of a long story, but I found her, and I told him about it the other night. He seemed a little messed up about it."

Julianne nodded, suddenly understanding his absence. Maybe it even sort of explained why he'd gotten drunk. She closed her eyes, wishing away the thought of him and Emily kissing.

"I guess I know he got drunk two nights ago. Emily told me," she said quietly. "Apparently he kissed her."

Harrison shook his head. "Wait, what?"

"Like I said, I don't really want to talk about Logan right now." She looked at Harrison, and she could see he wanted to say something else, but he stayed silent.

"So are you okay? About your mom?" she asked.

"Honestly, not when I was there," he said, fidgeting with the wrapper on his bottle. "I flew down to Houston to see her. I reacted shitty. But I think I was able to come to terms with it. I've never needed her, not the way Logan did."

"Had you been looking long?"

"I didn't look for a long time; I was worried what I would find." he replied. "I guess I assumed I'd find her dead, but instead I found her remarried with a daughter. It was just a punch to the gut I didn't expect."

"I'm sorry," she said. Her heart hurt for him. She couldn't fathom how a mother could do this. She had two amazing sons who she just abandoned. She wanted to offer more support, but she wasn't sure what else to say.

"Don't be," he said. His expression softened.

"It's her loss, you know," Julianne said.

The corner of his mouth quirked up as he leaned back and closed his eyes.

Julianne felt the scorching rays on her skin and knew it was good she'd grabbed the bottle of sunscreen inside. "Would it be totally cliché of me to ask you to help me put this on?" she asked, handing him the orange tube.

She hopped over to his chair, sitting on the end. He rubbed at her neck and shoulders. His hands felt amazing as they continued to travel down her back.

"Good?" he asked when he reached the bottom of her back.

She nodded, quickly going back to her own chair. While she craved for his hands to finish the job, she knew she could do the rest. She finished applying the lotion on her chest, stomach and legs. Julianne could feel Harrison's eyes on her as she rubbed the last bit of lotion on her thigh.

"I never got to finish talking to you earlier, at the club," he said. "You told me 'not right now' when I asked if I should try for you or not. I really want to be the good guy and listen to you. But I'm going to be honest, Jules..."

She cursed the damn tingle in her stomach—even though everyone close to her called her Jules, she'd never heard Harrison say it before, and it felt more intimate.

"You can trust me, but I'm not really the good guy, and I keep trying to convince myself that Logan isn't the right man for you. I feel like there's something here that I haven't felt before, or at least haven't felt in a really long time."

"Harrison—" she began.

"Let me finish," he said, looking down at his hands. "We're in a crazy situation right now. We both can admit that."

Julianne gave a small laugh. "Well, yes."

"Maybe . . . maybe we could we try this . . ." Harrison stumbled through his words.

She'd never seen or heard him like this; Harrison was nervous. She wanted him to finish what he was saying, but she was also worried because she knew where he was going with it. And she would have just seconds to decide on an answer.

"Just while we're here, not in the real world," he said. "Being the on-the-run versions of ourselves. When we go home, you can forget it ever happened if you want. It'll be our secret."

Julianne watched him closely as he spoke. He looked dead serious, vulnerable even. It seemed so out of character for him. His suggestion felt crazy, but at the same time, it felt more right than anything that had happened in the last twenty-four hours. Maybe it was time to send rational Julianne on her way.

She felt a little breathless as she spoke. "And what do you mean by *this*?"

21

Harrison got up from his chair and leaned over Julianne. His eyes were darker than she'd ever seen them. His lips went to her neck first and she felt warmth spread through her body. She fully anticipated him moving to her mouth next, but she suddenly found him going in the opposite direction as his tongue traveled over her breast. His hands slid behind her back as he straddled her with his legs resting over the sides of her chair. He threw her top to the ground, his teeth gently teasing her nipple while his hands worked further south toward her swim bottoms.

She gripped the arms of her chair tightly as her body took over for her brain. She half-heartedly thought about jumping up and saying she couldn't do this, but she'd known the moment his warm lips had touched her skin that she wanted to be his, even if it was just for right now.

"I've wanted to taste you for so long," he said, his voice husky.

Julianne focused on her breathing as he kissed her navel,

his lips moving painfully slowly down to where she throbbed.

He looked up and met her eyes for a moment and grinned before sliding his finger in the top of her swim bottoms and tugging them down toward her ankles.

He slowly teased her with short, small kisses on her swollen lips. His stubble rubbed her delightfully, and her hips arched toward him. He kept going, his kisses becoming longer, his tongue caressing her. He let up for a moment and she gritted her teeth.

"Harrison," she whined quietly. She needed him to keep going.

"Oh, you like that, baby?" he teased, his voice sexy as hell before his tongue pressed into her again.

Her hips rocked against him. She gripped her chair hard while she felt her body coming undone.

"Harrison!" she moaned loudly this time as her body settled into pure relaxation.

He helped pull her bottoms back up before grabbing her off of her chair and throwing her gently onto the sand beside them. She laughed as he jumped down next to her, pulling her on top of him so that she rested her head on his chest. She could feel his erection hard underneath her.

"Apparently your body was in agreement with my suggestion," he mused.

Julianne pushed her face further into his chest in embarrassment, but he pried her chin up with his fingers, his lips meeting hers.

"You're beautiful," he said. "And you taste like the ocean."

She scrunched up her nose. "I'm sure it's salt from sweat. I really need to shower."

He shook his head with a small laugh. "Let's go in the ocean and clean off then."

He helped her to her feet. She went to grab for her top but he stopped her. "I like you like this."

She pulled an arm over herself self-consciously. She wasn't embarrassed by her body, but she wasn't exactly comfortable being naked like this.

"Here, I'll be equal," he said, turning around and sliding off his swim trunks before running off into the ocean.

She watched, wide-eyed at his incredible body diving into a wave. She made her way into the water, her arm still covering her up, and walked closer to him.

"Come here." He smiled, grabbing her arms and pulling her up so that her legs straddled his hips. She could still feel him hard between her legs and she wanted so badly to give into what her body was telling her and take him inside of her. His voice was warm and hot in her eat. "I could make you scream my name all over again."

"This is crazy," she mumbled into his shoulder. "I . . ."

He let her down so they were standing facing each other and put a finger to her lips. "Don't overthink any of this. If you let guilt wash over you, you're ruining it all."

Julianne sighed. She still craved his body, but her brain was catching up with her.

"It's just . . . Logan."

Harrison's eyes darkened before he looked away. She knew she'd made a mistake as soon as his brother's name left her mouth, but she couldn't take it back. It wasn't like Harrison didn't know he existed as a barrier between them; she'd just reminded them both of it. But Julianne knew she'd picked the worst time to do that, because his eyes weren't just dark, they were hurt.

"I think we should probably get inside soon anyway, or at least get dressed," she said. "Ruby might be home soon, and I don't want her to see us like this."

"If that's what you want," he said, stepping back so there was now a physical distance between them matching the emotional one Julianne had created.

Julianne felt cold suddenly and wished she could pull him back toward her, but she didn't. She followed him out of the water and accepted the towel he handed her and wrapped it around her body. She grabbed the bikini top that was laying on the sand and put it back on before looking at Harrison, who had tugged his swim trunks back on.

He had become quiet, and she honestly couldn't blame him. She wasn't trying to throw around mixed signals; she was just so confused. She wouldn't have let things go where they had if things with Logan had been good before Elizabeth had taken her. But finding out about the bet, and him spending time with Emily, had put a sour note between them. It didn't make what was going on with Harrison right, but she could no longer deny she had feelings for both Williams brothers, and she wasn't sure which one she wanted more.

Logan was the safe choice in terms of having a similar lifestyle. But he came with the history of being a playboy. Harrison was dark and mysterious, and that made him an exciting choice. He didn't seem to have the trail of women behind him like Logan, except a wife. But even if Harrison wanted something serious with Julianne, would he be around enough for it to be worth it?

When they got inside the house, Julianne showered and

dressed in a pair of denim shorts and a white T-shirt. Harrison was on a landline phone when she came out of her room.

"I'm going to go up to Miami," he said to her. "I got a lead on where Ernesto will be tonight, and I need to make sure Lucy is still holding up her end of the bargain."

"But you might be recognized and get arrested," she said, her eyebrows scrunching in confusion. "I thought we were lying low here. What changed?"

"I can't sit around anymore and wait," he replied. "And like you said, we have no way to get ahold of Lucy, so for all we know she's dead in a gutter right now."

Julianne couldn't help but feel he was doing this because of what had happened out in the water. She felt so mad at herself for how it all went down. She wished she hadn't started something she hadn't intended to finish. She cared about him more than she had ever realized, and the thought of him leaving now hurt.

"If you go, I'm coming with you," Julianne said, her hands on her hips. "You're in this mess because of me."

He shook his head. "No, you're staying here. No arguments."

Julianne glared. "You don't get to make that decision."

"Actually, I do."

She was about to retort when they both heard sirens in the distance, growing closer by the second. Their eyes met, and Julianne saw fear in his. He grabbed Julianne by the arm, pulling her toward the front window, pushed them both flat against the wall, and looked outside. A lump formed in her throat while fear and adrenaline coursed through her body.

"Shit," he muttered. "This is unbelievable."

Julianne craned her neck so she could see too. Two police cars and another unmarked car had pulled into the driveway of Ruby's house.

"We . . . we can explain to them, right? Maybe they'll understand?" she asked.

They looked out the window again. The motorcycle was right out front, making it impossible to get to it.

"You like to run, right?" he asked.

Julianne looked at him and nodded.

"Find any pair of shoes you can that you can run in and put them on. We're going out the back door."

She found a pair of pink and black Nike shoes by the door and slid her feet into them, thankful that Ruby's feet only seemed to be a half-size bigger than her own. Harrison had quickly thrown on a shirt and tucked his own feet into a pair of worn and dirty white tennis shoes that appeared to be his own, or some guy's at least. Harrison opened the door, pulling Julianne toward a row of bushes that were out back. He slid her down and pushed through the bush to make a small hole to see through.

"They haven't sent anyone out back yet, so we can go," he said. "We're going through the neighbor's yards, so just go as fast as you can and try not to draw any attention."

There was a row of bushes that started and stopped between all the yards they went through, giving each home-owner access to the beach. She figured he'd picked this route because running right on the beach would make it much easier to spot them.

They were two houses down when they heard some commotion behind them. Harrison grabbed her hand, throwing them both onto the sand behind one hedge.

"Did they see us?" she whispered, trying to catch her breath.

"Stay here."

She tried to object, but he'd already crawled off, leaving her alone. She looked around the beach in front of her to see if anyone was coming. It was quiet, luckily.

Harrison was back a minute later.

"They had two men out in the back of the house. They'll be coming this way soon," he whispered. "We need to keep going, but I think we need to make it to the alley that runs in front of the houses. When I say go, I need you to run as fast as you can past the blue house up there until you get to the dumpster. You're going to wait for me there."

She stared at him, wide-eyed. "Why aren't you coming with?"

"It will be easier to see two people than one," he replied. "Plus, if they do see us, I'll distract them and you'll keep going."

"I'm not leaving you!"

He pressed a finger to her lips. The warmth of his skin calmed her enough to listen to him. "We will be okay," he said, holding her gaze. "Remember, you're strong."

She nodded.

"Okay, now go!"

She scrambled to her feet, sprinting as fast as she could. She refused to look over to see if anyone was watching. It would slow her down. She kept her feet pounding the ground in front of her as she ran. She saw the dumpster and dashed over to it, quickly crouching down next to it. Her heart pounded furiously in her chest as she waited to see if anyone was coming for her. When she didn't hear anyone, she relaxed—until she realized Harrison wasn't anywhere to be seen. She tried looking back toward the hedge they had been behind, but she couldn't see him.

Suddenly she heard a commotion a house down and some shouting. She scrunched her eyes shut. If they caught him, she had no idea what she'd do. Should she keep running? She knew she'd never make it on her own as a runaway, not without Harrison. She grabbed a palm branch that was on the ground by the dumpster and slammed it against the dumpster several times until she heard the commotion pause and head in her direction. Julianne said a quick prayer she hadn't made the wrong decision.

Hands suddenly grabbed Julianne from behind and her heart sank. Harrison spun her around and relief flooded through her. She threw her arms around him, but he was rigid so she let go, looking up at his face for instruction.

"Thanks for the distraction," he whispered, looking around them. "It was stupid, but it worked."

Julianne rolled her eyes at the backhanded compliment.

"We're going to run again. Go as fast as you can and don't stop. I'll be right with you, unless you outrun me."

She nodded before they took off, sprinting as fast as she could. She might do more running than him, but he had at least six inches on her, and his body was pure muscle, so he was hard to keep up with.

When they made it about eight blocks, they'd left the residential area and were near a few white industrial buildings.

"Let's try the second one up here," he said as they kept jogging.

There were no cars parked near the building and only one semi-truck in the lot.

He led them to a door. He tried the handle, but it was locked. He tried kicking it in with his foot, but was again unsuccessful. He walked over and found a rock, slamming it down into the door handle until it broke and they were able to open the door.

It appeared to be a warehouse of some sort. Luckily no one was inside.

"How long do you think we're safe here?" she asked him as he looked around.

"I don't know."

"How do you think they found us?"

He sighed. "I don't know that either. Maybe someone reported the motorcycle. I should have hidden it better. Dammit."

Julianne rubbed his arm. She definitely didn't blame him. If anything, she wasn't even surprised they'd been found. If felt more like a *when* to her than an *if*.

"Maybe we can wait here until it gets dark out?" she asked.

"Yes." He nodded, walked over to a box, and sat down. "And then we need to find a way back to Miami. We need to end this."

Julianne nodded. It sounded like a terrible idea truthfully, but hiding out forever wouldn't work either.

They went to look around the warehouse. The main floor had rows and rows of boxes and forklifts. On the second floor appeared to be offices. They took the stairs, looking for any water or food that was around. They found a small break room with a mini-refrigerator that had two diet sodas, a cheese stick, and a plastic container with some unknown pasta dish. There was a half-full water tank nearby with small paper cone cups. Julianne grabbed one, filling and drinking it several times before she felt hydrated. Harrison had cracked one soda and was sitting on the floor.

Julianne sat next to him and wished desperately for their closeness from earlier. She'd been right to slow things down, but she didn't want it all to fizzle out to nothing. Now she didn't know how to get any of it back. She nervously reached for his hand, forcing her fingers between his own. She felt relief when he squeezed her hand hard. Julianne looked up at him and found him staring back at her.

"I don't regret anything that happened back there on the beach," Julianne said. "It all just happened so fast, I needed time to think—"

"I know," he replied. "In all fairness, you warned me not to try. But you're too perfect to not fight for."

"I'm not perfect," she said, her mouth agape.

He let go of her hand, taking her face between his hands before kissing her. What started off slow between them quickly escalated. Harrison leaned over her, his body weight pressing her into the floor below.

She moaned as he found the spot on her neck that made her body shiver. She responded to him differently than she'd ever experienced.

"Why do you always smell incredible?" he murmured between kisses.

She felt her face flush, sure he was once again mistaken. She was still sweaty from their run for their lives.

Julianne reached up, pressing her hand into his face to stop him for a moment so she could look at him. He was so damn handsome she sometimes had to take a moment to drink him in.

"You're not overthinking again, are you?" he asked, that knowing smirk on his face.

She shook her head. "I was just thinking about how much I like you."

He laughed, taking her hand off of his face and moving it back to the ground, trapping it with his. "I like you too, Julianne Davis."

"You're different from who I thought you were," she said.

He bit down gently on her earlobe, whispering into her ear. "Oh yeah? How's that? Am I not dangerous enough for you anymore?"

Oh lord, she couldn't think when his mouth was on her. She tried to regroup her thoughts before speaking. "You can be so hard and dark and impossible to read, but then when it's just us, like this, you're affectionate and loving and—"

She felt flushed talking to him about this. He was staring at her so intently, his hands moving on her body so that her brain was having a hard time keeping track of her words. "You make me forget about everything else."

"That was my plan," he said.

"I want you right now," she said softly as he dipped down toward her mouth.

"You don't know how good it is to hear you say that," he said, his voice deep and soft. He pulled her up and placed her in his lap so she was straddling his legs, facing him. "And I so badly want to take you on the floor in this horrifically ugly break room, but I would be way too distracted to keep you safe when someone could walk in downstairs any minute."

She closed her eyes, leaning her head against his chest. He was right, but her insides were begging her to convince him otherwise.

"If you decide when this is over, you want to forget about this, us, I promise I'll let you. But I feel like we could be so good to together. Just don't forget this moment. Okay?"

She nodded. She wasn't sure anymore what she wanted to do. At first she'd thought of their tryst as a temporary escape, but her heart was so attached to him she wasn't sure she'd be able to let him go. Somehow she was falling in love with Harrison Williams.

There was a noise downstairs that startled them both. Harrison stood up quickly, holding his hand for Julianne to stay in place.

"Stay here," he said. "Do not come out of this room no matter what. Do you understand?"

"Y . . . yes," she stuttered before standing up. She reached out for him before he could leave, pressing her lips into his. "Please be careful."

He closed the door behind him, and she found a lock and hit the button. She planned to stay put, but her mind raced with thoughts of what could happen, worse than getting arrested. She undid the lock and cracked open the door so she could hear what was going on.

"We know you're in here," a voice called out from below.

Julianne opened the door further, trying to hear better. The voice sounded similar.

"We just want to talk," said another voice, this one female.

Julianne recognized them now—it was Ernesto and Elizabeth. She hadn't been expecting them. Her heartbeat increased. The police felt like a safer bet. She pictured Alex lying dead on the plane and felt her stomach churn again. She looked around the room. There were a few plastic knives, but nothing that could be used as a weapon. She knew

Harrison was unarmed, and while she had faith in him, there were two of them, and they were most definitely not without weapons.

"So listen," Elizabeth spoke loudly. "our friend, Lucy, is being a real pain in the ass. I thought maybe we could regroup now that we're all being honest about what's going on here. We all agree to kill Lucy, and I tell the police I was wrong about you killing Alex. You can go home, keep your mouths shut, and it's all over."

Julianne gasped. She couldn't let them just kill Lucy, but she really wished this could be over. She wished so badly Harrison had a plan to end this.

"I know you two are here, so you might as well just show your faces now," Elizabeth said. "Ernesto here is a bit testy. Lucy tried to turn him into the DEA, and his favorite motorcycle was stolen last night. Do you two happen to know anything about that?"

Elizabeth's voice was the only noise Julianne could hear. She didn't hear any footsteps from Harrison, so she had no idea if he was still upstairs or had made his way down.

"Come out, come out, wherever you are," Elizabeth sang.

Julianne heard a loud screeching noise, followed by a giant crash and thud. Seconds later she heard the loud, thundering sound of a gun going off several times until silence ensued again.

22

J ulianne ran out of the room, tripping over her own feet on the way out. She stumbled back up and rushed to look over the railing. She saw a huge piece of metal equipment the size of an automobile now sat on the floor. Elizabeth's leg appeared to be trapped underneath. Her gun had been flung out of her hand and lay about fifty feet from her.

Next she saw Ernesto. He had a gun pointed up toward where the railing was now absent from the equipment taking it out on its way to the floor below. Julianne followed his gaze; she didn't see Harrison. She got on her knees, crawling in that direction so Ernesto couldn't see her.

She spotted Harrison moments later, sprawled out on the ground.

"No!" she yelled, throwing her hand over her mouth to silence her screams.

She rushed over to him, aware that Ernesto would come up any moment now that he'd heard her, but there was nothing she could do.

"Harrison, Harrison," she said. She reached for his neck to check for a pulse. Her hands shook as she waited, and she finally came across a weak one. He was alive.

"Harrison, can you hear me? You're going to be okay. Can you open your eyes?"

It looked like he'd been hit in the shoulder. The blood was coming out so quickly that the floor beneath him was now sticky and red. She ripped off her shirt, tearing it with her teeth to try to get something to tie over the wound. As she worked to treat his wound, she heard footsteps coming up the stairs. She quickly moved the fabric underneath his arm, tying it tightly. They were next to a small office, but she knew she wouldn't be able to drag him into it without help. He weighed too much.

The steps got closer, and Julianne looked at Harrison, tears running down her cheeks. She knew if she went into the office by herself, he would definitely kill him. She couldn't leave him, even though she knew she would die too.

She laid her head on his chest, unable to stop the sobs coming out of her mouth that were muffled by his chest.

Julianne heard a second set of footsteps now coming up the stairs. The first set had to be almost to her. She looked up at Ernesto and watched in slow motion as he pointed his gun at her. She blinked several times and flinched at the crack of a bullet cutting through the air. She watched as his body crumpled to the ground in a heap.

Julianne stared straight behind where Ernesto had stood moments before, looking right into the eyes of Lucy.

"Lucy!" Julianne yelled as Lucy ran over to her, throwing her arms around her on the ground where she knelt next to Harrison.

"How did you—" Julianne began.

She heard the commotion below and looked down to see multiple DEA agents and police officers entering through the door.

"I lead them here," she said. "I was able to get a tracker on Ernesto last night. I didn't have any idea they'd be coming after you. They must have followed the police. Is he . . . ?"

"He's alive," she said. "But barely. We need to get an ambulance here; can you have someone call?"

"Yes, stay here," she said. "I'm so damn glad you're alive, Julianne Davis."

Julianne let out a nervous laugh. "I still feel like I'm not."

And it was the truth. She'd never known how it felt like to almost die until that moment. There had been no flash of her whole life before her eyes; it was just like any other second she lived, except that she'd thought it would be her last. Now she had to help save Harrison so it wouldn't be *his* last. The shirt was helping stop some of the bleeding, but he'd lost so much before she'd been able to help him. She kept checking his pulse, waiting anxiously for someone to show up to help.

A police officer approached her and it was just then that Julianne remembered she and Harrison were still wanted criminals.

"Julianne Davis?" the officer asked. He was in his forties with a fitting police officer mustache and patrol hat.

"Lucille Aldridge filled us in on what happened when Elizabeth kidnapped you and Harrison Williams. We have Elizabeth under arrest for the murder of her husband, Alex, and for being an accomplice in the drug operation run by Anthony Lawrence. We'll need you to come down to the precinct before you leave to clear a few things up, but just know this is over."

Relief rushed through her. "Thank you." She kept holding pressure on Harrison's wound. He had to survive this. They were free; he had to live. She looked back at him. He was pale and his pulse was still weak. "Do you know how close the ambulance is?"

"I'll go check on that for you," he said, tipping his hat and leaving them alone.

She lay down next to him while she kept pressure on his shoulder and kissed his cheek. A few minutes later, the EMTs came up the stairs and loaded him onto a stretcher.

"I'm coming with," she said to them.

"Are you family? We really need you to just meet us at the hospital."

"I'm . . . yes, I'm family," she lied. There was no way in hell she was going to wait for Harrison's family to arrive to get updates on his status. That would involve calling the only family member she knew of his, and that simply couldn't happen right now. Or was she being selfish by not calling him? It was his brother, and if the worst happened and Harrison didn't make it, Logan would be devastated about not being able to say goodbye.

She bit at her nails as they took him out the door. Julianne went to find Lucy, who was talking with a few of the officers.

"Luce," she said, grabbing her arm. "Do you think you could give me a ride to the hospital? I want to meet Harrison there."

"Of course."

"Also, I need to use your phone. I think I should call Logan."

"I have a shirt you can borrow too," Lucy said. "Not that you can't rock that look."

Julianne looked down and groaned, realizing now she'd been standing around in only her bra.

"Hello?"

It was weird hearing Logan's voice. It hadn't been that long since she'd seen him, only two days, but it felt like a lifetime.

"Logan? It's Julianne."

There was silence on the phone and for a moment she thought maybe they'd gotten disconnected or, worse, that he'd hung up.

"I hope I'm not your one call from jail, Davis," he said, finally breaking the silence.

She smiled. She needed a bit of humor. She dreaded having to break the news to him.

"No, no, everything's okay. I'm officially no longer a wanted felon." She looked over at Lucy, who was driving her to the hospital. Lucy gave her a supportive smile and reached out and patted her leg.

"I called . . . I called to tell you Harrison's been shot," she said.

There was silence again, so she kept speaking.

"He was shot in the shoulder, but he lost a lot of blood and he isn't conscious. He's on the way to the hospital now by ambulance. Lucy is driving me. I just thought maybe you should know, in case, well . . . I mean, I don't think he's going to die, but you're his only family I could think to call," she blurted out.

"Where are you guys?" he asked.

"Key Largo."

"Well, I guess you could have picked a worse place to make me come to. Are you holding up okay? I literally do not understand what the hell you're up to, just so you know."

"I know," she replied. "But yes, I'm okay. It's been an insane couple of days. I'll fill you in on everything later. We're just pulling up to the hospital."

"Be safe," he said before hanging up.

Julianne handed Lucy back her phone, glad the call was over. She'd been so relieved he hadn't asked her anything else —anything about them. She wasn't prepared to talk to him about it yet. She knew in heart what she had to say, but it felt impossible to do, especially hearing his voice. It brought her back to a place from just a few days before.

"How's it going with the two boyfriends?" Lucy asked, giving her a wink.

Julianne threw her hands up over her face and let out a frustrated scream. "It sucks."

Lucy smiled. "I don't know, they're both good-looking. It can't suck too bad."

Julianne sighed. "I don't want to hurt anyone, and I really don't want to cause those two to hate each other any more than they already seem to. But I . . ."

"I saw your face, with Harrison," Lucy said. "You're in love with him. Are you in love with Logan?"

Was she in love with Logan? She and Logan had never been pushed into the situations she and Harrison had—it had brought her feelings to light so much faster. But she took a moment to think about her time with Logan—their talks, the secret rendezvous in the closet, the night they'd spent together in her room. She'd been on the verge of it before everything happened, but she couldn't answer that right now.

"Thanks for the ride," Julianne replied. "Are you coming in?"

"I would, but I need to go meet with the officers about a few things. I'll stop by and see you later. Oh, and just remember, when you're trying to figure out which guy to choose—we're young. Don't take yourself too seriously."

Julianne walked inside and checked in at the ER desk. She spotted Ruby seconds later.

"Julianne!" Ruby said, pulling her into her arms. "I'm friends with Derick who's on the local squad, and I came here as soon as I heard."

"Have you seen him yet?" Julianne asked.

Ruby shook her head "They said they were taking him straight to surgery, so I guess now we wait."

She sighed. It was annoying be on the patient side in a hospital. If they'd have been in Minneapolis, at least she could have found someone to ask for more details. No one knew her here, nor would they care she was a surgical resident thousands of miles away.

"I'm so sorry this happened," Ruby said. "It's always been safe at my place. I don't know what went wrong."

"Apparently we took Ernesto's motorcycle—my guess is he had someone looking for it, and we'd stupidly left it out in the open."

Ruby nodded. "Well, Harrison is strong. This isn't his first bullet."

Julianne raised her eyebrow. "Do you mean that literally or figuratively?"

She gave her a knowing smile. "Definitely both."

"Was he like this when you were younger?"

Ruby laughed. "Oh, girl, he was so much worse. I fell so hard for the bad boy. I shouldn't have been surprised when he left to go off to do god knows what. But some parts of him haven't changed. He was always loyal to those close to him. There's nothing luckier than being someone Harrison cares about."

Julianne smiled.

"I can see he cares about you," Ruby said.

Julianne tried to keep her simple polite smile, but she knew Ruby was watching for a reaction so she said, "Yes, we've become good friends lately."

She raised an eyebrow at her. "You sure that's it? Because I know he said you're dating Logan, but I feel like there is definitely something going on between you two."

Julianne sighed. "Things are complicated."

"They always are with the Williams brothers," Ruby replied. "But just so you know, my allegiance is with Harrison, so if you hurt him, you better watch out."

Julianne could see from her expression she was serious, even if she tried to make it seem like it was a joke. "I don't think I'm capable of hurting Harrison."

"He's human. So just for curiosity's sake, and yes I'm being nosey, is there something between you two?"

"Yes," Julianne replied without hesitating.

"So you're stuck between two brothers."

"Can I be nosey too? Can you tell me more about their

feud? I heard it was about some time when Harrison got Logan into some trouble?" Julianne asked.

Ruby sighed. "From what Harrison told me, Logan was pissed about the time they got arrested. But if you ask me, that wasn't all it was. I think it brought up some unresolved issues between them. Honestly, I think Harrison was upset that Logan was so mad at him for what happened. He didn't understand where Logan was coming from. I think Logan might have berated him and his life choices pretty badly when it happened. So there was Harrison who felt like Logan was turning his back on him as a brother, and Logan who felt like his life was being screwed up."

Julianne listened, taking it all in. It was nice to get the story from a neutral party.

"Thanks," Julianne said, offering her a small smile.

Julianne got up and returned with two cups of coffee minutes later, and they sat in silence, flipping through magazines for the next two hours. Julianne was just beginning to doze off in her chair when she heard someone speak.

"Mrs. Williams?" a young doctor said, walking up to them.

Julianne and Ruby looked up. Julianne wondered if Ruby really still went by Harrison's last name, or if she'd just given them that name so she could be more convincing as his wife to receive information.

"Yes?" she said. "How is he?"

"The surgery went well. We were able to get him a blood transfusion after stopping all the bleeding and retrieving the bullet. He hasn't woken up yet, but we expect him to soon."

Julianne let out a breath. It was definitely the best news she'd gotten today.

"Wonderful," Ruby said. "Can we see him?"

"Sure. You can come back shortly once we get him into his recovery room."

Another hour later they both followed a nurse to his room. He was laying in his bed, and his color looked much better than when she'd seen him last. It was reassuring to see him looking more like himself.

"I felt like I needed to see with my own two eyes that he was alive," Ruby said. "But I think I will go. I'll stop by later and say hi to him. Take care of him for me."

Ruby gave her a quick hug before leaving. Julianne pulled up a chair close to Harrison's bed. It was odd just sitting here, watching him sleep. For having just been shot, he looked rather peaceful. That most likely had to do with the IV in his hand supplying his pain medication. She knew he'd need it.

She took a moment while he was resting to grab the phone on the table next to him and call her mom. Julianne hadn't had a chance to let her know she was okay, and she couldn't even imagine what a mess her mom would be.

"Hello?" Her mom answered on the first ring.

"Mom, hi! It's Julianne."

"Oh my god, Julianne. Are you okay? What is going on? The news has been out of control on this. I-I . . ."

"Mom, please calm down. I am okay. None of it is true, and it's all over."

"Do you even know the trouble you're in with your residency program?" she asked her. "Julianne, they might kick you out for this."

Julianne swallowed. Her throat felt dry and parched. She'd been trying to avoid thinking about this and wished suddenly that she'd never called her mom.

"Mom, I'm sure it will all be resolved. Everything was seriously not my fault and a big misunderstanding."

"Really, Julianne?" she asked. "If you hadn't had gotten involved with that friend of yours, Lucy, to begin with, this wouldn't have happened."

"You sound like Dad. I'm sorry for trying to be a good friend."

Her mom sighed. "I'm sorry, sweetheart. I didn't mean to throw this at you all you at once. But you have to imagine, as your mom, what I've been feeling these last two days."

"I know," she said. "I'm so sorry, Mom. Just please . . . please try to be calm. I'm safe and will be home soon, I promise."

"Okay," she replied. "I think you should know before you come back, your father is irate. He's chewed my ear off a handful of times—I think he blames me for this mess, as though you're fifteen and I should be controlling you. He's been talking to your residency program director to sort this mess out. You need to go see him as soon as you get back regardless of how you feel about him."

Julianne groaned. Just what she wanted to go home to. They said their goodbyes and Julianne hung up the phone and looked over at Harrison. Her heart skipped a beat when she saw his eyes open and staring back at her.

"Jules."

23

Julianne grabbed his hand, giving it a gentle squeeze.

"Hi," she said softly, smiling at him. "You're up."

He tried to return her smile, but grimaced. "I feel like hell."

Julianne gave a small laugh. "Well you were shot, so that's probably why."

"You're okay though?" he asked, looking her over carefully.

She nodded. "Yes, I am totally fine."

He closed his eyes, laying there silently for so long Julianne thought maybe he'd fallen back asleep.

"But not because of me," he said, opening his eyes again. They looked sad.

Julianne shook her head in confusion. "You got shot because you were helping me, Harrison. I'd say that, yeah, I'm fine because of you."

"I guess we don't see things the same way."

"Can we just focus on you being alive?" Julianne said, trying to keep his mood from spiraling downward.

Julianne filled him in on what had happened with the machine trapping Elizabeth's leg and Ernesto getting shot by Lucy. She left out how close they both came to being shot. She would never blame him; he'd literally pushed a two-ton object over a railing and had taken a bullet to save her. Just because someone else had to finish the saving didn't make him any less of a hero in her eyes.

"Ruby was here. She says hi."

He nodded.

She knew she needed to say more about how she'd felt in those last moments—her realization of her feelings for him. But she wasn't sure if it was the right moment. She'd given him so much information to process already. She knew when patients first woke up they were typically a bit out of it. If she confessed now that she'd fallen in love with him he might not even remember later.

She was still holding his hand when there was a knock on the door. She looked up, expecting to see his nurse coming to check on him, but she saw a face she hadn't been expecting. Not yet. As she let go of Harrison's hand, it reminded her of the time Harrison had once seen her and Logan holding hands. And now this . . .

"Logan!" she said, overcompensating for her nervousness. She wanted to shove her foot into her mouth. The last thing she wanted Harrison to think was that she was super excited to see Logan. But she couldn't deny seeing him was calming after the last two days of chaos.

Logan pulled her into his arms, burying his head into her where her hair hung over her shoulders. She hugged him back, but pulled away after a few seconds.

"I didn't think you'd make it here so fast," she said, looking at him.

She wished she'd have told Harrison now that she'd asked Logan to come, because she could see by the look on his face he was very irritated by his arrival.

"I stopped at the airport after you called to see if there were any open seats on any outgoing flights to Miami, and I got lucky," he said, his baby blue eyes wrinkling in the corners from smiling. "Good lord, Davis, I didn't realize how good it would be to see you."

She heard Harrison clear his throat from the bed, and they both turned to him.

"Hey there, brother," Harrison said, his tone as irritable as his face looked.

Yikes. She really wished this meet-up could have happened after he'd had more rest.

"Hey, man," Logan said, walking up to him and laying a hand on his shoulder. "Glad to see you didn't die after all. I guess now I just get to enjoy some sunshine with my girl."

Silence. Julianne wondered if maybe she could pretend she hadn't heard him. She thought after their casual phone call there was an understanding that they were . . . neutral, maybe? She really hadn't anticipated him thinking they would be able to just jump back into where they were without even discussing what had happened before she'd left.

She looked at Harrison, but he was just staring at the wall, unreadable. She smiled at Logan. They definitely needed to talk, just not in this room.

"Well, get going then," Harrison said, finally breaking the silence. "I'd hate for you to miss out on your tan, bro."

Julianne wished he'd make eye contact with her so she could try to give him some type of reassuring look, let him know she hadn't just decided they were over. But still his eyes stayed on the wall, staring at a poster with smiley faces for a pain rating scale. Julianne definitely could relate to the last face.

"Harrison, we can stay if you want?" she said, hoping that would help.

"Your boyfriend came to see you. You should go," he said, still not looking at her.

He wasn't even giving her a chance. "He came to see you, not me," she said, her own tone sharp now.

"Actually, he's mostly right," Logan said, somehow oblivious to Harrison's attitude. "I mostly wanted to see you, Julianne, but you did give me a pretty damn good excuse to miss work tomorrow."

"Fine, we'll stop back later. You need to rest anyway." She rested her hand on Harrison's arm for a minute before following Logan out the door.

As they walked down the hall toward the parking garage where his rental car was parked, it felt like she'd suddenly gone back in time. She shook her head to clear it, trying to just focus on what she had to do. "It's good to see you. It feels like it's been forever."

He smiled at her, grabbing her hand. "You have no idea."

"I haven't really eaten today. Maybe we should go find somewhere to grab food?"

"Sounds good, girl," he said with a wink as he reversed out of his spot, laying on his classic Logan charm.

They found a spot with an outdoor seating area on a patio that faced the beach. It was early evening, so the sun was just starting to set, which made for the most perfect ocean view. They ordered two mojitos that showed up with two sticks of sugar cane, a handful of mint leaves, and sliced limes floating in the drinks. The server brought a basket of plantain chips that they snacked on while Logan caught Julianne up on what she'd missed at the hospital. Apparently she was all anyone could talk about. Logan had been doing his best to downplay the drama there, but it was impossible to explain to every single person what had been going on in the past couple of weeks with Lucy.

"So that lady drugged you and dragged you onto a plane?" he asked her after she summarized to him what had gone on in Miami.

"It was insane, all of this," she said, taking a sip of her second mojito. The alcohol was making her feel relaxed, and she found herself enjoying Logan's company more than she had planned to. Her plan was to confess she had feelings for Harrison—but she realized she should have started with it. Every second that went by, it was becoming harder.

"If only she would have kidnapped me instead of Harrison," he said, smiling up at her from his drink as he stirred the mint leaves around.

She stopped to think about how it would have changed things if she had done that. She was pretty sure they would probably be dead, unless Logan could have charmed their way out of everything. It wasn't impossible. "We need to talk," she finally said.

He nodded. "I had a feeling this would come. Listen, about Emily . . . god, it was so stupid, Julianne. When she suggested this bet, or whatever, I honestly thought we were just joking at first. And I don't mean making fun of you, like, I just didn't know she was serious about it. Anyway, when she got you to the bar, I realized she was keeping it up, and I felt dumb about it. I literally was going to buy you a drink and tell Emily I was done, but then you smiled at me and accepted a crappy beer you didn't even want to drink.

"Suddenly you weren't just unattainable Julianne, you were within my reach. Literally. I should have had the balls to tell Emily I wasn't hanging out with you because of the bet, but, well, you know our history, and I was a chickenshit, and I'm sorry for that."

She pushed her lips together, taking in his explanation.

"There was something else," Julianne said. "You hung out with Emily the day after we agreed to give us a shot. And you kissed her. Do you know how that made me feel?"

He sighed. "I was drunk, and whatever she told you, she kissed me and I stopped her right away. We're just friends, Julianne. I swear."

"Yeah, friends who were literally sleeping together a week before. Like, how does that seem okay?"

"Okay," he said. "If you don't want me to hang out with her anymore, I won't. I like you, Julianne, like, I really like you. But you can't just run away or not take my calls when you get mad. You need to tell me, so I know. I'm not a mind reader, and I told you before I'm not going to be great at a relationship, not right away at least. But I want to be, for you."

She put hands over her face and groaned.

"What?" he asked, pulling her hands away from her face. "Please, just tell me what I said that was wrong."

"Nothing and everything. Logan . . . I feel like . . . no, I-I've been confused about how I feel about you. Sometimes I think we're perfect for each other, but then I feel like it's not the right time. You know? Like, I don't want to not trust you. But I find myself in that situation too often. And I know this is all new to you, but ..."

He let go on her hands and looked down at the table. He looked so sad that her heart was breaking for him.

"And I'm not being completely honest. I'm also struggling with my feelings for you because I have feelings for someone else too."

She watched him sigh, but his face didn't look surprised or enraged.

"I know," he said, his voice soft. "I saw it the moment I walked into that hospital room. I just hoped maybe you would change your mind."

"You're not mad?"

He looked at her. "It sucks, but I'm not going to be mad at you. I told you before he might be your better choice. And like you said: this might not be the time for us."

He pulled his chair close to her, throwing an arm around her shoulder and pulling her in. She felt tears falling down her face.

"Maybe someday," he said into her hair as they sat quietly, both looking out at the ocean. "I wish so badly it could be me. You were the first person I ever wanted to be different for."

"Be different if it makes you happy, but not for me, or anyone else," she said, resting her forehead against his.

They sat together watching the sunset. Julianne didn't even know what time it was until Logan showed her his phone that said it was already 9:00 p.m.

"Do you have a place to stay?" she asked him.

"No, I guess I never got that far."

"If it makes you feel any better, I don't either. I think we could go to Ruby's though. We stayed there last night."

"Ruby Kennedy?"

Julianne nodded. She'd left out the part of their story where they'd ended up at her house last night.

"I think I might just drive back up to Miami and try to get an early flight out," he said. "But you should go."

She knew it would be a smart move to go with Logan and fly back as well. She had her parents and the residency program to deal with. But she had to see Harrison again before she left, so she'd stay the night and work on getting home tomorrow.

Logan dropped her off at Ruby's house. She'd decided to not go to the hospital tonight. She was desperate for sleep, and she knew he wouldn't be up, anyway. Ruby opened the door seconds after she knocked.

"Hey." She smiled and opened the door wide to let Julianne in. "Did I just see little Williams drop you off?"

Julianne sighed. "Yes, he came, he's leaving. It's been a long day."

"I get it, lady," she said. "If you want to go straight to bed, I understand."

Julianne smiled at her. "Thanks. Did you go see Harrison tonight?"

She nodded. "He was in a chipper mood."

Julianne could sense her sarcasm. "He'll be better soon. He's just angry he got shot and that I could have—"

"Ah, yes. He always feels it's his duty to protect. And I'm guessing his little brother visiting didn't help?"

"Not at all," Julianne said.

Julianne said goodnight and fell asleep quickly in her bed.

The next morning, she showered and took the time to get ready so she would look decent for Harrison. She borrowed a cute black maxi dress from Ruby, with a pair of gold sandals and a floppy sun hat. She ate breakfast with Ruby and waited for Lucy to come pick her up. Lucy had texted her that morning that she would swing by because she was going to be heading up to Miami soon to fly back to Minneapolis. Julianne asked her if she wouldn't mind waiting so she could talk to Harrison, and then she'd ride with her and try to get a flight out too. As much as Julianne wanted to stay in Florida to be with him in the hospital while he recovered, she had so much trouble at home she had to resolve.

"Good morning, sunshine," Lucy said beaming, holding out a paper coffee cup.

Julianne took a sip, fully expecting a cup of hot coffee, but found something else entirely. She laughed at Lucy. "Is this a mimosa?"

Lucy laughed. "We're celebrating, Jules! This mess is over! Think it's too late for us to get back on our half marathon training program?"

Julianne laughed again. "We'll see."

"Now, I know I told you this before, but seriously, if I go ever go missing—"

Julianne held her hands up. "You're as good as gone with me. I promise. This trip has definitely taught me a lesson that I am best fit in the hospital."

"I don't know. You did well, actually," Lucy said. "And you're definitely not that same Julianne I once said needed to loosen up. You're not who I tried to make you either. You're you, the real you, and I love it."

Lucy and Julianne finished their mimosas in the parking lot of the hospital before Julianne ran inside. Lucy had filled her in on the things she'd taken care of at the police station, including wrapping things up for Julianne so she wouldn't have to go in herself. Overall, she felt great—really great. She had her life back. She was no longer stuck between two guys. She had her best friend again. Things were looking up for once.

She stopped at the front desk in the unit Harrison was staying at to check in.

"You said you were here to see Harrison Williams?" the nurse asked.

Julianne nodded.

She saw the nurse look hesitantly at another nurse sitting nearby. "She's here to see Harrison Williams?"

They both seemed to sit there staring at each other.

Julianne threw her hands on the desk. "Is there an issue with this?"

The nurse looked back at her. "He's well . . . Harrison's gone."

24

"Excuse me?" Julianne asked. She didn't let them answer; she walked past the desk to his room and threw open the door to find an empty, unmade bed.

A nurse had followed her to the room and was coming up behind her. "He left this morning, completely against medical advice."

Julianne's mouth dropped open. "He was shot yesterday and had surgery. You all just let him walk out of here?"

"Have you seen him?" the other nurse asked. "There was no way we were stopping him."

Julianne sighed in frustration. "This is unbelievable." This was so irresponsible of him. There was no way he was in any condition to leave the hospital. "I suppose he didn't mention where he was heading?" she asked. She couldn't imagine how he would get home in his condition. She knew he wouldn't be going to Ruby's either, knowing Julianne would be there.

They both shook their heads.

Julianne left the hospital, throwing Lucy's car door open in frustration.

Lucy stared at her. "Uh oh, that didn't go well."

Julianne groaned. "He's gone."

"He died?" she asked, horrified.

"No, that idiot left the hospital. He could die, Lucy. There was no way he is any condition to just walk out."

"But, he clearly did walk out. He doesn't exactly seem like the type to be told what to do, huh?"

Julianne shook her head. "Just drive me to the airport. It's time to go home."

The flight home was uneventful. She'd gotten a few hours of rest, even though she had a dreadful feeling in the back of her mind the entire time. Harrison was out there somewhere. She wasn't sure which felt worse—worrying if he was okay, or the realization that he'd willingly abandoned her.

Julianne took an Uber back to her condo from the airport. She wanted to have access to her own car if she needed to leave her father's place in a hurry. When she got to his house, she saw her mom's car was also in his driveway. Her parents were hardly ever alone in a room together. She hoped no blood had already been shed.

She knocked on the door and waited. Lauren answered the door and immediately took Julianne into her arms. Julianne did her best to not pull out of the embrace too quickly. She looked around for her parents, expecting to find them bickering and glaring, but found them instead sitting at the dining room table laughing and talking. They looked up at the sound of the door and became silent. Her dad's face changed immediately.

"Hi." She waved. "Listen, I . . ."

Her mom walked up and pulled her into a hug. Julianne settled into her arms. She breathed in the warm smell of oats and honey. It smelled like home, and it made her for one second forget that everything wasn't okay.

"I'm so glad you're back," her mom said, letting her go. "I've never even thought to worry about you. I took for granted that you've always had your head on your shoulders."

Julianne sighed. "I still do. I just had to help my friend."

"Since when do you almost give up your whole career to help a friend?" her father asked, his voice full of contempt.

"I didn't think it would hurt my career. I didn't plan on getting kidnapped by a psychopath."

"Yes, but—"

Julianne cut him off. "If you really must know, it's because she reminded me of Ella. And she was the first real friend I've had in, god, years. I've had enough to deal with the past two days; I don't need this right now. So if this is just a lecture, I will go."

Her mom held her hands up. "No, you're right. I'm sorry, Julianne. Of course I'm proud of you for trying to help a friend. No parents ever want to hear their child is in danger."

"Everything's been taken care with your residency program," her father said, his face still very stoic. "They weren't happy about any of this. But they agreed, considering what happened, and it seeming to not be at any fault of your own, to keep you in the program and pretend this didn't happen. But, keep in mind, this might follow you for some time."

"I know. And I'm willing to work even harder to prove myself. But thank you. It's a relief to hear this." She knew it wasn't a time to push the fact that she'd recently told him she didn't need his help. This was one situation in which she was willing to take it.

"Is your friend okay?" her mom asked.

"Lucy? Yes, she's back home now too."

Her mom shook her head. "No, not her, the one that the news said was shot. Harrington, was it?"

"Harrison," she corrected. "And honestly, I don't know. I went to the hospital to see him this morning and he left AMA."

Her dad looked at her, shaking his head. "What an idiot."

"Yeah, I know." She hated to have to be agreeing with her dad on this, but she'd been so happy he'd survived getting shot, that they'd both survived, and then he'd left and risked his life all over again. And for what? Did he just hate being in the hospital, or was it as she feared, that he didn't want to see her?

"Listen, Julianne, I wanted to talk to you about the other day at the house," her father said. "You were upset, and after talking more with your mom, I understand why."

Julianne looked at her mom, who gave her a small apologetic smile.

"I'm sorry I couldn't be there more for you in the way you needed growing up," he said. "And I realize you blame me for things you think are wrong with you that aren't wrong at all. You're driven. You're smart. But if you think I would have risked my entire medical career for a friend, you're out of your damn mind. That would be your mother one hundred percent."

Julianne and her mom smiled at each other and relief washed over her.

"I can't take back the last twenty-five years," he said. "And

I know moving to Washington is a big change, and it's a change that isn't for you, and maybe I didn't think about how that would make you feel."

She saw her mom nod at him to keep going. Julianne knew this conversation had to be hard for him. And in her heart she knew her dad moving wasn't to spite her. She just wished it could have all happened differently.

"I love you, Julianne," he said. "I always have, and I always will. I don't show it, I know, at least in a way you might understand. But believe me when I say I always did what I thought was best for you. At first, when I found out what happened this week, I was enraged, but then I realized you did something for a friend, a selfless act. And I realized maybe I can learn something from you too."

Julianne gave him a hug. He was still rigid. Her dad was definitely not a hugger, but she felt like for the first time in her adult life maybe she'd have a real relationship with this man outside of the hospital.

"I'm still going to find my own place," Julianne said. "And since my lease is up on the Lexus soon, I'm going to get my own car too. I need to do things on my own."

He nodded. "I fully support that."

She smiled briefly at both her parents. "Sorry to leave so quickly, but I need to go see if I can find Harrison."

Her mom nodded, and Julianne gave her a quick hug before grabbing her bag and heading back out the door to her car. Her plan was to drive to Harrison's house and see if he was home. It was the only place she could think to start.

She pulled up to the quiet street in front of his house and ran up to the door. She pounded on it loudly, waited a few seconds, and then tried again. The door opened finally after her third attempt.

An older man opened the door. He was probably seventy. She looked him curiously and then back at the house number. She was definitely at the right place.

"I'm sorry . . . are you a friend of Harrison's?" she asked.

The old man sighed. "You're looking for Harrison Williams, huh? Well, you'll have to go check out his other place. He's not here today."

"I don't think I understand. Isn't this his house?"

"He rents it to me for dirt cheap," the old man said. "In return he uses it sometimes. I don't ask a lot of questions, not for the price he charges me."

Unbelievable. What else did she not know about this man? She couldn't believe he'd brought her to his fake house. "Do you happen to know the address of his other place?"

"Sure, wait here a moment."

What felt like an eternity later, he returned with a sheet of paper with an address jotted down on it. "Here you go," he said. "I don't normally give this out, but you're awfully pretty, and I'm certain that he wouldn't want to miss out on you showing up."

Julianne smiled politely at the man. "Well, thank you."

She looked at the address. It was located downtown. When she arrived, she pulled her car up to the valet of the skyscraper in front of her. She'd say she was shocked at Harrison living at this place, if it wasn't for all the other craziness she'd been dealt recently. This was clearly just a cherry on top of the shitstorm sundae.

She handed her keys over to the valet attendant and

stepped inside the luxurious condo building. She stopped at the front desk. "I'm here to see Harrison Williams."

The man glanced at her and then looked down at something on his desk. "I don't see that Mr. Williams is expecting any visitors," he said when he looked back up.

"Well, he is," she snapped. "Can you please direct me to where he is?"

"I'm sorry, miss. If you'd like, I can try to call up to him and see if he'll give permission to let you up. These are the rules for everyone."

She huffed. This was worthless. She was about to give him a piece of her mind when a couple of young men entered behind her, being way too rowdy for his liking based on his expression.

"Will you excuse me?" he said to her, stepping up from behind his desk.

Julianne hoisted herself over and looked at his book, which had Harrison's name and unit number listed on it. She pressed the button that was located on the desk and she heard a click of the door nearby. She turned to see the man was still busy, so she quickly darted toward the door and found an elevator. She hit the twenty-fifth floor, which was the highest floor in the building.

She thought for sure with her luck the elevator would stop on the way up, but when the elevator opened to the twenty-fifth floor, she breathed a sigh of relief. Apparently Harrison lived in a penthouse in downtown Minneapolis. She wondered if Logan knew—no, she knew he didn't know. But he had warned her Harrison was dangerous. Heck, Harrison had warned her of that. What was he hiding in here? Hopefully not *another* wife.

She knocked on the door. She honestly didn't expect anyone to answer. But the door opened and there he was, looking exactly how she'd expected—like hell.

A muscle in his jaw twitched as he stared at her. "How did you find me?"

She glared at him, walking past him and inside. She took a minute to look around. It was insanely beautiful. She'd never seen anything like his place before. She turned to him, her hands planted firmly on her hips. "This is where you live? What the hell, to so much."

"The front door staff needs to be fired," he grumbled, shutting the door and following her into this penthouse condo.

"Why did you leave the hospital? Do you know how insane and stupid that is? I can see blood through your shirt, Harrison."

She reached for his white T-shirt so she could get a better look at his wound, but he grabbed her wrists, stopping her.

"It isn't anything for you to worry about," he said. His lips drew back in a snarl.

"Really?" she said. "Why would I be here right now then? Why are you being so stubborn and just an . . . asshole? Yes, you're being an asshole, just so you know."

He sighed, walked over to a chair nearby, and sat down. "So you came here to yell at me?"

"I came here to see if you were okay! And you're obviously not. Please, just let me at least look at your wound, and then if you really want me to go, I will."

Harrison didn't say any more, so she started pulling off his shirt. He lifted his arms a bit to help her, but she could see he couldn't move his left one much from the pain.

His skin was hot against her fingertips. He had a white gauze taped over the wound, but when she took it off, she could see he'd ripped through his stitches.

"I don't suppose you have any sutures lying around here?" she asked.

"In the bathroom. Down the hall on the right," he replied. "Bring whiskey too."

She looked around as she walked to the bathroom. To her left were huge windows that looked out onto the city. The interior was a modern mix of whites, grays, and blacks. Inside the bathroom there was a clear cabinet with a large first aid kit. She found what she needed and started walking back, remembering the whiskey request. She spotted a bar area across the way, so she went over, grabbing a glass and filling it up half way. This would definitely hurt.

He was still sitting in the same chair she'd left him in, his eyes closed.

"Here," she said, handing him the whiskey. "Sorry, this probably won't feel good."

He took a long sip before she came closer with the needle.

"And since I am sitting here with a needle, I think I deserve some answers."

He groaned. "Just stitch this up. I'll answer what you want after."

"Fine." She wondered if he meant it, or if he just wanted to shut her up.

He grimaced as she began. She tried to keep her hands steady, she'd done this plenty of times, but never on someone with whom she'd been intimate. Just smelling his skin as close as she was to him was making her brain do loops.

He took another drink after a few seconds. It took several

minutes of this until she was finished. She grabbed the new bandage and placed it on his chest. She could swear she felt his heartbeat increase for a moment while she worked on ripping a piece of the tape with her teeth. She looked at his glass. He'd finished almost the entire thing.

"Much better," she said, looking approvingly at her work. "If you go to the hospital, I'm sure you could get some pills for the pain."

He shook his head. "I don't want any."

"Alright," she said. "So . . ."

His eyes met hers for the first time since she'd arrived. She found herself able to read his emotions through his eyes, and at the moment all she could see was sadness.

He got up and walked to another room in the house that had a large white sofa. He sat down on it, staring off into the distance. She sat down near him hesitantly. For the first time, she considered the possibility that maybe he didn't want to see her not because of Logan, but because Harrison didn't have any real interest in her. Maybe he'd really just wanted them to be a fling in Miami. He could have lied— after all, he had lied about where he lived. And about what he did for a living. She'd seen his office, and him living here made no sense. "Why did you hide this place from me?" she asked.

He shrugged. "I didn't do it on purpose. I had been staying at the other house for another reason, so that just happened to be where I was when you needed a place to stay. I wasn't hiding it."

"How do you afford this place? I mean, what else do you do? Do I even want to know?"

He sighed. "I run a global security business. I started it

years ago, and it's done fairly well. It's why I have conne͟
all over the place."

"But the office you brought me to. What was that? I feel
like you hid this all from me. This . . . rich you. Not that I care
either way, but I feel you might have mentioned, 'hey, I run a
global company.'"

"I work from here. That office I took you to was my orig-
inal office. I guess old habits die hard."

Julianne sighed. He had answers for everything. "Okay,
why did you leave?" She knew this question would be harder
for him to answer.

"I don't do hospitals."

"Really?" she asked. "And you just decided to leave and
not even stop by Ruby's and tell me you're leaving?"

"You seemed preoccupied."

"I wasn't," she said.

"Well, then I'm sorry," he replied. "But as you can see I'm
fine, so you can go now."

"Seriously?" she asked. "Why are you being this way?
You're making it hard for me to want to be nice to you."

"Then don't be."

"But I want to be."

"Where's Logan?" he asked. She'd been waiting for it; she
just didn't know how long it would take to get there. She'd
wanted to go to Harrison when he was in a good mood, tell
him she'd ended everything Logan and that she wanted to be
with him, but his attitude annoyed her and couldn't get
herself to go there.

"You would know if you hadn't left," she retorted. "I'm so
mad at you, Harrison Williams. If you could just stop being a
jerk for five seconds, you'd have found out that last night

when Logan came to visit we ended things. I went back to Ruby's to get some much-needed sleep. And when I came to tell you this morning . . . you were gone. And now, honestly? It's my turn to leave. So, good luck with everything."

She stood up and rushed to the door. She hit the elevator button and was glad it was still close by and hadn't been all the way at the first floor. When the elevator doors shut, she felt warm, salty tears running down her face.

She wiped them off with her sleeve as she drove home. She'd fallen for someone who just wasn't who she'd thought.

25

The next day Julianne went back to the hospital and returned to her normal life. She'd decided to not tell Logan about what had happened with Harrison. It would just be another axe between brothers, and, even worse, she didn't need Logan to charm his way back into her heart. She was swearing off guys for the time being.

After work, she met up with Lucy and Molly at one of their usual running club meeting locations. Molly had joined the club again after the news about what had really happened with Katie and Angela came out. About twenty new runners had joined the group just in the last week because of all the press the group had gotten after not only what had happened with Katie, but also with the arrest of Theo Goldberg, and to run with the infamous Julianne Davis, who half of them still believed had indeed killed Alex.

After they ran, Lucy had agreed to go with Julianne to hunt for an apartment.

They pulled up at the apartment complex and walked inside. It looked like a nice building. The apartment staff had to open the door for them to enter, so security, check. It was about ten stories high and had an updated gym on the bottom floor with a lounge area nearby. As Julianne and Lucy took the elevator up to the seventh floor with the leasing agent, she thought moving out with her own means might not be so impossible after all.

"I think you'll be very impressed with this unit," the leasing agent said as they walked toward the front door.

And Julianne definitely was. She signed a lease on the spot and would move in that weekend. She squealed as she and Lucy ran out to her car.

"You're officially a new woman," Lucy exclaimed. "We're going out to celebrate, right?"

Julianne sighed. She would, it sounded fun, but she desperately needed rest. She hadn't been sleeping well, so she said goodbye before heading home.

The rest of the week went about the same: hospital, run, pack, sleep, repeat until Sunday arrived.

Lucy pulled up the curb minutes later, and Julianne was surprised to see Logan and Pete climb out of her car after her.

"Lucy says if we help you move we get free pizza and beer," Pete said, jogging up to her. "And you know we're not going to refuse that."

Julianne looked at Lucy, raising her eyebrows.

"What?" Lucy asked. "You know you needed some muscles. You weren't going to move your bed on your own."

She wished Lucy had asked anyone other than Logan, but it was nice to have help. Julianne had recently introduced Lucy to Pete after a rotation one day, and they'd seemed to hit it off. Apparently so much that she was already asking him for favors.

"Hey," Logan said, walking up to her. His hair had been recently cut, and it was much shorter than she was used to seeing it, but it looked good.

"Hi." She smiled. "Thanks for coming. You really didn't have to."

"I know. But friends help each other, right?"

"Right." She nodded.

They watched Pete and Lucy flirting over by the front door.

"I think you might have set up a good pair there," Logan said.

"Who knew?" She laughed. "She might be a little wild for Pete though, don't you think?"

He laughed too. "I think Pete can handle himself."

Logan followed her to the front door of her building, where they had lots of boxes sitting. She pointed to a few of the heavy ones she needed help with. They made small talk about the hospital as they brought the boxes back and forth, and she felt like the morning was going well until he asked the next question.

"So I'm guessing Harrison would be here helping if it wasn't for getting shot a week ago?" Logan asked, trying to make a light joke, but it read as more curious than anything.

Julianne pushed the box she was holding into the back of the truck.

"We're actually not talking at the moment," she replied, refusing to make eye contact with him. She knew what he'd think—*I told you so*. She just didn't want to hear it.

"What?" He grabbed her arm, stopping her from heading back for another box.

"I really don't want to talk about it, Logan. Let's just keep moving."

"Why aren't you two talking?"

She put her hands on her hips. "It's not really your business. Let's go, please."

Julianne noticed Pete and Lucy were staring at them, so she lowered her arms to not look so defensive. She didn't want them to think they were fighting. She grabbed Logan's arm, pulling him further inside the building where no one could see them.

"I just need you to be my friend and let this go," she said. "Please."

He stood quietly. "I knew he was an moron, just not this big of one."

She gave him the briefest of smiles before walking back to where Pete, Lucy, and her parents were standing. The guys helped carry the big furniture, and it was just after twelve by the time they got everything loaded up.

"You know, it's not too late to let us hire some people to unload all of this," her mom said, nudging her with her elbow.

Julianne could see she was joking, which made her happy that her mom still supportive of her decision to do things on her own. Julianne was even more impressed her dad had showed up to help with her move. She guessed he was dying inside, having to do physical labor, but he said nothing.

Julianne left to go get the pizza and beer that Lucy had promised, and they all had lunch before driving out to her new apartment and unloading everything. Everyone was exhausted by 4:00 p.m. when the last of the boxes had been cleared out of the truck.

Julianne stopped for a moment, taking in the group of people who sat in her apartment, and she felt a tear escaping her eye. But this tear was a happy tear. She had friends. Her parents were there, and they were actually getting along. It almost felt unreal—she was so used to just being solo Julianne. This was everything she wanted, well, almost everything. She felt Logan watching her out of the corner of her eye. She knew it would be so easy to tell him she'd changed her mind and wanted him. But it felt like a step backward. She could feel in her heart Logan wouldn't be her forever. And keeping him as a friend seemed like the more logical choice. Plus, just because she wasn't with Harrison didn't mean she had to be with someone else. Looking at the people who'd showed up to support her was more than good enough for now.

After everyone left, she stared at all of her possessions, which would take her weeks to unpack. She had no desire to start tonight, so she grabbed the bottle of wine she had bought earlier that was chilling in her fridge and opened it with her wine key she'd made sure to not have packed away. She realized belatedly that she hadn't had a clue where to find a wine glass, so she settled on a plastic cup.

She was sipping her second glass when she heard a knock on her door. She got up and looked through the small peephole. She expected to maybe see Logan or Lucy, but it was a man she didn't recognize. She hesitantly opened the door just slightly. "Hello?"

"Ms. Davis?" the man asked. "Mr. Williams has sent a car for you."

She looked at him as if he had just spoken a foreign language. "Excuse me?"

"Harrison Williams. He sent me to pick you up."

She looked down at her gray sweats and softball T-shirt she'd had since high school. He was sending a car to pick her up . . . in this? She wanted to laugh at the guy and shut the door in his face.

"He said to give you these if you said no," he said, holding out a huge bouquet red roses. "He also said I'd be fired if you didn't come, so I'd really appreciate if you would come with me."

Julianne swallowed. Fine. She'd go, but only tell him off. How dare he think he can just show up, wait, have someone else show up with flowers, and everything would be okay. She wasn't changing either. She shoved her feet into her running shoes and set the flowers on her counter before following him out.

They pulled up to his penthouse about twenty minutes later. She couldn't believe she was back here. She went into the front door of the building again and grimaced at seeing the same man at the front desk. Maybe he wouldn't see her on the list again and she could leave.

"Ah, Ms. Davis, right?" he greeted her immediately. "Please go on in."

When the elevator door opened to the twenty-fifth floor, she walked nervously to the door. She'd felt strong this whole time, like she was ready to kick some butt, until this moment. Now her nerves were getting to her, and she turned back around to the elevator. She hit the button, impatiently waiting for it to open back up. She heard the door open behind her while she waited.

"Julianne?"

She spun around. Her stupid heart fluttered a beat. Harrison looked much better than the last time she'd seen him. He'd shaved. It was probably the cleanest cut she'd seen on him. He was dressed in a pair of jeans and a black T-shirt, typical Harrison attire. He must have been healing because he didn't seem to be grimacing in pain anymore either. Also, as usual, he looked like the most beautiful human she'd ever laid her eyes on.

"Hi," she said. "Sorry, I was . . ." The elevator door opened. "Leaving."

"I see that," he replied, a small smirk on his face. "Would you come inside instead?"

She followed him in, once again astounded by his home. She still couldn't get used to it. She was sure you could fit four of her apartments into his.

"You look better," she said once inside.

"I feel better," he replied. "I had a pretty and stubborn doctor stitch me up."

He stepped so close to her she could smell every inch of him, and he smelled wonderful. She closed her eyes, trying to muster the spirit of the woman in the car who had been so sure of what she'd say to him.

He reached toward her face, tilting her chin up so she was looking at him. At those same dark eyes she'd seen before and knew so well. "I've missed you so damn much."

She moved back. "No, we can't just . . . we can't just go back, Harrison."

He sighed. "I was mad, and I messed up. I felt my heart crack in two when you walked out the door of my hospital room with Logan. I didn't want to feel like that again, ever, not even for a second."

"But you jumped to conclusions without even giving me a chance," she said.

"Is that really that crazy?" he asked. "You were in love with my brother."

"I was never in love with Logan. I was in love with you."

"You were? Are you not anymore?" His smile was slow as he once again moved closer.

"What made you decide to finally reach out to me?" she asked. She felt her skin heat under his gaze. Her body was trying to betray her.

"I've been thinking about it all week," he said. "But I've . . . I know you won't believe this, but I've just been scared. I knew I messed up after the last time you left. And I played out this moment in my mind so many times, and each of those times you left again. Also, Logan called me this afternoon and had a few choice words for me."

Julianne shook her head, bemused. Of course Logan had. She could still see the fear in Harrison's eyes that she was going to leave. She still felt like she might. Her heart was racing.

"I'd take another bullet if it meant this pain, right here, would go away," he said, placing her hand underneath his shirt and against his heart.

She looked up at him, her fingers carefully staying where he'd put them even after he'd removed his hand. She could feel his heart racing like her own. When he bent down toward her and she felt his warm lips on hers, she melted into him.

"I love you, Julianne Davis," he said, lifting her into his arms.

She looked at him, wide-eyed. "Are you sure you should be carrying me?"

He grinned. "It'll take a lot more than a bullet to stop me from doing this." He carried her to the master bedroom, which she had yet to see. It was gorgeous, just like the rest of the place. A fire was lit in the large stone fireplace against the back wall.

"Can I tell you a secret?" he asked, tossing her down onto the bed. Her body folded into the softest comforter she'd ever felt.

"Yes," she whispered.

He got onto the bed on top of her, straddling his legs over the sides of her knees.

"You look really sexy in your sweats," he said, murmuring as he kissed her neck.

"That's your secret?" She laughed, her voice a little shaky from his kisses.

"Sorry." He smiled. "You're so distracting. No, I was going to tell you that you're the first woman I've ever had in here."

She looked at him in surprise. "How? You're like . . . gorgeous and clearly also rich. I'm sure every woman in the world would want to be here."

He'd pulled off her T-shirt and threw it to the floor. She was glad she'd worn at least a decent bra, a black lacy one that matched her black lace thong, which was also visible as Harrison slid off her pants and discarded them next to her shirt.

His lips moved slowly and deliberately. He'd remembered what she'd enjoyed from last time. He paused for a moment, looking up at her.

"Maybe every woman would want to be here, which I'd say is most likely an exaggeration," he said, his dark eyes twinkling at her. "But I've never wanted any of them here. This has always been my personal sanctuary, I've never felt like sharing it with anyone before. But you, my Julianne, I never want you to leave."

He was so close to where he'd made her unravel before, but she stopped him, sitting up and pushing him onto the bed. She didn't want this to be all about her tonight. With his help, she pulled off his shirt. Her fingers lightly traced his bandage before working her way down to his jeans. She could feel him rock hard underneath the bulging fabric. She unbuttoned them, lightly tugging at them before he finished the rest. He looked as glorious as she'd remembered back at the beach. Only this time she could look longer, crave him inside of her, knowing that this time there was nothing holding either of them back.

She heard him take a deep breath as she dragged her tongue down his length. Her lips traced the head slowly before she took all of him in her mouth, relishing in the soft moans she heard from him.

"Sweetheart, this feels . . . hell, it feels unbelievable. But if you keep going, there is no way I will last more than a minute, and I really want to be inside of you."

He'd somehow managed to get her bra and underwear off in the mean time. He reached for his nightstand and pulled out a foil packet. His hands caressed her and her hips arched up to him. She wanted him inside of her so badly it hurt. Seconds later he thrust into her. It was slow as first, and she shuddered as his growth filled her. His movements picked up quickly, each thrust causing her to move closer and closer to ecstasy.

"You feel amazing," he groaned, his voice deep.

She opened her eyes and saw him watching her with hunger.

They'd both came minutes later. Harrison collapsed on the bed beside her. She looked over to find him grinning at her, and she felt her entire face turn red.

"I promise that will last longer next time," he said. "But damn..."

She laughed, laying her head on his chest. She looked around the room again, taking in the sleek modern furniture and fixtures. Through the open closet door, she could see his black wardrobe. "I have a feeling being with you is going to be quite the adventure," she said, turning back to him.

She didn't know what to expect, but she knew it wouldn't ever be boring. Not if they could do that every day. But she wasn't naïve, and his job wasn't the safest. This might not be the last time he got shot. And it terrified her, but it terrified her more to think about being without him.

"Maybe," he whispered into her hair, his eyes now closed. "But I promise it'll all be worth it."

As she fell asleep in his arms, she thought about what he said. And how she felt, in that moment, utterly content and most definitely loved. She would take his word for it.

ABOUT THE AUTHOR

Jamie Everlee is a stay-at-home mom of two (soon to be three) who enjoys writing in her spare time. She currently resides in Wisconsin with her husband and children, along with two cats and a yorkie. This is her debut novel. You can find out more by visiting her Instagram or website.

Instagram: @jamieeverlee
www.jamieeverlee.com